Magic Mysteries Of Gullah Island

BY

JAQUARY D. MOTON

Table of Contents

Chapter one

In the Beginning, There was Greed!

The air in the room filled my nostrils with a stale, dry scent. Accompanied by a fresh breeze in the air. It changed to a mysterious floral scent. Our new client must have arrived already. She was two whole hours early, and Beatrice hadn't started the ritual spell on Amaya, our rainbow serpent. I sat staring at myself in the mirror as the doorbell rang. I got up and walked out of the bedroom. Beatrice was still in the shower, she hadn't heard the doorbell ring.

I walked over and knocked on the bedroom door. Beatrice responded, "What's wrong"? She said through the door. "Nothing, but our first appointment is here already." Beatrice annoyed, "What already? "Her check-in time isn't until 10 am. Well, can you go ahead and show her to the room". I sighed, "sure, I got it." I walked over to the door, I peeked outside first. A medium build woman who appeared to be in her forties with big curly hair. Yellow skin and brown freckles. She was staring back at me with huge big brown eyes. She had this big silly grin on her face.

She waved hi as she smiled, I gawked at her through the window. She begins to speak. "Hi, I'm Ellie May Williams. I have a 10 am check-in. For the rainbow youth resort". I just smiled back. My brain was somehow frozen today. I hadn't slept in a few days. And who the hell would name their child Ellie May in this day and age. I stood back and unlocked the door. I extended my right hand. I opened the door wide. I smiled, "welcome to the rainbow youth resort. You're early".

She shook my hand with a firm grip. While she positioned herself through the door, She dragged her luggage and looked up at me. "I know, my flight got in early. I took a cab right over". I smiled, "It's ok, you can follow me to your room." As I guided her down the hall. I smelled that floral scent again. "Nice perfume." Her eyes lit up. "Why? Thank you, I made it myself. With fresh essential oils". I smiled as I opened her room door. "Oh, let me guess, rose oil, otto, of course, jasmine oil, patchouli with a dash of." I stopped and inhaled her scent once more. "Vanilla bean." Her smiled melted into a blank stare.

"Well…that's impossible, I mean… How could you know my signature perfume? I made it myself"! I smiled again as I opened her bedroom door wider. "This is your suite. Your procedure will begin tonight around midnight. If you have any questions in the meantime, Beatrice and I will be happy to answer. We have an office right down the hall, room 1111. We have a full house today". I handed her the key and walked out of the room and closed the door behind me. My Grandmother had an eight-bedroom ranch. She left it to me in her will. She would rent the rooms out. It was a bed and breakfast. I remembered so well from my childhood.

She loved this house. She was so proud to run her own business.The bed and breakfast dried up. After the big hotels and resorts came and took over Gullah island, they even tried to buy Grandmother out several times. But she wouldn't budge. This was her property, and she was proud. The property was right on the water with the beautiful sand and palm trees. You could even see dolphins.

In the water from our side of the island. Out of all the grands. She left the bed and breakfast for me. She would always tell me how special I was as a child, how I reminded her of herself. We looked alike. Both of us were very fair-skinned. We both had long dark hair. And dark brown eyes. We shared a special marking. We both had the same special mark right above our elbow. It looked like a raised mole. But, it wasn't, it was something else. I didn't find out what it really was until I was a teenager.

Beatrice walked over and pulled me out of my memory. "Hey Ty, are all the rooms stocked with towels and extra bedsheets?" I smiled, "Take it easy Bea, I handled all that last night. Since you were late getting in from

Atlanta,". We both walked towards the office. We went in at the same time. Beatrice smiled, "look, I'm sorry, I have a husband and child who needs me. It's hard for me to slip away for the weekend".

I sat down at my desk, and Beatrice sat down at hers. We turned the old den into an office. It was decorated with huge rare crystals and exotic plants. The whole house looked mystical. Of course, we remodeled and added hardwood floors, stainless-steel appliances. As much as people were paying for this procedure, We had to make it as upscale as possible.

Beatrice typed away on her computer. She smiled and rubbed her hands together. "Ty, come over here for a minute," I climbed out of my office chair and walked around to hers. "What's up"? Beatrice pointed to her computer. "look at the spreadsheet, if everyone shows up today. That's eight procedures at $10,000 apiece. That's eighty grand in one day"! I smiled and walked back over to my desk. "Yeah, well, it should be a great day. Only one thing, we need to go and condition Amaya". Beatrice sighed, "Oh yeah, forgot about that. I wish you would handle that Tituba".

I frowned, "Ty! My name is Ty, thank you"! Beatrice smiled. "Your mother named you Tituba. I'm going to call you Tituba". I frowned again, "Anyways, Amaya is not just my responsibility. It's safer if we are both in the room. Just in case something happens." Beatrice poured herself a glass of wine. The bottle was sitting on her desk. "I guess you're right, for safety purposes." She poured a second glass and handed it to me. Beatrice raised her glass. "Here's to eighty grand in twenty-four hours." I smiled and raised my glass. "To, eighty grand in twenty-four hours."

We made a toast. I gulped down my wine. We proceeded to go downstairs to the basement. I opened the basement door. It was always so dark and damped down there. I reached over my head. I pulled the metal chain to turn on the light. We both went down the steep stairway. "Beatrice, I need you to light the green candles and get the snake tooth out. It is now 9 am, and the spell will only last 24 hours. So, we need to start now." I went over to an old dresser drawer and pulled out a book. Not just any book. The Book of Nigron. I found it over a year ago when I inherited this place.

My mind went into a flash black after my grandmother's funeral. I decided to have a girls getaway. Right here, at the bed and breakfast. Just me and the crew. To relax on the beach. I went to the house before anyone got there. I begin to go through my grandmother's old things. I walked into her bedroom, and I noticed a letter taped to her mirror. It looked like a map, no words. I stared at it a little more. It was actually a map of the house.

I flipped the map over, and a riddle was written on the back, Between the map and the riddle. I figured the message out. Whatever she wanted me to find was in the basement. I always hated the basement of this house. It was so dark and damp. I went down there anyway.

I followed the map to a wall. The map said to knock three times. I did, and a small door popped open. It was a small crawl space. It was dark so I used my flashlight to peek in. I saw a metal lockbox. I reached my arms inside and pulled the box out. I placed the lockbox on my lap. I put in the secret code, and it popped open. Deep inside of grandmother's old lockbox was a black book. Glowing, with mystery.

I slowly picked it up. I opened the book, and the glowing light became brighter. It almost blinded me. I rubbed my eyes and looked again. My mouth dropped with amazement. There weren't any words, just pictures, and drawings. But, they jumped off the page as if they were three Dimensional. It was breathtaking. The crazy part was, I actually understood the different shapes and heliographic. It played through my mind, as If I was watching a film. Now I didn't understand every single thing. But, I understood most, and what I didn't know, I researched.

Beatrice tapped me on the shoulder and pulled me back into our realm. "Ty, we don't have time for you to be zoning out, you ok"? I totally got lost in my thoughts. "Yes, I'm sorry, let's get this show on the road. So, you got the green candles"? Beatrice shot me a smart smirk. "Um, yes, they are already burning, earth to Ty"! I looked over toward the crate and the green candles were lit. "Ok, Beatrice, let's put our padded gloves on, and

I'll play the flute this time. Grab the book of Nigron, and recite the words. The spell only lasts twenty-four hours, and we have a full house".

Beatrice's eyes lit up again. "Yes, got a lady in from Russia and another from Australia. Pretty soon, we are going to be known all over the world. We may be millionaires by the time we hit our forties". I still had my glass of wine, and I sipped it with a refreshing smile. "Would be nice." I put my drink down. Beatrice and I gloved up. Together we pulled Amaya's crate out of the corner. We removed the blanket that was lying on top of the crate. I bent down and slowly unhinged the lock.

I begin to play the flute for a full two-minute session. We both took a deep breath, and Beatrice projected the magical words from her mouth. Amaya's gated crate door opened. We both stood there frozen. The tip of Amaya's head began to sway out slowly as her alluring body slithered seductively out of the crate. We kept our eyes glued to her. Amaya was an ancient rainbow serpent. We purchased her from one of Beatrice's friends.

Amaya was originally from Africa. The shaman who sold her to us told us she was over one thousand years old. She was a pretty penny, but, because of Amaya, we were filthy rich. She was about six feet long when she was uncoiled. Her main color was green. But, rainbow holographic bounced off her green skin when she moved. You could see a radiant glowing rainbow.

We had to be very careful that we didn't fall under her mystical spell. Snakes had a magical way of moving to music. Not music heard by the ears, but music heard only in mind. It was mesmerizing, and if we let her take over, we'd be under her spell. So, we had to be strong and move quick. Amaya's body was now floating in the air, almost like she was being projected from a five Dimension screen. She begins to morph into a human; her eyelashes grew long and extended out. Her nose became full, and her thin lips became lustrous. Her slithery tongue became wide. Amaya's beauty was ancient, rare and breathtaking. The top half of her body was human, and the bottom half was a serpent form. Amaya's tail rattled as her body swayed.

I looked into her eyes, I could tell, she was under our spell. Beatrice looked over at me and gave me the nod of acceptance. We both begin to speak, synchronized. "Oh God of nature, grant my slithery companion and my everlasting friendship." I pulled out a snake's tooth I had in my pocket. I waved it over Amaya three times. We both stated out loud, "ASE' It is done"! Amaya shrunk back small, and begin to go back into her crate. She was conditioned, and all set to go. Beatrice and I slipped off our padded gloves.

We locked the crate door. And, threw the blanket over it. Beatrice and I carried it upstairs and into our office, where we performed the procedure. We placed her gently on the desk. "Ty, should I call the first client of the day." I went and sat at my desk and grabbed the first client's file, and glanced at my computer. "Sure, it's 9:45, Her appointment is at 10am". I opened her file and began to look through it. "Looks like we have a woman, mid-forties, bags are starting to protrude under her eyes. Breast are beginning to sag, can't seem to lose weight, yadda yadda yadda. Typical client." Beatrice sipped her coffee, "yeah, pretty much, I'll buzz her now."

Beatrice picks up her phone and dials her number. "Hello, good morning, Mrs. Williams, we are ready for you in room 1111". Beatrice hung up the phone. "Hope this one is not squeamish." I sipped my wine and then my coffee. I had to balance the high and the low. "They are always a little squeamish at first. They get over it fast. Once they see what they are getting in return". At that moment, we heard a knock at the door. "Come in," I said as I gathered her file.

Mrs. Williams walks through the door with a big smile on her face. I could tell she was nervous. "Have a seat on the couch, Mr. Williams." She gave another nervous grin. "Why yes, sure." She walked over to the couch and sat down. She took a deep breath. I begin to read off a few of her symptoms. "Let's see, saggy boobs, bags under eyes, double chin, wrinkles, and fine lines. Are these your biggest concerns"? She placed her hands together. "Why yes, it's been bothersome to me. Looking at all these tight bodies and youthful faces". She begins to tear up, a single tear stream down her face.

She begins to speak. "I just recently got a divorce. The papers were final yesterday". Beatrice and I looked at each other. Beatrice got up and poured Mrs. Williams a cup of coffee. She added a little cream and sugar. "Here, have a cup," Beatrice said with a concerning smile. Beatrice placed the cup in her hands, and Mrs. Williams begins to sip. I cleared my throat. "I'm so sorry to hear that. I know divorce can be life-changing". Mrs. Williams sniffled a bit and pulled a tissue out her purse. She wiped her tears. "I feel stupid, breaking down crying, I'm…I'm really sorry."

"No, No, it's ok," I said to her, as I placed my cup on the desk. Mrs. Williams took a few more sips. She scratched her head. "He um, left me for a younger woman, of course." Beatrice sucked her teeth. "Typical, typical man." Mrs. William's sad face became angry. "This is the ultimate revenge! Get my body back, become youthful and live… forever"! Beatrice nodded her head, yes. "Now that's the spirit we are looking for. If you're ready, we can get into the details and start the procedure".

Mrs. Williams placed her coffee cup on the desk. "Well, I'm as ready as I'll ever be." That floral scent of hers filled my nostrils. But, it smelled different this time. I couldn't quite figure it out yet, but I was concerned. Beatrice opened her folder and began to speak. "Well, I'd like to ask you, what do you know about this procedure, Mrs. Williams"? As Mrs. Williams begins to speak, their voices become mute to me. I got up and lit a bowl of white sage.

I wafted it in the air with a peacock feather. I walked around the room. Now, I knew what was different about the floral scent. It was mixed with fear. Fear had a particular scent. It sets off a chemical in the body. It mixed with her oils and sweat. It began to stink. The smell was becoming more and more potent.

This wasn't a good sign. I walked around the room as I wafted. Mrs. Williams glanced at me with concern in her eyes. I looked over at her and interrupted the conversation. "Mrs. Williams, are you sure, this is what you want"? Her eyes lit up, "Of course I'm sure, I need this! This is my ultimate revenge". Beatrice shot me a dirty look of disapproval. Beatrice was different these days, and she let money harden her. She was always a sweet soul. But something so different had come over her. I decided to stop my integration, and let Beatrice finish.

"So, you do know that we use natural alternative methods, correct"? Mrs. Williams nodded, "Yes, um I used your products with the snake venom, which lasted a good 3-4 weeks. Better and cheaper than Botox, but I really wanted to try this permanent fix. I follow you guys on Facebook and all the other social media sites. I love your work and what you have done for people. Now, I'm ready for this next step". I sat down and began to speak. "well, Mrs. Williams, with this procedure, we kind of…use the full snake".

Mrs. Williams's eyes lit up again. "Ok, well, I heard, I eat some type of rare exotic snake". I interrupted, "not necessarily, you will be consuming the eggs". Mrs. Williams face transformed from a confused look to a great big smile. "Like caviar, but only from a snake, not a fish"? I nodded, "Yes, but". I took a deep breath and exhaled, "The snake has to lay the eggs in your mouth."

Again, Mrs. Williams's facial features turned to concern and then back to excitement. "Well, I'm willing to try anything at this point. I explained that in my application". I glance into her eyes. "And that's the reason we called you back. We get thousands of applications for the program, and well, everyone is not a good fit.

So, allow me to tell you about the step by step procedure." I stood up from my seat and handed her a form. "Read along with me, step by step." I cleared my throat. "Now, number one, gag reflexes. How good are your gag reflexes"? Mrs. Williams glanced down at the paper and then back at me. "My gag reflex is not that good. My husband use to always complain about that". Mrs. Williams let out a jolly laugh. "It was a joke, well, not really." Beatrice and I looked at each other and laughed.

I looked over at Mrs. Williams. "Well, we have lidocaine to numb your tongue and throat. So, that area in your mouth will be relaxed more". Mrs. Williams kept nodding her head nervously. "Ok, do I have to swallow the snake as well"? I smiled, "Let me finish going over the steps.

This way, you'll know, gradually, on what to do". I cleared my throat again. "Now, once your mouth is numbed, we will summons Amaya out of her crate." Mrs. William's interrupted, "Um, Amaya"? I smiled again out of nervousness because she kept interrupting.

Beatrice could see I was getting a bit annoyed. "Amaya is the rainbow serpent. Basically, when her eggs are consumed, they become the fountain of youth and immortality". Mrs. Williams took a deep breath. "Well, how do you know, she will lay eggs every time"? I turned around in my chair. "Amaya has been conditioned. Because she is a mystical creature of youth, she never goes dry of eggs". Mrs. Williams shook her head. "I see". I glanced back down at the paper and continued the steps. "After Amaya is summoned, we will need for you to, Open your Mouth. At that point, Amaya will enter. She will swirl around several times. Until your body is transformed. At about sixty seconds on the clock. She will lay her eggs. At that point, you will swallow the eggs. You will wait for Amaya to exit, before making any sudden movements.

Don't move your head. While Amaya's in your mouth, you must not bite down. Or gag while she is in there. Do You understand Mrs. Williams"? She nodded her head yes. I could smell that odor getting stronger. The floral scent was completely gone. Even though she was calm, cool, and collective. Fear was overcoming her, which wasn't a good thing. Of course, all of our clients are a little scared at first. They seem to calm down and lose the fear. I took a deep breath. "Mrs. Williams, are you sure you're ready? Do you understand the rules?" Mrs. Williams swallowed deeply and said. "Yes, let's get this over with." I smiled; she seemed a little more confident.

Beatrice begins to mix the Numbing spray, I walked over towards Mrs. Williams and reached for her hand. She looked confused. "Where are we going"? I smiled, "Oh, Nowhere. I'm just moving you to our special procedure chair. Over there in the corner". She looked towards the corner. "Oh, it looks like a dental chair." I giggled a bit, "It's funny you should say that it was a dental chair. We started using them on our clients. So, it would be a little easier for them to keep their heads still."

Mrs. Williams walked over and sat comfortably in the chair. She moved around a bit and made herself comfortable. I walked over to the chair. "Relax your head a bit". She reclined her head back a little, and I positioned the padded fore headpiece. I looked at her, "Comfortable"? She nodded her head, "Yes." Beatrice walked over with the numbing spray. "Open your mouth, please." She said with a great big smile. "Mrs. Williams opened her mouth wide. Beatrice sprayed her tongue and mouth with the mixture. "let's give it a minute, and we will spray again, Ok"?

Mrs. Williams nodded her head, yes. She made a bitter face. "Yuk taste awful". Beatrice looked over at her. "Yes, the idea is to numb your mouth. Not to taste good. Can't offer any water; it will delude the effects. Do you feel any numbing"? Mrs. Williams nodded her head. "yes, yes, I do." She said with a slur. Beatrice picked the bottle back up and walked over to Mrs. Williams. "Great, your slurring, one more round." Mrs. Williams opened her mouth. Beatrice, sprayed one last time. Beatrice placed the bottle on the desk. "Now, you may not be able to talk at this point.

We will start the second stage of the procedure. Ty, can you dim the lights". I walked over to the lights and dimmed them. Amaya did not like bright lights. Although she was under our spell, we didn't want to trigger her. Beatrice cleared her throat. "Now, we will pull Amaya out of the crate." As Beatrice talked, I could feel Amaya's mystic presence. She was ready to come out. The lights were dim, except for a spotlight on Mrs. Williams. Beatrice continued.

 "When Amaya gets in position to enter your mouth. You will open wide. Remember, hold still, Amaya will swirl around. She will get in position herself. Then she will lay the eggs. At that point, wait for her to exit your mouth. Then, you may swallow. The whole procedure of Amaya being inside your mouth will take approximately sixty seconds".

Beatrice rubs her palms together. "Let's begin,"! I walked over and pulled Amaya's crate out of the corner. I positioned it on the desk in front of Mrs. Williams. I pulled the blanket off the top. I pulled the latch down, opening the crate. Beatrice and I stood back as Amaya slithered her way out of the crate. Amaya projected into a beautiful half woman half snake. She begins swaying. Mrs. Williams's eyes became enlarged. She looked afraid. But she was captured under Amaya's spell. Amaya coiled back down into a small snake. She slithered and swayed as she got closer and closer to Mrs. William's face.

Amaya was ready to enter. Beatrice stepped forward and said. "OPEN YOUR MOUTH". Mrs. Williams opened wide. Amaya entered slowly. Enchanting music played in the background as the procedure took place. It keeps Amaya calm, along with the dim lights. Amaya's whole body was now inside of Mrs. Williams's mouth. Mrs. Williams closed her eyes as if it were unbearable. Beatrice looked down at the stopwatch. "Sixty seconds, and she was free to go." She whispered. Amaya swirled and swirled inside of Mrs. Williams's mouth until her whole body was coiled inside.

Amaya's head was now visibly turned forward inside of Mrs. Williams's mouth. You could see her eyes. They begin to glow green. This was a good sign. Thirty seconds left on the clock. Mrs. Williams grabbed the arm of the chair. She started to sweat. Beatrice and I looked at each other with concern. Beatrice swiftly but quietly walked over and grabbed Mrs. Williams's hand. She did this to calm and support her. Saliva started dripping down the corners of Mrs. Williams's mouth.

She started tapping her right foot, out of nervousness. I walked over quickly and put my hand on her knee. I glanced at Beatrice; this had never happened before. I glanced at the stopwatch, twenty seconds left. This whole one minute felt like Eternity. Amaya begins to rattle her tail. The sounds pierced through my ears with delight. This meant she was about to lay her eggs. A sigh of relief comes out of Beatrice's mouth.

I glanced at the stopwatch, fifteen seconds left. Mrs. Williams left leg started tapping out of nervousness. I put the stopwatch in my mouth. I used my last free hand to put pressure on Mrs. Williams's left knee. I started to sweat. I looked up at Beatrice. She was now holding both Mrs. Williams's hands. At that moment, we heard gurgling noises coming from Mrs. Williams's mouth. She was starting to gag. Beatrice started to panic. "NO, Mrs. Williams, please, five seconds left!" "PLEASE, you can do this"!

At that point, Mrs. Williams started shaking her head, no and gaging more and almost ejecting Amaya out of her mouth. Mrs. Williams shook her head from side to side. She was trying to vomit Amaya out. Amaya fell into the left side of Mrs. Williams's mouth, and Amaya's eyes became red. I looked at Mrs. Williams's face. Her color was being sucked out of her! I stood up, "Beatrice do something"! Beatrice grabbed her gloves in preparation to pull Amaya out. I panicked and turned around frantically to grab Amaya's crate off the desk as I turned back around to bring the crate over. I heard Beatrice scream. I dropped the crate out of fright.

I turned around and saw Mrs. Williams's face. I almost fell over. I put my hand over my mouth. Mrs. Williams's face was a pale gray with tiny black streaks. The life was being sucked out of her. Beatrice yanked Amaya's head out of Mrs. Williams's mouth. I came out of my trauma and grabbed the crate. I opened the crate door, and Beatrice throws Amaya inside. I slammed the door tight and locked the metal door. Beatrice took the protective gloves off. She quickly checked for a pulse in Mrs. Williams's neck. Beatrice looked at me. She had devastation in her eyes. She couldn't find a pulse. I left Amaya inside the crate. I ran over and quickly grabbed her wrist. I frantically tried to find a pulse, nothing!

Beatrice started breathing heavy. A tear trickled down her right eye. "She's dead"! I stood back and dropped her cold, lifeless hand. I begin to cry, I couldn't speak. Beatrice and I looked at each other. Both our faces were flushed, and the tears Wouldn't stop pouring down. I licked my lips. "We have to call the ambulance." Beatrice looked over at me with amazement in her eyes. "What? We can't! "They will take us to jail, Ty! What the hell is wrong with you?

I couldn't believe what I was hearing. "Beatrice, it was an accident! We didn't kill her,"! Beatrice shushed me. "Shhhhh, keep your voice down! These walls are thin. you can't be screaming the word, KILL!" I looked into her eyes; she was afraid. I had known Beatrice since I was five-years-old. I had never seen that type of fear in her eyes. I gulped deeply, "Then what, do we do Beatrice"? She looked over at me and started tearing up again.

She started shaking her head, no. "I don't know, but we can't call the cops Ty. We just can't! Nobody will understand this. You know that, Ty"! I took a deep breath. "We can lie and say she got bit by a snake or something." Beatrice rolled her eyes, "With no bite marks? Yeah, that's smart. Look Ty, I have a husband and a son who needs me! I can't go to jail, I just can't! I looked over at Mrs. Williams, her body was slouched over. The only thing that was stopping her from falling out of the chair was the forehead piece we used to keep her head from moving.

I was confused; I had to clear my head. How could this happen! One hundred and eleven procedures in one year. Nothing like this had ever happened. Beatrice started pacing back and forth. After about four laps. She looked over at me. "We got to bury the body. We have to get rid of the evidence. You worked in a crime lab, Ty. You should know what to do". I shot Beatrice a dirty look. "I ran DNA samples, Beatrice, not help cover up murders!" Beatrice turned around fast. I guess my comment infuriated her. "Are you fucking serious, Ty! We didn't kill anybody! If anything, this was her fault.

We gave her instructions, and we told her what to do! She said she was ready; this is not our fault Tituba. And we are not going down for this"! She always knew how to hit me in my heart — calling me by my full name. Beatrice was like my sister. We grew up together. She accepted me for who I was. She was my best friend. I didn't want to lose her. I sighed. "How do you want to do this." Beatrice started tearing up again. "We can either bury her or throw her body in the island water." I shook my head. "Water is out of the question. Her body will wash up somewhere".

I thought really hard. Beatrice looked at me. "What about burring her body in that old abandoned cemetery? My eyes bucked. "I'm not burring her on my grandmother's property, I won't do it"! Beatrice sighed, "that fine, we just have to move, and fast, we have seven other appointments today." I looked over at her. "Well, we can't move her now, Beatrice. We will wait until its dark. We will just have to hide the body for now". Beatrice started shaking her head. "We can't move her out of this office right now. We have clients here". I took a deep breath. "The only thing we can do. Is put her body in the closet until today's sessions are over".

Beatrice started to tear up again. "This is a mess". I wiped my face. "We don't have a choice right now. "We have to get through these next seven procedures. People paid their money". Our clients need us." We both looked at each other. Beatrice walked over and put her arms around me. She begins to cry. I embraced her; we both looked over at Mrs. Williams's lifeless body. Beatrice wiped her face. "Let's get this over with." We both walked over. I grabbed a box of latex gloves. I handed a pair to Beatrice.

We both gloved up. I walked over first and unlatched the forehead strap. Her head dropped down to her chest. Mrs. Williams was a chunky lady. "Ok, Beatrice, you get her legs, and I'll get her top.? Beatrice nodded, yes. I got in front of Mrs. Williams and pulled her arms. Her body rolled completely onto the ground, which produces a loud thud. My eyes widened, "Um Beatrice, you were supposed to have her legs." I whispered. Beatrice grabbed her forehead. "I'm sorry, it just all happened so fast. I have her legs now".

I took a deep breath. "On the count of three, ok"? Beatrice nodded yes. "One, two, three". We lifted her body and semi dragged her over to the closet. We had to stop and take a break. Beatrice was breathing heavily. "Oh my God, she feels like a ton of bricks." I caught my breath. "I know, we are almost done. We just have to get her inside the closet and position her correctly". The closet was empty. We never stored anything in there, just our coats.

Beatrice opened the closet door. We slide her body inside. We folded her arms so they wouldn't hang out. We closed the closet door. I grabbed the skeleton key from the desk and locked it up. We both felt relieved for the moment. Beatrice turned to me. "Did she pay cash or credit card?" I walked over to my desk. I pulled her file up on the computer. My eyes widened. "She used a credit card, Beatrice." Beatrice slapped her forehead. "Shit,"! Beatrice started to think. "I mean, we can cancel the services. And, say she never showed up". I looked more into her file on the computer. "Beatrice, we really need to think this through. I agree with reimbursing the funds.

This way, it won't look so suspicious. Credit cards leave a trail. She was the first person here this morning. Nobody saw her but us. If we refund the money and say she never arrived, then there shouldn't be an investigation". Beatrice stared into space. She slowly begins to come out of her stupor. "I hope your right, Ty". We both became silent and just stared into space. There was no need for words. We were both afraid. I hoped we could get away with this.

We finished all the procedures that day with Mrs. Williams's rotting corpse in the closet. We had a successful day, for the most part. Everyone completed the procedure. We had some guest that were staying overnight. Until their flights departed in the morning, that night, we did rounds in the hallway to ensure all the guests were inside their rooms. No one was out on the beach. We had to make sure the coast was clear. We had a pully chart that we used to help people bring in large sums of luggage.

I discretely pulled it into the office. I closed and locked the door behind me. Beatrice was putting her gloves on. I grabbed a pair as well. "Good idea about the cart Ty." I shot her a semi smile. "Well, we got options here. We can put her body on the pulley. Then, we walk a mile through the woods to the abandoned cemetery. Or, we can put her body in the back of the trunk of the bed and breakfast van." Beatrice thought for a minute, "I think it would be best to pull her through the forest. This way, nobody sees the van leave. Our clients are our alibies. They will say the van and other vehicles were here all night."

I sighed, "Well, we better get this show on the road. It's almost midnight. Let's load her up on the cart. And, get her out of here." Beatrice opened the closet door. She uncrossed her arms and grabbed her hands this time. I bent down and grabbed her legs. The stench from the closet hits my nostrils. It hadn't even been twenty-four hours. I could smell the death eroding from her body. I had the gift of olfactory. I could smell body chemistry. Fear, death, sickness, happiness, you name it, I could smell it. Each emotion gave off a particular scent. I was always sniffing and smelling things as a child. I'd always say, "What's that smell"? When entering a room.

And people would say, "what smell?" As if I were crazy. That's when I realized they couldn't smell what I could smell. I didn't know it was a gift until my grandmother told me. Being able to smell scents that others couldn't, was a gift and a curse. When I was nine, my aunt Teresa came to stay with my grandmother and I. Along with Taylor, my cousin who was only ten months old. Aunt Tereasa was about eight months pregnant.

Unfortunately, her husband had been abusive to her. The day she arrived, I inhaled her scent. Of course, I smelled fear and sadness. But most of all, I smelled death. She was alive and well. So I knew, the baby she carried in her stomach, was dead. I smelled it; death had a pungent odor. Nothing in this world smelled exactly like it.

It was a distinctive smell. Not from this realm. I wanted to tell her, but I didn't know how. I was only nine. I didn't know how quite to put it in words. I mean, I knew what it smelled like. No words could ever replace that scent. My aunt went into labor three weeks later. My grandmother rushed her to the hospital. I stayed at home. I waited by the window sill, that day. My grandmother returned with sadness in her eyes. She looked at me and said, "Why didn't you tell me. I needed to know so, I could have been prepared". I looked up at her big brown eyes, and I said. "I didn't want her to hate me. So, I kept it a secret". She rubbed my head and began to hug me. "She'll be ok, once the suddenness leaves. Sadness is only a temporary emotion. She'll forgive herself and move on".

As I hugged my grandmother, I could smell something new on her. Her chemistry changed. I broke free from the hug, and I looked into her eyes again. "Grandma, please go to the Dr. soon…please, promise me you'll go". She smiled down at me. "My dear child, I'll head out first thing in the morning. I don't' want you worrying your pretty little head over me". I smiled and hugged her tighter. I visualized in my mind. All the sickness I smelled coming from my grandmother's aura. I saw blackness lifting out of her body. Black clouds begin to lift. I could tell, this was healing her, just a little bit. And it was real. She was all I had. I wasn't going to lose her.

Not to any sickness, person, or death! I could keep her strong and healthy. And I did, for many, many years to come. A sound of snapping fingers pulled me back into my current realm. Beatrice was standing there, snapping her fingers. "Earth to Ty! We don't have time for these fading spells. We have to get this body out of here". I shook the dizziness off. "I'm sorry, sometimes I get pulled in." Beatrice slightly smiled with understanding. "Past or present Ty"? I pushed the cart closer to the closet door. "Past, back to grandmama."

Beatrice shot me a look of concern, "I miss her too, Ty." I felt my face become flushed. "What do you think she would say? What do you think she would say about, what's happening tonight"? I couldn't compose myself. I let a tear run out of the corner of my right eye. Beatrice sighed, "Ty, she wouldn't want you to rot away in a jail cell. Over a mistake, that I know. Please, we have to move now". We lifted Mrs. Williams. "On the count of three. One, two, three." We got her body onto the luggage cart. She was much easier to move around on wheels.

We covered her up with a blanket. I quietly opened the door and looked outside. The coast was clear. We pushed the cart out of the office and towards the emergency doors in the back. Beatrice switched off the alarm. We pulled her lifeless body outside. Into the crisp cool air. It felt whimsical upon my skin. So cold and refreshing. Like sipping cold water on an extremely hot and humid day. I took the first round of pulling the luggage cart.

Beatrice took the second round. We moved briskly through the forest. It was dark outside. The sounds of the crickets and other insects filled my ears. All the delicious scents of fruits and vegetables filled my nostrils. We must have passed through a deep forest garden. The moonlight fell upon us, guiding the way. I was never afraid of these woods. Beatrice and I spent a lot of time in them as kids. We knew them like the back of our hands. You could blindfold me, and I could still find my way home. All I had to do was touch the trees and inhale their scent. Each one smelled quite different. Giving off different patterns of waves.

I'd, later on, found out. Those waves that I could see and feel were called vibrations. As we were running through the forest, I could still sense and smell every single last one of them. It had been a while since my receptors connected with theirs. Oh, how I missed being one with the trees. The dirt, the moon, the rocks, and the crystals. Even though we were doing a horrible thing, nature was upgrading my soul and connecting to me as I passed through. It felt amazing. Of course, as a child, these feelings were more intense.

As we get older, we forget the little things that make us happy and feel good — just a brisk walk through the forest on a late-night adventure. The wind magically ran its fingers through my hair. My scalp begins to tingle. The space between my two eyes begin to tingle. Beatrice looked back at me with a big smile on her face. I could tell she was experiencing the same joy. We approached the abandoned cemetery as we came back to reality. We stop pushing and pulling the luggage cart.

Beatrice caught her breath. She was short-winded from the brisk walk. She was huffing and puffing as she spoke. "I am completely out of shape." I started laughing, "Yeah, skinny and out of shape does not mix well." Beatrice shot me a dirty look. "Ok, Ms. Vegetarian, let's find a spot and fast. We got a whole lot of digging to do". We both started looking around. I peeped an empty spot. Or what appeared to be an empty spot. "Over there, to your right." Beatrice turned around and saw what I was looking at." We pushed and pulled the body over closer.

Beatrice stopped pulling and rubbed her hands together. "I hope this is a good spot…well, let's dig in and get the hell out of there". We both took out a shovel from the luggage cart. Beatrice took her shovel and with all her might, drilled the tip into the ground. A bunch of dirt splattered into the wind. We both started digging like our lives depend on it. How in the hell did we get ourselves into this? The night wind howled loudly, and the crickets and locus sound filled our ears. As we dug and dug and dug.

Chapter 2

BEFORE THE STORM!

Flash forward.

That morning I decided to pack my things. We have another girl's getaway this weekend. Of course, at my grandmother's old bed breakfast on the island. I decided that before I packed. I'd go inside the ethers and meet with my spirit guides. I had been so confused about so many different events going on in my life. Meditation and going into the realms gave me clarity. I would wake up with answers. Right now, I needed answers. I got off my bed and walked into my crystal room.

It was an empty room in my condo, that I decorated like a botanica. It was full of exotic crystals, big and small — lots of beautiful rare plants. Money trees and bonsai's, to name a few. On my desk laid my wands and huge amethyst crystals. Tons of essential oils, potion bottles, herbs, dried roses, and pounds of white sage. The room was magical and enchanting. All the energy that beamed from this one room. It was electrifying and relaxing, all at the same time. I sat down at my desk.

I took a small amount of white sage from a bundle. I put it inside my rainbow shell and lit it. I inhaled the alluring scent deeply but lightly. The white smoke filled my nostrils and cleared out my negative thoughts and feelings of doubt. I felt renewed and refreshed. As I watched the smoke swirl and come towards my face. A small stream of smoke brushed my left cheek. As it danced and moved, it was putting me under its spell. White sage always had a way of seducing me. I took my psychic oil off my desk.

I opened the dropper and squeezed a small amount on my fingertips. I rubbed it on my forehead, between my eyes. The oil helps open the third eye a little bit. I got out of my seat and grabbed circular crystal quartz from my window sill. It was a special piece of quartz. I used crystals to help advance me to higher realms quicker. I needed to tap in fast today. Lately, it's been rush, rush, rush. With work and other things, I had ongoing. The extra help was nice. I stood up from my chair and walked around the desk. I laid down on the floor. I put the crystal quartz on my forehead. I closed my eyes and looked inside. I saw the violet flame quickly. I knew I was already at my crown chakra and ready to go further.

I inhaled deeply and held it for as long I could. I let the oxygen fill my head, my heart, my stomach, my kidneys, liver, and spleen as my physical body was being nourished with the air. I traveled further up, outside of my body. I exhaled slowly, I waited a few seconds and inhaled deeply again. I nourished my body once again with the oxygen. I floated higher and higher into the subconscious. I finally felt that familiar warmth Of love, I was floating; everything was black. Small stars lit the realm.

My spirit guides slowly appeared to me. I had two, Ioleon, and Elta. Their names were a little different from our earth names. I also had a dragon, and she appeared shortly. She was black, with beautiful mystical skin, almost like glitter. She shimmered, I'd ride her at times. Her name is Ciseally. These are the guides that watch over me daily. They keep me from harm. They guide me through life. It took me a while to get to know them. And, have them reveal their names to me. Lots and lots of mediation and connecting to the spiritual realms. Or as they call it, the ethers. Here in the ethers, you had to be careful. Sometimes, if you went too far, you see lots of other things. Lots of other unexplainable things. Things you only see in Science fiction or fantasy movies. As a kid, you're told that these things, these beings, these animals, don't exist.

But, actually, they do. They are just in different worlds, different realms, they've always existed. I exhaled as their celestial faces filled my vision. Some nights it was really hard for me to enter the realms, especially after not sleeping and drinking a bottle of wine. But, I made it back and seeing them made me tear up. Ioleon walked over to me. She was unusually tall; her skin was bronze. Not like a human, but like a crayon. She had what seemed to be little tribal lumps around her eyes. Above and underneath. They trickled down her nose in a straight line.

Her hair was long, and it hung down to her knees. She wore two French braids mixed in with her curly hair. Her eyes were a solid black. She wore black leather-like tight pants. With a long black veil as a shirt. She smiled as she saw me. She walked over towards me and hugged me. Elta was next in line. Elta, wouldn't reveal herself to me for a long time. She didn't think I would understand. I begged and begged and begged. Until one day, she said, I was ready.

One day she appeared to me in the ethers. Her skin was a pale blue, and she had cat-like features. But, she also looked human. It was kind of hard to explain. Elta had long dreadlocks. She kept the top half in a bun. She wouldn't reveal herself to me until I leveled up in dimensions. Which I did, it took some time, but I got it. I learned that being with nature, upgrade your DNA. So, I started spending lots of time at the local waterfall. She was proud of me. They both walked towards me with Cisealy right behind them. They both hugged me at the same time. I embraced all their love. My heart chakra felt lite and glowed green.

Oh yes, amazing things happen in the ethers. I felt Cisealys breathe on my forehead. I reached out and petted her stout. Ioleon pulled back and looked at it. "Where you been, stranger,"? I sighed, "working my ass off, extremely tired." She smiled, "You can't make it to the ethers, sweetie, without rest." I sighed again, "I know, I just have to find time to meditate daily." She touched my face, "the more you come, the easier it is to get here." I smiled, "I know". They walked me over, into the white light. There was no longer darkness. The scenery changed, there was a blue sky and green grass — kind of like a meadow. I sat down on what appeared to be a rock.

Elta smiles at me. "So, what seems to be the problem"? I took a deep breath. "I've just been confused lately, I'm thirty-three and still, no husband, no children." Eta smiled, "It's coming, no need to worry about that stuff. It's the least of your problems". I raised my eyebrow.

They always had a way of making me think deeply. "I know you guys are with me, and I see 333 almost daily, sometimes three, four times a day. I know you are with me, no matter what". Ioleon smiled at me. "I know why you're here." She walked over and placed her hand on my forehead. Everything went black, and I woke up back in my crystal room, on the floor.

It happens like that at times. I won't remember the conversation, but I'd wake up with all the answers. I slowly pulled myself up off the floor. I decided to take a long shower before packing and getting on the road. Grandmother's old bed and breakfast was about four hours from Atlanta. It was left to me in her will. My grandmother and I had a special bond. I grew up with her. My biological mother abandoned me. She ran off with my dad. Or so I was told. I never had the chance to even lay eyes on her. Grandmother and I spent years looking for her.

We figured they were either dead. Or just didn't want to be found. So, we stopped the hunt when I turned eighteen; it didn't matter anymore to me. Grandmother was my mom. We had a special bond. We would meet up in the ethers sometimes and explore different realms. Grandmother's old bed and breakfast sit on an island. It is now called Hilton Head in South Carolina. Grandmother had to fight for her land. They offered her loads of money to buy the land. But, Grandmother wouldn't take it. She was proud to own the bed breakfast. It was passed down from generation to generation in our family.

She always told me she would never let it go. The hotels and resorts were built up around her small ranch bed and breakfast. Once the big franchises moved in. It was hard for my grandmother to make lots of money. But, she still held her ground. Grandmother's prices were a lot cheaper than the hotels. Plus, you got a delicious hot breakfast that came along with your stay. Her prices and food kept her in business. People were always looking for a deal while on vacation and business. Grandmother left the bread breakfast to me. It closed down after a while when she got sick. I was living in Atlanta at the time and had just bought a condo.

Grandmother was ninety-two years old. She had kept her financial situation a secret from me. She didn't want me to worry. Bed and breakfast was paid off, but the upkeep was getting too much for grandmother in her old age. I always felt guilty about the situation. Here I was living my life in Atlanta as she struggled on the island to keep things afloat. I needed my peace with the situation, but I just never found it. Work was very demanding at times. I got my bachelor's in forensic science. I worked in a crime scene lab where we ran DNA to determine if accused murderers really killed their victims. Not a hard job, just very demanding. Due to the fact, there were not enough lab specialists. We had a lot on our plates, and people's lives depended on our results.

I couldn't complain, my salary was awesome. Just long hours and bombarded with work. I stepped into the shower and turned the water on. I was still in a daze from being in the ethers. I forgot to warm the water up first. The cold water was a shock to my system. It was quite invigorating at the same time. I decided to let the ice-cold water cleanse me. It was summertime and very hot. I was meeting the girls for our monthly weekend getaway. Beatrice, Lilly, and Zorah. Every once in a while, Patrice would show up. Patrice was what I would label as a frenemy. She was close to Lilly, Beatrice's older sister.

She only came around to show off new cars, jewelry, etc. and was often caught talking about all of us behind our backs. I never understood people like Patrice. She wanted so desperately to be our friends. When we finally decided to be around her, she's just showing off new items purchased — bragging on fake achievements just to make us feel inferior. Her energy was bad, and it smelled awful. Usually, people with hateful energy had foul odors. It smelled like dead meat. I never understood why we kept her around.

I saw no reason or pleasure in having fake friends. It was something I just never understood. Beatrice and I grew up together in South Carolina. She was my best friend. Like the sister I never had. All the way back to kindergarten, and we've been so close ever since.

Beatrice also lived in Atlanta. We moved here together after college. We were roommates for a while. Until Keith came along. Beatrice married Keith, they bought a home and had one son together. Cameron was Keith and Beatrice's sons. He was only six and stole my heart the moment he was born. Beatrice, Cameron, and I had a special bond.

He was almost like my son too. And I lavished lots of love onto him. During our time together. I soaked up some of that loneliness I had. I was longing to be a mother one day. I loved it when Keith and Beatrice had date nights. That meant Cameron and I could spend time together. And fill the missing pieces that only a child could replace.

Flash Back to Gullah Land

I got my first taste of motherhood, back when my aunt Teresa showed up with Taylor. I was about seven, and aunt Teresa was so broken from the abuse. Aunt Tereasa just laid around the house all day, staring at the wall. Grandmama was spending all her time nourishing Teresa back to health, using her herbs, crystals, and secret potions. Potions, she would one-day hand down to me.

With Grandmama being so tied up, that left me to take care of Taylor. I was only seven, but oh I how Loved that baby. I fed her bottles and changed her diapers. She was like one of my baby dolls; grandmama had bought me for Christmas. The first day she brought her into the house. I could smell her scent a mile away.

The fragrance was like nothing I had ever experienced. It was almost intoxicating, as soon as the scent hit my nose. It set off several receptors in my brain. As well as different centers of my brain. Tingles upon tingles upon tingles hit my gray matter like a ping pong game. I could tell my dopamine levels were rising. Almost like a drug, but a good one. My eyes zoomed in on the baby's pores. The scent was leaking from the sweat glands. The alluring mix of love, excitement, and warmth, times ten thousand. That is the best way to explain a baby's bouquet. But then, the aroma of love is hard to explain if one does not have the gift. At that moment, I knew why people got baby fever, repeatedly.

She was a delight and oh so special to me. When My aunt Tereasa got better and finally had enough strength. She took Taylor, and they moved to New Orleans. She got a new job she couldn't refuse. That day I watched her pack Taylor up and took her away. I cried myself to sleep that night. I felt like a piece of me was leaving. I guess my grandmother heard my cries. Or she knew what I was feeling at the moment. Grandma and I had a special bond. We were both empaths and could easily pick up on each other's emotions. She came into my room that night and rubbed my back. She comforted me until I felt better and went back into her room.

Years went by, and I would see Taylor over the summers. I'd hug her and kiss her and indulge in all of her love. She was growing up to be the sweetest little girl, and very pretty. The Jones girls were all so very pretty. We all had long dark hair, wavy, and high cheekbones, Golden sun-kissed skin, long eyelashes, and juicy full lips. My grandmother was quite the catch back in her day. One summer, when Taylor was in town, we were playing as we usually did. I was about twelve, and Taylor was five. We suddenly heard weird noises coming out of my grandmother's special room. Grandmother's special room was full of enchanted flowers, plants, crystals, and herbs. Grandmama was a healer. All the Gullah people and townspeople came to her when they were sick, Or when they needed something, like money, or love. The sounds got louder and louder. We went right over and put our ears to the door. Grandmother was in there with one of her clients.

Grandmother did magic, and it wasn't a secret. Her nickname around town was madam (She-Wolf). Grandmother had a special connection with the wolves. She had several pets growing up. Most Gullah people did magic. Well, the ones who hadn't been converted to Christians. But, grandmother's powers were the most powerful of all Gullah land. All the townspeople would come to her with their problems, and she would fix them. Whether it was something herbal or magical, grandmama would always fix it.

We listened in a little closer and heard more weird sounds. The smell coming from underneath the door was horrific. I had smelled that scent before; the client in the room was ridiculed with Anger. Grandmother was administering one of her revenge spells. We heard someone get up and move out of the chair. We hurried back into the living room and watched the door. Out came a heavy-set woman who had seem to be crying, but now, she had a smile on her face.

I left Taylor on the couch. I took the opportunity to walk into my grandmother's special room. She was cleaning up the mess she made. She started clearing out the energy of the room with white sage. She stopped clearing and looked up at me. "What do you need child, I'm just finishing up?" I swallowed deeply. "Gram, I thought we were good witches. I know what you did in this room. I could smell the ingredients to the spell". She took a deep breath and paused, from walking around the room, wafting the smoke. "Come here, sit down for a minute, let me talk to you." I walked over to my grandmother and sat down at the table.

"My child, we are good witches, we… are of the light. Sometimes light has to fight the darkness. Every day we are dealing with spiritual warfare. Good versus evil, light versus dark. This battle will never end. The Gods and Goddesses gave us these powers to use. They need our help at times. Now, we are both light and darkness, but balance is needed between the two. Without one, the other doesn't exist. Some entities look like humans, but they are not really humans. They are demons in the flesh. One day, you will watch a demon suck the life out of someone you love. And, at that point, you will have to decide if you will be that person's karma.

At that moment, while looking at your loved one suffer. That darkness will rise in you and come through you. Like a raging force, use it as you will. Help rid the earth of these disgusting parasites. All they want is a host to suck dry until they are gone. If we let these negative beings destroy our good, then what help are we to humanity? Our brothers and sisters need us, all humans. All this, Do no harm, in magic. Just another trick, so we won't retaliate against the dark ones.

The great Martin Luther King once said. The hottest place in hell is reserved for those who remain neutral in times of great moral conflict. We have to fight back. You will understand once you experience a demon in the flesh. You will be equipped to deal with it. You will feel that anger rise in you, but never hopelessness or despair. Because you'll know exactly what to do."

She looked into my eyes and leaned over and kissed me. My grandmother was the sweetest woman in the world. Her long wavy hair sways from side to side at her waist while she continued clearing the room. That summer, Taylor left me again, and again I was saddened and heartbroken. I didn't see her for many years after that. We kept in contact via letters. As time went by, we started sending each other emails and text messages. I got a call one day when Taylor was about twenty. I was twenty-seven and living in Atlanta. It was Taylor's mom, my aunt Teresa. She called me hysterical and crying.

She told me that Taylor had met some guy and ran off with him. They were still in New Orleans, but she couldn't find her. Word on the streets, the man, who she ran off with Strung her out on heroin and was selling her body for drugs. Aunt Tereasa cried her eyes out to me; she begged me for help. At that point, Grandmother was going through Alzheimer's and couldn't remember much. "Please, Ty, you have to come and do something! Mama taught you all her tricks and magick. He's going to kill her if I don't get her help, please! The cops won't help because she refuses to leave the man.

Almost like, he got something on her. I'd do it myself, but I became a Christian, about ten years ago. I never told mama because I knew it would break her heart. She wanted us to keep the tradition of Gullah island. Worship the ancestors, use herbs to nourish the body and magick for whatever we needed. I got lost in my marriage. I've lost myself, my heritage, EVERYTHING…Ty, I need you"! She broke down, crying again. At that moment, I decided to book a flight to New Orleans.

Chapter Three

Man Down!

My taxi pulled up to the airport. My heart was racing, I had been communicating back and forth with Taylor. I did not alert her of my visit. I texted her for days and told her I was sending her a package. I approached the kiosk and printed out my tickets. I walked towards the security line. I packed my most important crystals and herbs. I brought my male shaped candle — a poppet with a few other items I needed for the spell to work. I made sure my bag would be checked on the plane and not a carry-on. I had no time to explain to security what those things were for. After an hour, wait through security. I now had to find my port and board my plane.

Atlanta airport was always quite busy. The process could take forever. But, I made it through and found my port in the nick of time. I got to line and handed the lady my ticket. She smiled as she received it. At that moment, I glanced at her face. The smile froze for a minute and then started to shift. This often happened when I encountered different entities, and she looked like a human. But, only she wasn't. She stood there, frozen with a smile as she parted her lips to speak. "Thank you, Madame, your flight will be leaving shortly." She let out a ghastly laugh. Her words slurred as she spoke to me. Almost like a record being played backward. She was in slow motion. This happened to most clones, programming mishaps.

I smiled and walked passed her to board the flight. Clones always had a synthetic smell to them. Their body odor smelled like burnt plastic. Although they had human DNA, they didn't possess a soul, which made them reek of burnt plastic. Most had bad Body odor. It wasn't easy having my gift, knowing that in this world, Many, many different kinds of humanoids existed. You have your hybrids, different mixes of species. Of course, clones, who are genetically modified. Most humans were genetically modified. But if the motherboard could be fixed, Humans could possess all powers. Fixing the motherboard is a lot easier than most would think. Meditation, connecting to the earth, using earth's resources awaken the cells. The DNA repairs and most memory is brought back to the surface — also, powers and abilities. Just connecting to source energy can repair

DNA. But, it doesn't happen overnight, and it takes dedication. Just being in nature, can upgrade your DNA. I came out of my mental stupor as I felt a tap on my shoulder. I turned around; there stood a tall woman with red hair — also, a very tall man with blonde hair standing behind her. "Man, you're holding up the line. My husband and I need to get to our seats." I felt my face become flush. I forgot I was walking down the aisle of the airplane to find my seat.

I looked into her eyes. "Oh, I'm sorry". I moved to the side so they could get by. That happened a lot for people like me. We always got lost inside our heads. I was often called a space cadet as a child and even throughout high school. I checked the row number on my ticket and found my seat. I was by the window which I loved. I like decoding the clouds with my eyes. They never looked real to me. As I sat down, I started thinking about Taylor again. I pulled a photo out from my purse. I had been holding onto it for years. I smiled as I looked at it. Taylor was always a beautiful girl. A small tear trickled out of my right eye. I fumbled around in my purse until I felt my shades. I placed them on. I was a bit nervous.

But I was not afraid. I knew what had to be done. But, I had to see it for myself. This type of magic should not be used lightly. It should only be used upon demons that walk the earth amongst humans. My grandmother taught me a lot, such a gifted woman, Died at ninety-nine years old. She always told me she'd live to be one hundred. Three days before her birthday, she died. She told me that things were different for my generation, and we could live a lot longer. That was the reason why they were trying to destroy us, with diet and destruction.

The plane journeyed into the clouds. I decided to take a nap. The flight to New Orleans was short. As my eyes awakened, we were porting into New Orleans. It was very strange that I fell asleep. I never sleep on planes, and my spirit guides probably pulled me into a meeting about this trip. And, although I couldn't remember, all the answers I needed were uploaded.

Strange how that happens at times. As I started to wake up and stretch. I gathered my small items into my purse before the plane landed. Taylor and I had a special way of connecting mentally. Although I could feel a block lately, she wasn't aware that I was coming to New Orleans. The man who was selling her body was controlling her heavily. I knew her phone calls and text messages were being monitored. I told her I was sending her a package. Of course, she thought it was money for drugs. So, she gave me the address to where she was staying.

She was actually living in a hotel. How could this have happened to such a beautiful soul? I had nightmares about it. I saw her face in many of my dreams. She didn't look well. I loved that little girl. In my eyes she was still a baby. The baby I bottle fed, changed diapers, and rocked to sleep. As the plane landed, most of the passengers cleared out of the aisle. They grabbed their overhead luggage and moved quickly. I sat until the chaos cleared. I rubbed my hands together. I noticed they were wet. My heart was racing. I was getting close to seeing Taylor. I walked off the plane and went to get my luggage. I packed lightly, no need for a wardrobe.

I walked out of the airport in New Orleans. I hailed a cab and got in. She was staying in a hotel on the French quarters. I decided to book a room in the same hotel. I even managed to get a room on the same floor. Across the hall, so I could wait and make sure the demon was gone. I checked into my room. The rooms were very Victorian style with a splash of modern décor. I noticed I had a balcony. I walked out onto it and looked down. I saw the beautiful people and heard whimsical music that delighted my ears. New Orleans was always such a site and full of culture. I wish I was here under better circumstances, no partying for me. I had work to do.

I immediately got into a spy mood. I took off my shoes. I looked out the peephole. No one was in the hallway. I walked across to her door quietly. I put my ear to the door, and I heard sex moans. The smell that hit my nose made my stomach turn. Demons, I smelled them, inside her room. The sounds stopped abruptly. I quickly ran back to my room and quietly shut the door. I put my eye to the peephole. The door opened, a small, dark-skinned older man walked out. He stopped and straightened his tie and clothes. At that moment, I glanced at his eyes. They flickered red. A small frog was implanted in the whites of his eye. Reptilian hybrid it was. All reptilians were not bad, but this one leaving my cousin's room reeked of death.

As I watched him walk down the hall. I waited until he was out of sight. I then positioned myself halfway inside my room and halfway out. I waited until the coast was clear. I briskly walked over to her door. I listened to make sure she was alone. She promised me she would be at the hotel alone, at this time. I told her she had to sign for the delivery. So she must be present. As I neared the door, it was cracked, the guy who left didn't lock it. I looked around, the coast was clear. My heart was pounding as I entered her room. I looked around the room. Same fancy Victorian décor. It was quite different from my room. I didn't see her at first. Then I glanced down and there she was. Handcuffed to the bed lying on the floor. I checked the bathroom to make sure no one was there, and She was alone. I went back to the door and locked it. I ran over to her and kneeled on the floor.

Taylors lustrous long hair was dull and limp. It covered her face. I flipped her over and wiped her hair from her eyes. She was high and trying to come out of her stupor. She looked up at me. The glow from her face was gone. Dark rings plagued her eye pockets underneath her eyes. She stared for several moments. When she realized who I was. She smiled and tried to sit up and hug me. She had on a white lace dress with no underwear. There was a key next to her. I grabbed it and unlocked the cuffs. She sat up and smiled. Tears ran down her face. She finally realized who I was. She grabbed me and hugged me tightly. I hugged her back with all my power.

I gave off energy from my body and transferred it into hers. She was weak and drugged. Taylors grip became limp. She leaned back in my arms and looked at me. "What are you doing here?" She slurred, "You said, you were sending a package." I laid her head in my lap and rubbed her hair. "What happened to you Taylor, why are you living like this"? She sat up slowly, "I'm in love, I'm in love with this man." She was so brainwashed to believe that anyone who loved her would let her live this way. I became angry, "Where is this so-called man? Was it the one who left the hotel room a few minutes ago"?

She looked into my eyes as another tear trickled down her face. "No…it wasn't". I shook my head. "Why are you selling yourself? Why!?" Taylor started to shake her head. "Listen, this is the life God gave me. So, I'm doing the best I can". I became angered, "What God would want you to live this way"? There is nothing Godly about this situation; this is evil and demonic! No God would order you to live this way"! I felt a tear trickle down my face. "Let's go,"! I stood up and pulled Taylor upon her feet.

"Pack your shit; we are leaving now!" I felt her arm jerk away from my hand. "No, I can't,"! I glanced deeply into her eyes; she was gone, far gone. I grabbed her and held her tight. My body scanned hers. I needed to feel her. I hugged her so tight. I detected an ounce of her still left inside, my Taylor. And, at that point, I loosened up and wiped my tears. I smiled; there was hope. A small bit of my Taylor was still there. I grabbed her chin and lifted it. I needed to see into her eyes. "Then, you give me no choice." I helped her sit on the bed.

Taylor started shaking her head. "No, you can't, you can't work magic on him. You can't" She broke down crying again. I cleared my throat. "My mind is already made up." Taylor broke down crying again. My grandmother was right; one day, I would watch someone drain the soul out of someone I loved. And, that day, it was today! It was over for him. I hugged her tightly, "I'll be back." As much as I wanted to stay, I had to prepare. I went back to my room.

 I sat down on the bed. I took a deep breath. I grabbed my magic bag and pulled it closer. I sat it in my lap and stared at the wall.

It had to be done. He was destroying her, and why? I never understood evil. Evil is different from darkness. I learned that as a child. I embraced the darkness that was rising in me. I needed it to destroy this demon. I zipped my bag open, pulled out a black male figured candle, a picture of the demon that I copied from Taylor's Fakebook page, my sack of pins, my Hotfoot oil, and my war water, a packet of dried blackberry leaves, a bag of graveyard dirt, a black cloth and small shovel. It was Saturday like I planned. A perfect day for this kind of spell. I pulled out a small bit of white sage and lit it.

Grandmother always taught me to clear my space. And call upon your spirit guides, if need be, before any spell. I called upon them. The room was filled with that beautiful white sage scent. I just asked that my guides be with me during this moment. I asked that they guide me and give me energy and power. I moved all my items to the desk, and I sat down in the chair. I Toke the black male figured candle. I carved his name in it. I then poured the hotfoot oil into my palms. I rubbed the hotfoot oil into the candle from top to bottom slowly. As I was rubbing the oil, I put my mind to work. I visualized him in a car, driving. I visualized the car sparking flames and then finally blowing up. I stopped rubbing the oil. I took out his picture.

I pinned it to top of the black candle's head. I shoved a pin in his heart. I shoved a pin in his penis. I shoved a pin in his stomach. I shoved a pin to his right side. I shoved a pin to his left side. I took out the black cloth. I placed the candle on top of it. I mixed the graveyard dirt with the dried blackberry leaves. I sprinkled it all over the candle. I laid the candle down. I wrapped it up in the black cloth. I stitched it together with black thread.

I called out aloud his name. "Jeffery Wright, I send you back to the evil veils you rose from," I said it three times and visualized his car blowing up once again. I took out the hammer and hit it with all my might, three times. I gathered the mess and placed it inside my magic bag. The good thing about New Orleans is they had cemeteries everywhere. I waited till nightfall, of course.

I dressed in all black. I wore a black scarf around my hair and face. I tied it beneath my chin. I put on dark shades and wore my black crystals. Being in all black repelled negativity. My black crystals kept me safe and protected. Obsidian was my crystal of choice. I left the hotel and wandered straight into a cemetery. The night air was crisp and alluring. I looked around the graveyard. A few people were visiting loved ones. I found a spot where no one could see. I dug a hole quickly and buried that mess in the graveyard. I went back to the hotel. For seven days straight, I watered the mess with warm water. On that seventh day, I got a call from my aunt Tereasa. She was frantic, "Hello, Ty… You did it; he's gone"!

I had just awakened, it was early in the morning. My head was still a little cloudy. "Calm down aunty, how do you know this to be true"? Her voice became calm. "Turn on the local news." I pulled myself up from under the covers and sat up a bit. I grabbed the remote next to my hotel bed. The news reporter on tv was standing in front of Mercedes Benz Or, what was left of it. The car was still on fire and causing major traffic and delays. I smiled; victory was mine.

"Aunt Tereasa, let me shower and get dressed. I have to go see about Taylor". I ended the call and jumped into the shower. I got dressed and packed my things. It was time to go home. But, before I could that. I had to make sure Taylor was safe and detoxing from the heroine. I went over to Taylor's hotel room. Once again, the door was open. I cracked the door and peeked in. She was sitting on the bed. With her back turned to the door. She just sat and looked out the window.

I walked in slowly. Before I could get passed the door, she called my name. "Ty". She turned around and looked at me. Black mascara ran down her face. I went and sat next to her on the bed and hugged her. I scanned her emotions. She wasn't angry at all. Just sad and confused.

She looked into my eyes, "where have I been all this time"? I stared into her eyes. The power he had over her was gone. But, he drugged her, and that addiction still possessed her body. I had to deal with that before I left New Orleans. I lead her into the bathroom. She showered while I ironed her some appropriate clothes. I also looked on the internet to find a nearby herbal store. There were plenty. Taylor came out of the bathroom, wrapped in a towel. She got dressed and dried her hair. She was still weary and weak. She sat on the bed as she put her shoes on.

She glanced up at me and smiled. My heart warmed because I knew my Taylor was home. I brushed her wild mane and put it into a ponytail. I helped her up. We walked out of the hotel room hand in hand. I checked out of the hotel room. We stopped off at the herbal store. I let Taylor stay in the car. I picked up large sums of herbs she would need to detox. I drove Taylor to her mother's house. We got out of the car. Before we could even make it to the door. Aunt Teresa came flying out the front door. She ran over and hugged Taylor so hard I thought she would pop.

Aunt Tereasa then grabbed me with her other arm. We engaged in a three-way hug in front of the driveway. As our tears dried from our faces, we walked into the house. Aunt Teresa took Taylor to her old room. She put Taylor in bed and let her rest. I sat at the table. Aunt Tereasa walked in and made me a cup of hot tea. I started taking the herbs out of the bag. Aunt Tereasa sat down at the table with me. "I can't even begin to tell you how much I appreciate this." I smiled, "I know Aunt Tereasa. Really, the pleasure was all mine."

Aunt Teresa looked at me with concern. "A man is dead, Ty. You've grown cold throughout the years". I put my cup down, mid-sip. "A man? That wasn't a man. He might have been walking around in the flesh, but he wasn't a man. He had to go back to where he came from. He doesn't belong here. And, he defiantly doesn't belong to killing my cousin slowly. Would you rather it be Taylor or him"? I stared at her weak-minded ass, straight in the eyes. She was afraid. I made her uncomfortable, so I backed down a bit.

"Anywho, I wanted to make a few things for Taylor. I won't be here, so I want you to learn. A special tea, she should sip on throughout the day. And, a cleansing bath, she will bathe in, every night for 30 days.

opioids Be Gone Tea

- 5 grams of Kratom powder

- A slice of fresh ginger

- 2-3 tablespoons of organic honey

- 1 cinnamon stick

- A tablespoon of Passionflower powder

- A small pot of water, alkaline if possible

Put all ingredients in a pot, preferably a loose teapot. Slowly boil these ingredients together. Let stand for 15 minutes. Add more honey if needed. Strain any residue if using a regular pot. Serve and drink.

This special tea will help Taylor with cravings. Also, it will help with withdrawal symptoms. Like nausea, vomiting, and diarrhea. She needs to drink this daily for as long as she can. Don't let the ingredients in the house get low; always have plenty. Also, I will put together and show you how to make a cleansing bath. This cleansing bath will pull the drugs out of her system.

Opioids Be Gone Cleansing Bath

- A half a cup Kratom powder
- 2 tablespoons of Passionflower powder
- Half a cup of Epsom salt
- 1 tablespoon of Frankincense powder
- Half a cup of White sage dried leaves
- 2 tablespoons of Dried Basil leaves
- 2 tablespoons of Dried Rosemary leaves
- Half a cup of Baking soda

Put into a blue bag, burn a blue candle. Make seven bags using this recipe. Pour into your bath water and soak for twenty minutes or more. For 7-30 days, add more days if need be.

Aunt Tereasa, this will pull the drugs out of her body. Please, you must understand. She smiled at me. "Child, I am madam She-Wolfs daughter. I do remember a few things as a child. Before I was married and became lost. I smiled at her. "Why do you think grandma taught me all her secrets and not you?" She looked up into my eyes. She was unprepared for that question. She took a deep breath. "Ty…your, mom, and mama had a very special relationship.

When your mom disappeared, it almost killed her. You, mama, and my sister are the same species. I am different from you all. I think mama knew that when I was born. You all have B plus blood type. I don't, a different breed, so she never taught me. You can have different kinds of kids: different breeds, hybrids, and humanoids. I always thought mama was crazy when she talked like that. But, a lot of her knowledge has stayed with me."

I sipped my tea some more. I wasn't ready to hear my mother being brought up in a conversation. It was a touchy subject. I gulped down the rest of my tea. I have to be leaving soon. My flight leaves in a few hours. I'm going to say goodbye to Taylor. If you need anything, please call". I stood up and walked around the table. My aunt Tereasa stood up. We embraced each other with a hug. I scanned her body for emotion. She was still saddened, and I could smell a bit of fear. I didn't like scanning most people. To me, it was an invasion of privacy. But, my aunt Tereasa had a way of masking how she really felt.

I broke away from the hug, and Aunt Tereasa led me to Taylor's door. Aunt Tereasa went to her room. I knocked on the door. It was open, so I just walked in. Taylor was asleep on the bed. I shook her lightly; she rolled over. Her big beautiful eyes lit up. Due to being drained, she continues to lay. I sat down next to her on the bed. I rubbed her hair. "I have to leave, but I'm always a phone call away. And, if necessary, I can always hop on a plane. She giggled a bit. It was so refreshing to my heart to see her laugh.

She sat up and hugged me tightly. "Thank you; I mean that you saved me." She teared up a bit. I hugged her tightly. As much as I wanted to stay longer, I had to get back to work. I kissed Taylor on her cheek. "I'll call you, now get some rest. I left special teas and cleansing baths for you. I left the recipes and ingredients with your mom." She kissed me on the cheek back and laid back down. "I'll see you in my dreams" She smiled even brighter. I felt warm. "See you in my dreams". She closed her eyes and fell fast asleep. I covered her with a blanket and walked out.

Chapter 4

Girls Get Away

The cell phone rang. It startled me, but, pulled me back into my current realm. I glanced down at my phone. It was my job. I decided not to answer. They had a bad habit of calling me on my days off, always wanting me to put out fires at the lab. I would usually answer. But I was mentally exhausted and needed a break. I decided to text Taylor since she was on my mind. It had been a year since the incident, and she was doing well. I sent her text, just to let her know I was thinking about her. Sometimes just an emoji. I finished up my packing and loaded up the car.

I always loved those four-hour drives. I had some time to think in the car. We tried to have girls getaway at least once a month. Just to relax on the beach and get away from the city. The girls really enjoyed getting away from their husbands and children. The drive was tranquil and quiet. I liked getting arriving on Friday evenings. This way, I could freshen up the place before the girls got there. I made sure all the rooms had clean towels. I always went into my grandmother's room. It was still decorated with all her stuff.

I wasn't ready to change it. She died a little over a year ago. I thought about reopening the resort. Nothing wrong with making a little side cash. But, for now, it was a safe haven with all grand mama's memories and mine. I opened the door to her room. It smelled like fresh cinnamon and ginger, just like grandma. I knew for a fact she was still around. She often came to my dreams. But, most of all, her scent was still in the room. I sat in her rocking chair and looked out of the window. It was very dark outside. The darkness always had a way of making me sleepy. I decided to go to bed and wake up bright and early.

That morning I woke up refreshed and full of energy. Grandmother had so many crystals in her room. It was like being recharged when your batteries go low. I took a shower and got dressed in my bathing suit and put on my sheer beach pants. I was definitely going out on the beach. I needed some sun. My skin was super pale. I loved that golden sand look. Plus, soaking up the sun always made me happy. I often woke up at sunrise when I was there. I'd go out unto the sand barefoot and sun gaze.

The wonderful upgrades I received from sun gazing was awesome. It rejuvenated the motherboard. And administered downloads upon downloads of information. Sungazing also corrected any defects like depression, addiction, forgetfulness, etc. I walked into the kitchen and made sure it was stocked with lots of drinks. I also kept the champagne cooler full. And of course, the cellar was full of organic red wines.

The girls usually got in early to maximize their time. A few came late and only spent one night. Of course, Beatrice would stay for two nights with me. The doorbell rang. I walked from the kitchen and looked out the window. Of course, it was Beatrice. I opened the door, "Bitch what took you so long"? I chuckled out loud. "I only took a second, Bea, come on in." Beatrice walked through the door with one small suitcase.

We walked towards the kitchen. "I know its early, but you want a mimosa"? Beatrice smiled, "Now, you know I want a mimosa." I laughed, "Great I was just pulling out supplies to make a few for everyone. I didn't really feel like cooking, so it's a continental breakfast for everyone. You know the usual, gluten-free bagels, muffins, fruit, and juice." Beatrice grabbed a muffin and started to dig in. "Great because I'm starving."

Beatrice was tall, Mahogany skinned, and beautiful. She resembled a chocolate Barbie doll. We were the prettiest girls in high school. Both different in our way. Beatrice's parents were Gullah, as well. We use to run around on the beach together as children. We hadn't spent much time together lately. Beatrice was very active in her son's and husband's lives. She really enjoyed these weekends together. It gave her time not to be a mom or wife for the weekend. She smiled as she ate her muffin. "I brought some more samples from the cosmetics lab. We are going to make a fortune, Ty. Once we get the formula down pact, start some branding, and we could make millions."

Beatrice worked in a cosmetology lab. They made makeup and beauty products that kept you looking young — reversing the signs of ageing. Beatrice and I were in business together. We were in the midst of creating a cream that was better than Botox. I also had clients on the side, that I sold my herbal remedies to. I also did a little spell work from time to time. Just like my grandmother. But it wasn't lucrative, not just yet. Only had a handful of faithful clients. Work took up most of my time. Killing my creative side. I tried to have a better balance. Sometimes work was just so damn draining.

Beatrice pulled out a plastic bag. "Look at what I got". She laid the bag in front of me. Beatrice pulled out two little jars. She smiled as she looked up at me. "Now, we will take your herbs and crystals and mix it with this cream. Together, this chemical and those herbs will create the fountain of youth". I picked up one of the little jars to give it a closer look. The cream looked pink and sparkly. I looked at Beatrice. "What is this stuff"? I opened the jar and smelled it. Beatrice's eyes lit up. "It's basically Botox, but no injections, just cream. I've been playing around with chemicals in the lab. I designed this formula myself.

I've been using it on myself. I'm the Ginny pig and of course, Lilly. You know she's not turning down any free cosmetics. Even if they are experimental". We both started laughing. "Well, Bea, she is your big sister. Is she still getting that bargain-basement plastic surgery"? Beatrice takes a deep breath. "Girl, you know I warned her about getting those hotel booty injections." My eyes widened. "Wait, what do you mean, the hotel"? Beatrice takes another bite of her muffin and swallows. "She goes to see some women in a hotel who is unlicensed." My eyes grew even bigger! "That's just crazy. If my husband couldn't accept my natural body, then he would have to go kick rocks".

Beatrice nodded her head. "Girl, I wish Keith would come to me with that shit." I walked over to the refrigerator to get some water. I poured two glasses. "I wish you hadn't told me all this. It's going to be hard for me, not stare". I slid Beatrice a glass of water. She picked it up and sipped. "Well, that's not all. She's been reaching into Kim and Kimora's savings account". I almost spit my water out. "For what? Surgeries"? Beatrice sighed. "Yeah, girl. She really thinks all of this is going to stop John, John's whoring around".

I swallowed my water. "John! John's been a whore since high school. Plus, Kim and Kimora are both seventeen. Hope she left something in the poor kid's college funds". Beatrice cleared her throat. "Can you believe someone almost the same age as us, has seventeen-year old's"? I sat down on a stool. "Yeah, well, she started early. Plus, she's five years older than us Bea". Beatrice thinks for a minute. "Yeah, I guess, she's got three now. Had the last baby, because John John is rumoured to have an outside child". I slammed my hand on the counter. "Girl, get out of here"!

Beatrice nodded, "It's the sad truth. Of course, she hasn't told me. Eventually, she will, she always does". At that moment, we heard a loud bang come from grandma's room. We looked at each other. "Ty, what was that"? Beatrice whispered. I wasn't scared, I knew it was grandma, trying to get my attention. "Come on Bea, let's go see, don't be afraid." I started walking, "It's just grandmama; she wants my attention."

Beatrice walked slowly behind me. I opened the door. We both looked around. At first, everything looked about normal. And then, I looked down. The carpet was pulled up, exposing a small doorknob on the floor. I think Beatrice and I saw it at the same time. I bent down and got on my knees. Beatrice swatted down to watch. I immediately turned the knob and pulled upward.

It was like a small door. I pulled more, and it popped open. Beatrice moved back with fright. I leaned over inside the hole. There was a dusty black book inside. I got up from the floor and grabbed a lighter. I sat back down on the floor. I used the light from the lighter. The book had words on it. I still couldn't make out the title. So, I sat the lighter down and just picked the book up. It was super dusty. Once I pulled it out, I closed the little door. I dusted the book off. We both coughed from the thickness of the smoke.

I wiped the book and wiped some more. I clapped both hands together, to get the dust off. I could finally see the title. I read it out loud, "THE BOOK OF NIGRON." As I was holding the book, it started to shake. I dropped it immediately, and a brisk wind swooshed through the room. The book started to glow, and the pages started to flip. Beatrice crawled backward away from the book. She backed herself up against the dresser. I didn't move, and I couldn't. I knew this was a message from grandma, and I wanted to receive it.

The wind stopped blowing, and the book was still. I slowly reached for it. It was opened on page 333. I pulled the book close to me. I realized this was the book, the book I found in the basement when I inherited this place. Grandmother must have moved it. I began to read it. "Immortal Fountain of Youth Spell". I smiled, "See Beatrice, she was listening. This is a spell for immortality".

Beatrice crawled closer to look. She sat next to me and looked at the pages. "Ty, have you ever seen this book before"? I shook my head. "Yes, the first night I was here alone. After grandmother's funeral. It was in the basement. Not sure how it got here". Beatrice starred at the book and smiled. "I haven't done spells since we were in Jr. high." I laughed, "lies, you tell. So, let me get this right. You didn't put a love spell on Keith"?

Beatrice looked applaud. "Now, you know I believe in free will. I don't fuck with love spells. Ty, I thought you believed in free will as well". I smiled, "I do. If I did love spells, I'd have a man by now". We both started laughing. I stopped for a moment. "Why did you stop doing spells with me that summer Bea"? She sighed and looked at me with love in her eyes. "I didn't want to be different anymore, Ty. They called us those Gullah witch girls". They teased us. High school was a new start. I just wanted to fit in. You've always been stronger than me, Ty. You never cared what those girls thought about you. I always admired that."

I smiled. Beatrice was my best friend. "You still go into the ethers… I hope"? Beatrice smiled back. "Of course, all of that, magic, meditation, supernatural powers. That's all still apart of me." We both glanced back down at the book. Beatrice smiled, "Well, let's see what we got here." I put the book on my lap. I read a few passages and repeated them out to Beatrice. "It says here; this spell will make you immortally young forever"! I continued, "Never aging and never dying"! Beatrice's eyes got wide. "Oh my God". Beatrice took a deep breath.

"Well, what are the ingredients"? I glanced over the page again. My eyes widened as I read the main ingredient. I looked at Beatrice. "Well, it says here, we need a rainbow serpent snake." Beatrice's facial expression went blank. "Well, is that something we can pick up from a pet store Ty?" I scratched my head. "let's google it. Give me your phone". Beatrice took her phone off her hip and handed it to me. I typed in, rainbow serpent. Not very much came up. I read out loud. "It says here, this rainbow serpent can only be found in Africa. It also says the rainbow serpent is the giver of life".

Beatrice smiled, "Ok, we know that, what do we need to do with the snake"? I gave her back the phone and glanced at the book. I read more lines in the book. I could feel my eyes opening wide. I took a deep breath. "It says…we have to put it in our mouths." Beatrice busted out laughing. "This is not the time for dirty jokes, Ty." My face became serious, "No, look here, with me." I placed the book between both of us. The book read we must cast a spell on the serpent. Once the spell is cast. We must put the snake, in the mouth, of the person who wants to become youthful again or immortal. We both looked at each other and continued reading. Once the snake is in the person's mouth, they must wait until the serpent lays eggs. We both looked at each again and continued reading.

Once the eggs are released into the mouth, then the subject must, (we said it out loud, at the same time) "Swallow the eggs"! We both looked at each other. I said, "Wait, there's a warning here. It says while the snake is in your mouth. You must not bite down, gag or pull the snake out. Disturbing the snake while laying eggs will lead to death. It also says you can use the venom from the rainbow serpent to make a facial serum. This serum will turn wrinkled sagging skin back to youthful, smooth, clear skin.

But, it says here, it's only temporary." Beatrice smiles, "It looks like we have two products here. That could make us potential millionaires". I shook my head, yes. "Yeah, well, this all has to be tested, before we can do it on actual people, Bea." Beatrice sat up straight. "Well, we will do it on each other first. Like we use to when we were young". I laughed, "This isn't some self-love spell, Bea. We have to put a snake in our mouths and let it lay eggs!"

Beatrice laughed, "No shit Sherlock, I have a great gag reflex." I laughed, "I bet you do." Beatrice's smile faded, "What's that supposed to mean? Anyways, I've never known you to be afraid Ty, not even of death". I closed the book. "Were not fearless little girls anymore, Beatrice. And, I'm not scared, I'll do it". Beatrice smiled. Good, so let's, find out how and where we can get a rainbow serpent".

There was a knock at the front door. Must have been one of the other girls. I opened the small door. Put the book back into space. Inside the floor, and closed the little door. Beatrice and I got up and walked out. I closed the door shut. Beatrice got to the door before I could. It was Lilly, Zora, and Candice. The three rode down together, As they came through the door. Everyone hugged each other. I grabbed a tray of drinks I prepared before everyone got in. "You guys can go to your rooms and unpack. I'll be out by the pool with the drinks". I took the drinks outside, Beatrice helped me with the trays of food. I put everything under the umbrella to protect it from the sun.

Chairs were already set up around the table. I kept this place up really well after grandmother's passing. Aunt Teresa was a little jealous; she left the resort to me, but she understood. I was more like her daughter, then either one of her children Zora and Candice came out. They sat down under the umbrella at the table. Everyone started eating and drinking mimosa. We were all getting tipsy. Finally, Lilly came out of the house. She was wearing a very seductive bright red bikini with a sheer robe and red high heels. Beatrice cracked a joke. "Damn, you trying to catch a hot date or what"? We all started laughing.

Lilly often dressed in super sexy clothes. Her husband paid her no attention, and often, she wore tight or revealing clothes to show off her new body. Lilly smiled at Beatrice's remarks. "No, silly; look at my stomach." Lilly held her arms open out and did a spin around. We just sat staring at one another. Then back at Lilly. She huffed and puffed in annoyance. "I got a tummy tuck, hello, it's been three years since the baby." We all looked at her stomach. I said, "Oh, I see it now, not too shabby." Lilly smiled and walked over to the table. She joined the rest of us.

Lilly was a cute girl. But, she always lived in the shadow of Beatrice's ancient beauty. Lilly wore lots of loud make-up and long exotic weaves to look almost as beautiful as Beatrice. Beatrice was a natural beauty. She didn't have to overdue her face with makeup, and she wore her real hair. There was always a constant battle between the two. The party was going great. We all continued to drink. We got tipsy drinking mimosa's. Zora took a dip in the pool. We went out to the water and did some pedal boating. I swam for a little while as well. Saw a few dolphins, they came really close. I always loved soaking my body in natural water. We were sea witches my grandmother always told me that. We thrived and were more powerful out by streams of water — waterfalls, lakes, etc.

We all grew tired and headed back to the resort, which was only a few feet away. We went back and gathered around the table outside. Candice lit a joint. We all did a little puff puff give action. I wasn't your usual weed smoker. I loved wine and was sipping on a glass. But, when I got with the girls, I always had a few puffs. Candice looked over at Lilly. "So, Lilly, how are you paying for all these surgeries'? Lilly looked a bit annoyed. "What do you mean, how"? Candice smiled; she looked very high. "Well, I'm just saying, this is like your seventh plastic surgery. And plastic surgery ain't cheap"! Lilly looked annoyed.

"Well, John John does well with real estate, and he pays for a lot of it. I also put money down and can pay on it monthly". Candance looked surprised. "I didn't know you could do a payment plan for a boob job." Lilly shook her head yes. "Yes, you can, if you have good credit." Lilly's face was almost expressionless from all the cheap Botox. Her skin did not look well. Zora chimed in, "I'd kill to get my saggy boobs done. What's the doctor's number, who takes monthly payments"? We all started laughing.

Beatrice was really drunk and high. She started running her mouth. "Look, Ty, and I have the fountain of youth all figured out. We are working on something better than Botox and Boob jobs". Lilly's eyes lit up. "Really? Well, let's hear about this, baby sis". Are you stealing more samples from the lab"? Beatrice looked annoyed. "Hell No, we came up with our shit! Nobody will have nothing on us once we create this treatment and put a patent on it. We're going to be filthy rich" I put my hand over her mouth. I wasn't even ready to tell people. "Beatrice, will you please hush." Her eyes locked with mine, and she calmed down.

"We are actually still in the first stage." Zora shook her head and sipped her wine. "Ok, well, let me be the Ginny pig, for this creation, Ok"? I nodded, "right, after it's been through a few trails, ok"? Candance smiled. "Ok, just let us know." It was late, and everyone was high or drunk. So they retired to their rooms. I stayed up late and decided to go back to my grandmother's room. I opened the door, and I could smell that cinnamon, sage, and fresh ginger.

I closed the door behind me. I locked it. I grabbed a crystal from one of her shelves. Moldavite had a way of getting me to the ethers and fast. I took a jar of her ether oil from her window sill. I opened it and rubbed a few drops onto my forehead. Right on my third eye. It started to tingle immediately. I took the moldavite and placed it inside my bra. I kneeled and pulled the carpet up. I saw the little knob and opened the door.

I pulled the book out and began to search the space more. I turned the flashlight on, from my cell phone. I searched around inside the hole. I saw something, and I reached down into the hole. I pulled out a dusty zip lock bag. Inside it was folded up papers and old pictures. I cleared the dust off the bag. I opened the sip lock. I took the papers out and unraveled them. Then I took the pictures out. My heart was pounding fast. My intuition told me to go back and look inside that hole. I sat there with the folded papers and pictures in front of me.

I was too afraid to look. I took a deep breath and released it. I pulled the first large piece of paper from the pile. It was folded in half. I opened it, and it was a drawing of some sort. It was colored with crayons. So a child must have drawn it although it was very abstract. If a child drew this, they had to be gifted. In the picture, there was a waterfall with a woman underneath. The women looked like grandmother. But only, she had a mermaid's tail. I was so confused.

At that moment, I decided to not look at the pictures and other drawings just yet. I decided to go into the ethers for answers. I placed the drawing down. I laid on the floor. I took the moldavite out of my bra and placed it on my forehead. I closed my eyes, and I inhaled slowly. I traveled up and floated towards my crown chakra. I could see the purple amethyst light. I inhaled again and floated through the purple haze.

I exhaled and inhaled deeply again. I floated up and out of my crown chakra and into the darkness of the ethers. I exhaled and inhaled deeply again. I held it inside for a long time. I soared even higher. I opened my eyes, and I could see stars. I knew I had come far enough. At that point, I summons my spirit guides as I floated Inside the dark matter. My body begins to tingle, My skin became stardust black With star sparkles, almost like silver glitter as I merged with the dark glue that held the universe together. My body and mind transformed into a euphoric state.

It was invigorating, the tingles moved from my crown, down to my feet. All of a sudden, I heard them calling my name. I opened my eyes. We were in our meeting spot. I saw the mountains and blue skies. I was sitting on my favorite rock. As the mother ship landed and the metal silver doors opened. I entered the spaceship. There they all were. Waiting for me at the entrance. I was so happy to see them — the work and stresses of everyday life. Really kept me from my spirit guides. Although they surround me daily, and I can feel them. To actually be able to see them and touch them, was amazing.

They smiled as I walked through the doors. Ciceally, my dragon greeted me with a nudge of her wet nose. I hugged her stout. Although her skin was a bit scaly and moist, I became accustomed to it. Ioleon came over and hugged me, and so did Elta. I sat down in the center. The room on the mother ship was very futuristic. The technology they had was like, nothing an earthling had ever seen. Ioleon begins to talk. "My child, what do we owe this pleasure? You look frazzled by the way". I sighed, "I'm a bit confused; my grandmother has been visiting me. Today she revealed somethings to me that were quite confusing.

A gifted child drew an abstract drawing that I believe. A long time ago, the paper was pretty old, but it's still intact.

I know it's not mine, but somehow I feel connected to it." I looked up at Elta's face. She came in closer. She tapped my third eye with her quartz wand. Everything went completely jet black. I woke up laying on my grandmother's bedroom floor. I lay there for a minute. I felt a lucid dream coming on. I was awake but still in a dream state. My thoughts were pulled into a classroom with children. It looked like the early seventies, late eighties time frame due to the outfits that were being worn. A teacher was drawing on the board and giving instructions. It was an art class. I could tell by the smell of the paint. And all the art that was placed on the walls. The teacher finished giving instructions. She waited a little while and started walking around the room.

She smiled as she glanced at some of the artwork the children were making. The kids in the class had to be about five or six years old. She continued to walk around, smiling, and critiquing. She walked upon a little boy, and she glanced and smiled. She almost continued walking. But, she did a double-take at the drawing instead. The smile begins to melt from her face. I zoomed in on the little boy. I scanned his face. He looked very much like me. I scanned again, and I felt a connection. I walked closer to the teacher and child. I sat down at his art table. He had my eyes, and I stared into them deeply. Hoping to pick up a trace.

The teacher picked up the drawing. She gawked with amazement. She scratched her head. She begins to speak. "Tyrone… what, what is this? Can you explain this abstract art to me"? He smiled innocently and said. "Sure". I looked at the drawing. It was a little girl that resembled the teacher. An adult man was lying in bed with her. There were demons and dark entities drawn around the bed. He begins to speak again. "This is you when you were little.

You had an uncle that would sleep with you at night. He would tickle you in bad places. And it made you sad". The teacher's mouth dropped open. A tear ran from the corner of her eye. Her face became flustered and red. She wiped the tear away quickly and tried to compose herself. She was confused, and she looked down at him. "How could you possibly know this"? He turned to her and said. "Because you carry it here." He pointed to her heart and touched it. She looked down at her heart and began to cry.

The tears streamed from both eyes. She couldn't keep her composure any longer. She broke down and ran out of the classroom. The young boy, with my eyes, who she called Tyrone, wasn't aware of what he just did. He was just a child and he did what came naturally to him. He had powers like grandmother and I. Who was this being? I sat

51

and stared at him for a while. I tried to pick up his scent, and this was a hard task in a lucid dream.

Lucid dreams were like projections, on the walls, holograms to be exact. They could be past, present, or future. The scene of Tyrone in the classroom begins to fade. He was no longer sitting at the table with me. I was being pulled into another day. Another time, inside another classroom.

Tyrone sat in front of the class. A teacher walks in with a tall man and the art teacher. They ask to see Tyrone. The teacher dismisses him. This scene dissolves. I am then pulled into a room with white padded walls. It looked like a lab. Tyrone is sitting at a table playing with toys, being observed through a clear glass wall. Two people in white lab coats write on clipboards as they study Tyrone. I walked over and sat with him at the table. I see the art teacher walk in. She walked over to the tall man in the white lab jacket. I audio pierced through the clear glass wall and begin to listen. "Can I talk to you for a minute, please." The art teacher says to the tall man in the white lab coat. She seemed upset. The tall man in the white lab jacket walks out of the room with the art teacher.

"What in the hell, do you think you are doing"? The tall man in a white lab jacket looks confused. "I'm doing exactly what you asked me to." Her mouth dropped! "I did not ask you to do this! You come and take him out of school, put him into a white van, and bring him to a lab! No parent consent, nothing! I asked you to come and look at his pictures. Have him draw a special picture for you! And he did, revealing something that happened in your past! I just wanted to show you his special gifts! Not this! You've been taking him from the school. Twice a week. His parents don't even know!

What is this place anyway? I followed you here because I saw you last week, putting him into the van". The tall man in the white lab jacket was emotionless. "Look, he has special powers. We can use him when we go to war. He has powers already; we can enhance them times ten. We can turn this child into a force to be reckoned with. He has other powers, Ally". The art teachers' eyes widened. "This is a child, NOT SOME KIND OF A WEAPON"!

The tall man in the white lab jacket whispered. "Lower your voice; this is a government that ran the lab." The art teacher's eyes widened again. "Government…a government ran lab? Bill, are you crazy"? The tall man in the white lab jacket moved closer to the teacher. He whispers into her ear. "He has other powers… Ally". The art teacher pulls away. "I don't care,"! She walks towards the door to leave. She looks at the tall man in the white lab coat. "I'll tell his parents if you don't stop"! The tall man in the white lab coat looks angered. He grabs the art teacher by her upper right arm and pulls her back in. "I wouldn't do that if I were you.

I still have the tapes that your uncle made when you were a child. I'm sure you wouldn't want those to get into the wrong hands". The art teacher became silent. Her face begins to transition red. Tears filled her eyes. She yanked her arm back and walked out the door. The tall man walks back into the transparent room. He stands and talks to a lady with a clipboard. I was then pulled into another scene. I was standing on the lawn of a house. The house was old and odd. Although it seemed quite familiar. I was then sucked into the house through the walls. Tyrone, a man, and women who resembled him were gathered around the table eating. I stared at the man and the woman. I searched my heart and felt a connection immediately.

I had never seen these people before in my life as they were eating dinner. I heard a baby crying. The sound entered my audio zones. The mother got up from the table to tend to the baby as the women walked into the other room. There was a knock at the door. The man got up. Leaving Tyrone at the table eating alone. He peeked out of the front door window. His eyes widened. "Tyrone run"! Tyrone dropped his food. He ran out of the dining area towards the back of the house. The mom came running towards the front. Loud thuds hit the door. I stood in the dining room, watching, wanting to help, but I couldn't.

This was definitely something from the past, from my past. The door cracked opened so quickly — police officers in war gear with bulletproof shields enter the house. The woman, whom I assumed was Tyrone's mom, threw up her hands. At that moment, everything froze in time.

The cops stopped moving. The men busting through the
door came to a halt. It was almost like she stunned
them. So, they couldn't move. The man who looked like
Tyrone ran towards the back. The women's nose begins to
bleed. She had powers, just like my grandmother and I.

She grabbed her head with both hands. As if she had a
headache. Her powers were fading. She couldn't hold them
any longer. The police officers became unfrozen and broke
through the freezer spell. They began spraying bullets
with their machine guns and shot her in the head. The
crimson blood splattered on the walls. They ran towards
the back of the house. I heard more gunshots. All of a
sudden, silence filled my ears. The officers came from
the back of the house, carrying a glass crate. Tyrone was
inside, with a dart-like object stuck in his neck. He
looked like he was asleep. Must have been some type of a
tranquillizer. They loaded up the glass crate with Tyrone
inside. Into a military-style vehicle and drove off.

I walked towards the back of the house. The dad was shot
dead on the floor. All of a sudden, I heard someone
coming in through the back door. They quietly tiptoed in.
I zoned in on the face. It was my grandmother. Of course,
the woman was a lot younger. But it was my grandmother! I
knew her eyes as I pierced through them. She walked into
the bedroom through the back. She saw Tyrone's dad on the
floor, covered in blood. She wanted to scream but covered
her mouth. She closed her eyes and bypassed the body into
the living room. She saw the female lying on the ground,
drowning in her blood. She ran over to her and dropped to
her knees. She picked up her top half and began to hug
her and cry.

At that moment, the scream of an infant filled both our
ears. She stopped sobbing, gently placed the body down on
the floor. She walked towards the cries. She quietly ran
towards the back into another bedroom. I followed her
into a small sunroom by the back porch. We both stopped
and looked around. We saw nothing. The cries pierced my
ear lobes once again. My grandmother ran towards a
closet. I followed close by. She opened the door. I
leaned in and looked. Inside was a small baby carriage.
My grandmother's face lit up. She smiled and shouted.
"Thank the Gods and the Goddesses"! I moved closer.
Inside was a newborn baby girl, dressed in all pink. She

leaned in and picked her up. "Oh, Tituba, I'm so glad they didn't find you."

At that moment, I realized what she just said. I stared into the baby's eyes. I scanned her heart with mine. I felt the vibrational match. That baby was me! I stopped for a moment and caught my breath. I had a mom and a dad and a brother. Grandmother never spoke of my mom or dad. I always thought they abandoned me. But they were dead. I had a brother, somewhere, out there. If he was still alive, it was my duty to uncover the truth. Now, I see why grandmother never uttered a word about them. She didn't want them to find me.

She didn't want them to know I even existed. It was her way of protecting me. At that moment, I was pulled back into my reality. Back into Grandmother's bedroom. I slowly sat up on the floor. I was a bit dizzy. I had been inside the hologram for quite some time. Once I felt stable. I rose slowly to my feet. I walked slowly, a few feet, and collapsed in my grandmother's bed. I remembered we had just finished a girl's weekend. Tomorrow was a new day.

Chapter Five

The Book of Nigron

Finally arrived at my apartment after a long day's work at the DNA lab. It was Friday and Beatrice, and I was meeting me for drinks. I walked slowly up the stairs and took off my high heels, even though I was still in the hallway and approached my door. I slowly pulled my key out of my purse. Before I could get it to the keyhole. I felt a tap on my shoulder. I turned around quickly. It was Steve staring down at me. "Hey stranger, haven't seen you in a while." I smiled and tried not to look annoyed.

"Hey, Steve, how are you"? He shrugged, "I don't know, I guess I'd be a lot better if you actually answered my phone calls." I sighed and looked into his brown eyes. "Look…I just don't think it would be a good idea. I mean, we can be friends". His smile became a frown. "Ok…well, just wanted to stop and say hello. Since we live in the same building,". I smiled, "Thanks Steve, it's always nice seeing you." He put on a phony smile and walked away. I turned to my door. I took a deep sigh and finally turned the knob and walked in. My two cats, Gretta and Gisele, ran to greet me.

I dropped my purse and keys on the kitchen counter, to free both my hands. I gently rubbed both their heads at the same time. Both cats were Bengal breeds. They were tall and looked like tigers. Gretta had green eyes, and Giselle's were brown. Both beautifully exotic. I had a strange attachment to cats since I was a little girl. Always collecting strays, feeding them and keeping them safe. My grandmother told me that cats were my familiar. Sadly, I was more attached to them; then I was to most human beings.

I continued to rub them both. Musical vibrations entered my ears. Causing my third eye and body to vibrate. Nothing like a cat's purr, to relax the mind and loosen up the body. They were both very competitive for my love and affection. There was plenty to go around. A knock at the door broke the magical spell they were placed upon me. It must be Beatrice. I stopped petting and looked out my keyhole. All I could see was a bottle of red organic wine. I laughed as I opened the door. Gretta and Giselle fled from the kitchen. "Come in, silly". Beatrice walked in wearing a long raincoat, down to her ankles. I was quite confused as I stared with amusement. It was very warm and sunny out today.

I started laughing, "why the hell are you in that long raincoat"? She put the wine bottle down. She started searching my kitchen drawers for a corkscrew. "Well, Keith has been working really long hours lately." Beatrice popped the wine cork. And poured herself a small glass. She continued speaking. "So, I decided to stop by his office and give him some." She sipped her wine. I begin to laugh. "Oh, really, is that what married couples do"? Beatrice sipped more wine and smiled, "Well… the smart ones do". Beatrice grinned, "Speaking of giving somebody, some, I saw Steve in the hallway."

I laughed and grabbed a clean wine glass from the rack. I poured myself a large glass. I took a long sip. "Yeah,

he's borderline stalking me these days." I took another
sip. "Lessons in dating 101. Never sleep with a guy who
lives in your building". Beatrice almost spits out her
wine. "Yeah, I guess, how come you never gave him a
chance"? I placed my wine glass on the table. "Well, to
be honest, he's shallow, and his chakras aren't aligned,
and he stinks, self-doubt is a hell of a pungent odour."
Beatrice busted out laughing again.

"So, you're going to judge him based on his chakra game
Ty? You are completely hilarious; you know that?". I
smiled, "It's not just that, He's conservative and
bougie. Doesn't like nature, not in tune with his
spiritual side at all. He has no knowledge of self".
Beatrice sipped more wine. "Well, you know that stuff
takes time, Ty. And most men like that, all spiritual and
in touch with nature, are broke". We both started
laughing. "No, not necessarily, there's this guy at
work." I smiled as I mentioned him. "I picked up on
certain codes from his aura." Beatrice placed her glass
down. "You, didn't say that to him, did you, Ty"? I
picked my glass up and sipped more. "Say what"?

Beatrice swallowed, "That you, picked up on codes in his
aura"? I paused for a minute. "Of course not, I only talk
to you like that, and grandmother when she was alive."
Beatrice smiled, "Good girl, we need to find you a man
Ty. We don't need him calling you the big W". I rolled my
eyes. "Oh, what? Weird"? Beatrice sighed. I grabbed the
wine bottle and poured myself another glass. "I'm used to
it. Guys have been calling me weird all my life. They
like me because I'm pretty. But once we get into deep
conversation. They always drop the W bomb. Which is cool
with me, I could care less".

Beatrice could tell I was annoyed. "Ok, subject change,
where's the book"? I swallowed my sip of wine. "In my
bedroom, on the bed, let's go inside. I need to take off
these work clothes". Beatrice and I walked into my
bedroom. I headed towards the closet and began to
undress. Beatrice sat on the bed next to the book. I put
on a T-shirt and some sweat pants. I pulled my hair up
into a ponytail. Then I pulled my long hair through the
hair tie to form a bun. I walked over and sat down on the
other side of the book. I grabbed my notebook and pen off
the nightstand. Beatrice's eyes begin to widen. I looked

down at the book. It was starting to glow, a green colour.

Beatrice smiled, "Well, we always wanted to go into business together, Ty. This is our chance. Billions of dollars a year are spent on plastic surgery. Procedures, pills, and potions to look young forever, immortally". I smiled at Beatrice. "You sound like the old Beatrice I use to know." Beatrice smiled as well. "Well, we both became mad scientists, both work in labs." I sighed, "I'd work in your lab any day over mine." Beatrice laughed, "are you serious. Isn't it exciting dusting those crime scenes for killer DNA?" I rolled my eyes. "I don't dust the crime scenes, and I never leave the lab. I take the samples brought in and run them in the lab. They also bring in dead bodies sometimes. And it's really hard for me. Being a super sensitive empath!

I'll trade with you any day. Testing chemicals in makeup". Beatrice laughed. "Yeah, I work in a cosmetic lab. They create youthful products that reverse the signs of ageing. I really think that whatever this book can provide for us, along with stealing secrets from the lab, we could be rich, Ty". I sighed,

"yeah, that would be nice. I'm extremely tired of dead bodies". Beatrice sat up, "Well, let's look at that immortality spell." I rolled onto my stomach in front of the book.

I could feel the warmth blazing from it. It begins to glow again. Beatrice came closer, "Open it up, Ty. I can't believe your grandmother hid this book. Wonder where it even came from"? I touched the black wooden cover. The title glowed green. THE BOOK OF NIGRON. I ran my fingertips over the title. I slowly opened the book. The pages begin flipping by themselves. Beatrice's eyes lit up. The book finally stopped flipping. It opened right up to the page of the immortality spell. We both moved in closer, and I looked at Beatrice. "The book must have a spirit or possessed by a spirit. It can hear us; it knew exactly what page to turn to".

We both leaned in to read. I studied all the ingredients needed. We both glanced at the main ingredient at the same time. We were going back through the spell again. I pulled out a piece of paper. We needed to write down a

list. We had to be exactly right about what was needed.
I sighed, "Where the hell, are we going to get a rainbow
serpent snake"? Beatrice smiled, "I have a friend who
owns an exotic pet store, on the low. He use to be a
shaman. Not sure what he's up to these days. I smiled,
"what do you mean on the low"? Beatrice smiles, "Well,
you know, it's illegal to have some animals as pets. He
keeps them in his basement, and people contact him via
the internet through his website. He makes a fortune. A
lot of people seem to want weird pets. If he doesn't have
one, he will know exactly where I can find one."

I rubbed my hands together. "Ok, that solves one problem.
The other issue is, it says here in the book. That we
have to cast a spell on the snake. To get her to do what
we want. We have to be super careful Beatrice. I've never
handled a snake before, and neither have you". Beatrice
smiled, "we will be fine. I have complete faith in you,
Ty. Think of all the money". Beatrice was starting to
reek of greed. The smell was almost unbearable. The gift
of olfactory was not an easy one to have. I never really
considered it a gift. Until my grandmother explained to
me what it was and how I could use it for good.

We both begin to read again at the same time. I looked at
Beatrice. "Ok, so according to the book. The snake has to
be put in your mouth". I glanced back down and began to
read aloud. "Place the rainbow serpent in the subject's
mouth, who wishes to become immortal and youthful again.
The snake will lay an egg on the subject's tongue. The
subject must not move, gag. Or speak while the snake is
inside the subject's mouth once the egg is laid. The
rainbow serpent will crawl out. Then and only then should
the subject swallow the eggs." Beatrice made a gruesome
face. "Wow, so the egg is what makes the person
immortal." I sighed, "Yes, but remember, there is a big
caution! It's written in bold letters here. If the
subject gags, talks, or moves while the snake is in the
mouth. Death can occur". We looked at one another.
Beatrice rubbed her neck. "Damn, well, even when people
get plastic surgery, death can occur." I sighed, "Yeah, I
know, just something to think about; that's all."
Beatrice touched my hand. "look, I'll be the guinea pig
first. We will both do it before we unleash this on the
public". I swallowed, "well, let's not be too hasty. I

say we try it on a dummy first. You know, the spell part and making sure we can tame the snake". Beatrice rubbed her chin in thought. "Good idea TY, at least that part will be mastered.

Well, there's only one thing to do now. And thats call, Sergio". I exhaled, "He's open around this time"? Beatrice laughed, "he has an online store. He is always open". Beatrice climbed off the bed. Grabbed her purse off the floor. She fumbled around inside and found her phone. She jumped back on the bed. Laid on her side and begin to dial. I was nervous, and I could smell the funk coming from her glands. I could hear his phone ringing from Beatrice's phone. Finally, I heard a voice say hello. Beatrice put him on speaker and laid the phone on the bed.

"Hey, Sergio, it's Beatrice, how are you"? His voice had an alluring accent. "Beatrice, long time, what can I do for you at this fine hour"? He said. "Well, I'm looking for an exotic pet." Sergio continued, "O.k. Well, you've come to the right guy, what do you need"? Beatrice gulped, "I need a rainbow serpent, has to be a female, only." Sergio chuckled, "Well, I don't have one. But I can get one shipped in. The serpent is not what's expensive. Rainbow serpents are very abundant in Australia and Africa. To ship the crate with a live animal. It is going to cost you about $1000, and my fee is going to be $500. So, your total will be $1500. May I be nosey and ask what you need the snake for"?

Beatrice cleared her throat. "Well, we need the eggs for some cosmology testing. Nothing harmful to the animal, just some research. Sergio paused, "Well, it's none of my business. When would you like to get started"? Beatrice grabbed her purse and looked over at me. "We're going half on this." She whispered. "I'll put it all on my credit card. You give me half later". I nodded yes. "You guys take credit cards, right? Sergio laughed. "Of course, we do. Numbers off the credit card when you're ready". Beatrice gave him the credit card information. It was done, the rainbow serpent was on the way.

Chapter 6

Mystery date

The delivery for the rainbow serpent would take up to three weeks. Until then, back to work! Working in the DNA lab was sometimes exciting. Especially when a murder occurred. Other than that, it was boring, boring and oh so boring. There was this hot guy at work. I found very much to be eye candy status. He would flirt with me from time to time. A smile, a long stare, it was completely innocent. But, I had a way of complicating my life when I got bored.

Of course, he didn't work in my department. He was a lawyer with the DA's office. He stopped in almost daily for DNA results for his cases. He was quite breathtaking. I mean, I never flirted back. I just didn't live a normal life. My grandmama had a few men, here and there.

Grandmother was actually married five times. Back in those days, that was a lot for a woman. Grandmother was a healer, and when your healer. You seem always to attract broken ones. As grandmother grew older and got her wisdom, she realized this. In her early twenties, she had been with a lot of toxic men. Grandmother always told me, it's not our duty to heal these broken ones.

Sometimes they come with dark entities and wreak havoc in our lives. Grandmother taught me; sometimes, the dark ones are sent to us purposely. To keep us from our mission. To stop us from evolving. Grandmother always told me. A lot of us special ones, are in mental institutions, jail, special education classes, and addicted to drugs, just broken! They know who we are when we're born. They come for us early. Child molestation, abusive households. Grandmother always told me. That, if you were strong and made it through childhood. They would start throwing handlers into your life. And most times, these handlers are lovers, girlfriends, boyfriends, husbands, wives. They are strategically placed. To keep you from being your greatest version of you.

Grandmother also told me, they exterminate our kind at birth. We have a certain mutation on our genetic marker. It can be found on the sonograms. It can also be read on a blood test. A lot of times, they tell mothers who carry special children like us. That the child will be mentally or physically disabled, and the mother should abort the child. A lot of star children don't make it past the womb. These horrible things have stayed stuck in the back of my mind. Of course, I've had boyfriends here and there. Especially in high school and college. Nothing really serious.

I guess her words of wisdom are always sitting in my subconscious mind, locked away. I had to be careful. But, it wouldn't hurt, to date someone though. I just had to be careful of getting serious with a handler. As I sat at my desk that day, the smell of burnt plastic and bad cheese filled my nostrils. I turned around, it was mike, from the mailroom. I always knew he was a clone or a robotic of some sort. Not human at all. They had extremely bad body odour.

He was very robotic with his movements. Mike threw the mail into the port and picked up the outgoing mail. I turned to look at him. He felt my eyes piercing. He turned around very robotically and said. "Hello Ty, nice day out, isn't it?" He always said the same thing daily, almost if he was programmed. Which I knew he was. I lifted my coffee cup and sipped. "Yes, great day out".

He smiled as he pushed the cart and waved goodbye. I turned around and began checking my emails on the computer as I was checking my emails. A steady stream of confidence penetrated my nostrils. Confidence had a very enticing, alluring aroma. Anytime a person has confidence, that's a sign of self-love, and love always smelled like a hint of roses. I love the vibration and scent of roses. I wore pure rose oil as a fragrance. The reason I wore one hundred percent rose otto. Was because, just a whiff, would make me happy. Rose oil raises vibration times 10. That's why when a confident person walks into a room. Every one stares with amazement. It's because they actually smell it first. Before they even see the person visually. I came out of my trance and turned around. I wasn't surprised at all. It was Kent Walker, the sexy lawyer from the DA's office. Kent had a bewitching aura about him. His presence demanded attention. Kent was tall, slender, and rocked a goatee. Kent's body looked as though fine artisans with exotic tools chiseled it. His skin colour beamed of ancient Egyptian Gods. I could smell a warrior in his blood. Kent wore a grey suit with a blue tie and black shoes. His watch sparkled as he put his right hand into his pocket.

Glad I actually did my make up today. My long dark tresses were pulled back neatly into a long ponytail. I tried to not notice him at first. I turned back to my computer. I picked up my coffee and sipped it. I felt his shadow over my shoulder. The rose scent became seducing. I slowly turned my head. He was staring down at me. I smiled and said. "Hello," for the first time. He smiled back, "Hello…Ty" I had to control myself so that I wouldn't blush. He knew my name. Interesting, because we never formally met.

Kent continued talking, "I needed some help with a file. A client of mine needs DNA results. It's kind of a touchy subject. But, could you actually speed up the results for her case? I know it's a lot to ask. But, please, I need your help". I paused for a moment to take in everything that Kent was saying. I rubbed my hands together. "Well, I suppose I could help you. You know were super backed up here". Kent smiled, "Yes, I know. That's why it took me a while to ask you".

I smiled, "I suppose". I turned back to my computer. "What's your client's name?" He cleared his voice. "It's Dominque, Dominque Farrow." I paused for a moment; that name sounds familiar. "Oh, so you're working on the high-profile case. The politician who has all these rape allegations coming against him". He pulled up a chair and sat next to me. "Yes, Mrs. Farrow was the first; many more are coming forward." I glanced at the computer. "Let's see here; the samples just came in... yesterday!" I started laughing. "We are literally months behind, Mr. Walker." Kent's smile evaporated slowly. He started to look hopeless.

I felt bad, I mean, I had it within my power to help him, but it was unethical. I sighed, "OK, I can help." The smile on his face was resurrected with joy. "How... How can I return the favour?" I smiled, "well, I don't know yet. You are a lawyer. So, I guess if I ever need to be represented. You owe me one." He was so happy, he grabbed me and gave me a tight hug. "Oh my, I shouldn't have done that, I'm sorry." I smiled, "no, it's ok". He calmed down. "Well, how about dinner, to go over somethings about the case." I nodded, "sure, that would be awesome." He stood up from his chair. "Here's my card, can I get one of yours?" I grabbed a card off my desk. "Sure," I said with a big smile.

He glanced at my card. "Thanks, I hate to be brief, but I have to run." I rubbed my neck, "I'm sure your quite busy; it's understandable." He tucked my card in his wallet. "I'll be giving you a call; it was nice to meet you formally." He walked out slowly. That beautiful rose scent left with him. I looked at the time. It was almost time to go. I started packing up my things. As I sat in traffic for about an hour, I finally approached my building. I took the elevator up to my floor and entered my condo. My beautiful kitty greeted me.

I peeled off all my clothes got into something more comfortable. I decided to call Beatrice and tell her about my date. Since she's always on me, about a quote on quote "Getting some." She just doesn't understand. Being an empath, olfactory, telepathic being, just wasn't easy. I can smell my date fears. I can feel their emotions. Only if its weighed heavily upon their hearts. I smell foul, malicious intents. I see attachments in their aura's. It was just all so complicated. I started dialing Beatrice's number. The phone rang three times. She finally answered. "What's up, Ty"? I laid on my bed and smiled. "Got a date."

I begin to hear laughter on the other end. "Well, I'm happy for you. So, who is the lucky guy"? I smirked, "The guy I've been telling you about. My eye candy at work". Beatrice chuckled again. "Oh, so Ms. Anti-social finally spoke,". I smiled, "Not at all, and he approached me. I'm actually quite interested in how this will go. I rolled over on my back. "I'll keep you posted, call you later, ok?" Beatrice replied, "ok". I hung up the phone at that moment. Thoughts of my long-lost brother came into my mind. Any time someone or something just popped into my mind. I analyzed it as to why?

It took me a long time to learn this technique. Things didn't just pop into our minds for no reason. Either a message was there. Or someone you have recently met is tying into someone. Or something from the past. Well, I did just meet Kent Walker. I thought for a minute. What does Kent have to do with my brother? I decided to grab my laptop. I pulled it down from my desk. Unto my bed and opened it up. I googled Kent's name. Surprisingly, I found out Kent was from a long line of generational lawyers. Most of the articles that came up were of Kent's dad.

He was some big hotshot lawyer in South Carolina. I dug deeper and found an article from 1976. About a drug bust that went down with a family. A husband and wife murdered. And, a child who came up missing. I was in disbelief at what I was reading. The name of the dead woman was Ava D. Conyers. My mother's first name was Ava. They called her Ava D. Conyers must have been her married last name. My grandmother's last name was Jones. There were pictures of the lost child that came up missing.

I pierced the photo deeply with my eyes. It was my brother. The little boy I saw in my holographic realm. I begin to read more. Apparently, Kent's dad brought a lawsuit against the police, who were involved in the murder of the family. I immediately shut the computer closed. How ironic? How could this all be happening? At that moment, my text signal on my phone went off. I glanced down at my phone to view the message. It was Kent asking me to meet him for dinner at eight pm tomorrow. I sent him a message stating, "Yes." He sent me a follow-up message with the address.

I decided to get up and walk to the kitchen and have a glass of wine. I walked into my living room. I decided to clear my mind with a movie. I drank my wine and fell fast asleep on my couch. The next day, I slept in. It was a Saturday, and the only thing on my agenda was Kent. Nightfall came quickly. I begin to prepare for my date. I texted Kent to confirm. I glanced at the address again. It didn't look familiar. But I wasn't an Atlanta native. I haven't had much time to explore the city. I put on one of my best dresses. It was black and strappy. Came right above my knees. I put on my black pumps. I made up my face to perfection and let my hair down.

I drove to the destination using my GPS. I finally arrived. I scanned my mind and body for any negative feelings. My scan gave me the OK. No malicious energy was found. I used all of my senses. Especially being in a new environment, with a person I barely Knew. All systems were GO. I turned my car off and climbed out. This place looked like an abandoned church from the outside. It had mosaic stain glass windows. There was a big neon (Open) sign on the front of the building. No official name, just an open sign. A hand full of cars were parked out front.

As I approached the front door. A man was standing in a tux. He bowed his head and asked to take my coat. I took it off and handed it to him. He then took my right hand and led me inside the building. I had never been to a place like this before. He walks me down a semi-dark hall. Lit by only candles. We approached a door. He bowed his head and walked away. He hadn't said one word, which was odd. But, I've been in way more odder situations as I stood in front of the door. I begin to raise my hand slowly to knock on the door. Before I could, it opened as

I looked inside, the colour kind of changed, right before my eyes.

All the colours in the room faded to black and white except the coloured stain glass windows. I gasped at the alluring décor. I walked slowly and looked all around, I did a slow twirl and took in all the scenery. The most charming artwork in 4D on the walls, life-sized humans curved out of druzy crystals. The most captivating chandeliers made of tropical plants and crystals. It was unreal. Again, everything, black and white. Except for the colours that fell upon my body, from the stain glass windows. It was like a sanctuary. And the scent of the room was exhilarating. It smelled like something I've only encountered in subconscious realms. There were no words to describe it. Just a knowing! Only I was in the material plane.

   But How? Was this just in my mind? The only thing that could explain combining the physical and other subconscious realms. Was, I must have leveled up in dimensions. Again! I finally came out of my twirl. And my eyes landed on Kent. He was sitting at a candlelit table. There was only one table in this whole mesmerizing room. I walked over towards him. He was sipping champagne. He glanced up and saw me. His eyes widened, and his mouth almost dropped. He stood up and pulled out my chair. I got closer, he grabbed my hand gently and kissed it. I sat down in the chair. I was kind of speechless.

I smiled at him. "This is very extravagant for a first date, slash let's talk about work." Kent laughed. "Well, when you're a member of a secret society, rooms like this are very affordable. This place is not open to the public. It's by appointment only and only for members". I picked up my glass and sipped my champagne. I sat it back down on the table. "Secret society, huh?" He smiled, "it's not what you think. You get a few bad apples out there, and everyone thinks your down with the Illuminati". We both laughed. A man dressed like a high-class waiter walked into the room. He was carrying a silver-covered tray. "Appetizers," he said, as he placed the dish on the table.

The waiter uncovered the dish, and it was shrimp cocktails. Romantic music plays seductively in the background. Kent begins to nibble and dip his shrimp. He looked up at me as he swallowed. "You look absolutely amazing tonight." I blushed, "thank you". He sipped again quickly. "Well, I chose this place because I thought you would be bored with the usual dinner and a movie. So, I figured we'd do dinner here, something exclusive. I smiled. "Nice". Kent, raised his glass. "To our official date". I raised my glass and repeated it. "To our official date". We toast, and I sip more champagne.

More dishes were brought out by the wait staff. A silver tray was placed in front of me; it smelled amazing. I lifted the silver cover. "This scent is really delicious," I said as I picked up my fork. Kent smiled. "Yes, this is shrimp and grits with spinach. A special role that I like to call a soul roll. It comes with a special dipping sauce. The ingredients are a family secret".

My eyes enlarged, "You mean you made this"? Kent swallowed his food. "Yes, I actually cooked all of this myself." I put my fork down. "So, who taught you how to cook soul food." Kent smiled, "Well, growing up in the south, and I'm originally from South Carolina." I swallowed deeply, "So am I." I said slowly. Kent smiled, "really, what part"? I eyeballed my plate. "I'm from the sea island area" He nodded his head. "Oh ok, Gullah girl, huh"? I smiled, "yes, is that a good or bad thing?" Kent chuckled, "Well, it could be a bad thing for me, I hear you Gullah girls work roots." I begin to laugh, "Roots? You have a lot to learn, my friend. Honestly, my grandmother dabbled in the craft of magick. But nothing called roots". Kent started shaking his head again. "I mean, I think that's wonderful, knowing your true heritage, it doesn't scare me at all."

I sipped my champagne. "So, back to my question, who taught you how to cook"? Kent smiled, "Well, I was taught by the best, and nothing but the best. My father and grandfather owned a soul food restaurant when I was a kid". I was confused, a soul food restaurant? Kent saw the confusion in my face. "Well, they were both lawyers, my dad decided to retire around 1977 — early retirement, of course. So, my granddad and father opened a restaurant". I sipped my champagne, "why early retirement"?

Kent placed his fork down. "Well, to make a long story short. Let's just say my dad was prosecuting a bunch of crooked cops. They shot up a house with a family inside. The cops said it was a drug bust that went wrong. But after investigating, my dad found out differently. The neighbourhood demanded justice for the family. Neighbours claim, the family was quiet and hard-working individuals that the community respected. And, was no way involved with any drugs. To make the cases even stranger. The son who belonged to the couple, came up missing. So, as you can see, there was a lot of inconsistent material to this case".

I swallowed deeply and stuttered a bit. "Soooooo, did they ever find the boy"? Kent took another bite of his food and swallowed. "No, that's the crazy part. To this day, he is still considered missing. Still sitting in a cold case file". Kent started to stare at me weirdly. "Why do you ask about the boy"? I took a deep breath and tried not to look suspect. "Just wondering, just find it odd." Kent sipping water, "Yeah, who you telling? My dad found out some stuff about the police department. Because he had evidence, they decided to disbar him. He made up some bogus story.

It was a hot mess and all over the news. Once, he got disbarred. My grandad and dad decided to open the restaurant. I nodded yes and sipped. "I see, I see". I rubbed my chin. Kent glared at me suspiciously. "Did you know the family, Ty"? I took a deep breath. "I'm not sure yet." Kent looked me directly in the eyes. "What do you mean?" I gulped down the last two swallows in my glass. "The story sounds familiar to me. Might have heard about it, when I was a child". Kent nodded yes, "Well, I'm sure you have, high profile case."

The waiter came out and refilled our glasses with champagne. Kent smiled, "so back to the date." I took a few bites of my food. "This shrimp and grits is tasty, and so is the soul roll." Kent picked up the champagne bottle and topped off my glass. My eyes widened, "Are you trying to get me drunk"? Kent had a smirk on his face. "Not at all". I started laughing, "You have wonderful taste in music. I'm really feeling this song". I was actually getting quite tipsy. I think Kent could tell. Kent smiled, "Well, I use to play acoustic guitar, some years ago."

I decided to drink water, to mellow myself out. "Is this your work"? Kent chuckled, "No, no, actually he's and underground artist, I found his work on YouTube. I've been a fan ever since". We both were tipsy and becoming enticed by the melody. It had been a long time since I let myself relax around a man. I happened to glance over in the corner and saw a few buckets of latex paint, next to an exposed brick wall. I place my glass down. "Are they going to paint those brick walls"? I think they are ravishing, just the way they are". Kent glanced over and looked.

"Well, the paint is latex meaning, it was made to go on the skin." Did I hear him correctly? "Skin?" Kent noticed my face. "Hey, would you like to dance"? I smiled, "Sure, why not." Kent slowly gets out of his seat and slowly takes my hand. He pulled my body close and tightly wrapped his hands around my waist. I put my arms around his neck. We sway slowly and sultry to the music. Our eyes lock, and we stare intensely. I tried to scan his thoughts and got a block. Kent leaned in close, and his lips touched mine. Electric impulses started going off in my brain.

The kiss started off delicate and mild. Within minutes, mild became fiery. The kisses got deeper and deeper. And wetter and wetter. I was overwhelmed but in a good way. I decided to break free of the kiss. Kent smiled and pressed his forehead up against mine. He gazed into my eyes. The song ends, and we both catch our breath. We head back to our seats. I was confused, why I couldn't I read him? I sat back in my chair and gulped down more champagne. I had to cool off.

Another song begins to rotate in the background. I guess I looked a little uneasy. Kent grabs my hand. "Did I do something wrong"? I was actually overtaken at how powerful his kisses were. I could hear Beatrice's voice in the back of my mind. "Stop overthinking things and just go with the flow". I decided to let down my guard and just go with the flow. Kent was still glaring at me.

"Um no, no…not at all. It's just been a long time since I've kissed anyone. I was a bit overwhelmed. I'd really actually like to try that again". Kent putting his glass down. "Try what again? The kiss"? I smiled out of nervousness. "Yes, the kiss".

I fumbled for my words. Kent leaned in over the table and began kissing me again. Kent got overly aroused and stood up and flips the table over. Kent grabs me in his arms and presses my body up against the brick wall. Kent kisses my neck. My head leans back and touches the wall. Kent rips the top half of my dress down to my belly button. He unhooks my bra as he caresses my back with one hand. He throws my bra onto the floor. This was so unlike me. But, I had been on a hiatus for quite some time now.

I was finicky about who I shared my energy with. The last thing I needed was to lower my vibrations. Or receive some type of attachment from a handler. Last time that happened, it took me months to get the funk of that attachment off of me. Kent was different, and I couldn't read him. That could be a good or bad thing. I stopped thinking and started enjoying Kent devouring my nipples. He rips the rest of my dress, clean off.

He presses me back up against the wall. I closed my eyes, and pleasure zones in my brain started to tingle. I saw the purple flame, dancing around. Subconsciously my higher self was pleased. I opened my eyes and glanced up, and the vivid stain glass windows. I decided to let myself fall completely under his spell.

Chapter seven

Serpents and smiles

As I sat at my work desk and sipped my coffee. I got a call from Beatrice. Still looking at the computer screen, I answered the phone. "At work, make it quick"! Beatrice laughed. "Listen, I got the call last night. The rainbow serpent is here. We need to go pick her up from Sergio's. Can we make this happen after work"? I stopped typing and paused for a second. "I guess it's cool, what time"? Beatrice whispered, "Meet me at about 7 pm. I'll text your Sergio's address, don't be late". I placed my coffee down. "Wait, where is the snake going to stay"?

I heard Beatrice sigh on the other end. "Look, Ty, and I can't bring the snake home. If Keith finds it, he'll kill me". I rolled my eyes. "Um, earth to Beatrice. "I live in a condo, and you live in a whole house"! Beatrice sighed again. "listen, Ty, we can drive it to your grandmother's bed and breakfast this weekend, its Thursday. The snake will only be at your house, 24-48 hours tops"! I took a few deep breaths, why me? "I guess so, Beatrice, but we have to get her out of my place, ASAP"! Beatrice paused, "Of course, Ty, you have my word. Remember, if this works out, we are going to be rich"!

Beatrice had a way of talking me into everything. She was a good friend, my best friend. We always looked out for one another. We were in this, together as I was talking on the phone. More files were placed on my desk. "Beatrice, I gotta go, see you at seven, ok"? "Ok, Thanks Ty". I hung up the phone and got to work on my case. I opened the new file placed on my desk. I jumped as someone tapped me on the shoulder. I turned around wide-eyed. It was Kent, which was strange because I could usually smell him a mile away.

"Hey, stranger, called you the other day, no answer." I smiled, "Sorry I wasn't sure what to say." I looked around and began to whisper. "After…our romantic evening." Kent laughed, "Just a call to say hello, how's it going, maybe"? I laughed, "I'm sorry, I'm not used to casual sex." Kent pulled up a seat from another desk. "Not casual at all, I know you." We both laughed. "Well, I guess I'll call you more often."

Kent looked at his watch. "Just wanted to stop by and say hello." Kent scratched his head, "just wondering, any word on those samples yet?" I glanced into his eyes. He was afraid. I could smell it. "No, Kent, I'm sorry, I put a rush on the process. Trust me; I'm moving as fast as I can". Kent smiled as I saw a sign of relief come over his face.

He stood up from his seat. "Thank you, Ty, I'd like to see you again soon." He looked around when he saw no one. He grabbed my hand and kissed it. The truth was, I didn't call him back because I didn't want to get my hopes up about a possible relationship. I wanted to make sure he was genuinely interested. So far, it seemed like he was. I had to be careful; my grandmother always told me. Be careful of possible mates. That most were handlers. Not all, but a good percentage of them. Although I was a bit suspicious, as to why he asked me for help. And why he's in fear? I know it's something about his case. But there was more to it. My intuition is telling me so.

I continued working on my cases until 6 pm. I was exhausted and had to meet Beatrice before going home. I packed up my things and walked out of the lab. I got on the elevator and went downstairs. I entered the parking lot and walked over to my car. I opened my car door and got inside. I look around for safety and then locked my doors. I put my seat belt on and glanced down at my phone. Sergio's address lit up on my screen. I cranked up my car and put his address into my GPS. His place was only fifteen minutes away. I turned my music on and listened to some enchanting tunes. I was excited and afraid all at the same time.

Beatrice and I always wanted to start our own business. Of course, this meant more work for us. But, it also meant freedom and that was a goal we shared. I arrived at my destination and pulled into the driveway. The house looked very tropical. Palm trees surround the gate. I glanced down at my watch, and I was early. I didn't see Beatrice's car. I decided to wait. Plus, I didn't have the gate code. The camera above the gate motioned towards the direction of my car. At that moment, Beatrice's car pulled up. She parked her car behind mine. I glanced at the rearview mirror. She got out and walked around to my car. I rolled the window down. "Hey, you excited or what?" I laughed, "how about, or what? Why are we still outside of this gate"? Beatrice fumbled around in her purse. She found her phone.

At the moment, the gate doors begin to open slowly. Beatrice ran back and hopped into her car. She cranked it up. I drove through the gate first. Beatrice followed. We went down a long trail until we came to a tropical pink-coloured house. It was huge. We both pulled up to the front and got out of the car. We looked at each other and took a deep breath. We approached the door. Beatrice begins to knock. Before she could knock twice, the door opened.

There standing before us was a medium build man with a muscular physique. He had long black hair. With a few streaks of grey. It was pulled neatly back into a ponytail. He was only wearing swim trunks and nothing else. He held his arms out wide and greeted Beatrice with a big hug. "Beatrice! "So good to see you, it's been years. So, how's married life treating you"? Beatrice looked uncomfortable. I never had in my entire life, heard her mention a Sergio, ever. Beatrice smiled nervously. "Well, married life is, well… married life". Beatrice begins to laugh. I could smell embarrassment reeking from her pores.

Sergio extended his arm out. "Please come in". We walked inside, and I looked around, he had a very exotic place. Spiral staircase, lots of plants. Very jungle wilderness style. It was becoming more and more apparent to me that Beatrice and Sergio had past chemistry. I could smell it. But my question was, when? She had been with Keith since college. Sergio leads us down a hall and then down a flight of stairs. We walked towards an elevator and got in. We went down and finally arrived on our floor.

The elevator doors opened to a gate. Sergio dug in his pocket, pulled out a pair of keys, and opened it. It smelled like a zoo down there as we walked deeper into the room. I saw spider monkeys, baby lions, and tigers in cages. I also saw a few animals that looked kind of spliced. They didn't look real to me. My eyes widened as I shot Beatrice a look of concern. Sergio kept walking, it was quite dark, and only the cages had lights above them. Over in the corner was a medium-sized crate. Sergio led us to the crate. Sergio slowly pulled the crate out and lifted it onto a table.

Sergio smiled, "This is Amaya, according to the Shaman I bought her from, she is 1000 years old". Beatrice's eye's widened. "How is that even possible"? Sergio smiled, "I only go by what the owner tells me." "He also told me, because she is very old, that her powers are strong." I glanced at Beatrice with big eyes again. Sergio grabbed some protective gloves off the table and put them on. "You guys ready to meet her"? I shrugged my shoulders. "I guess". I laughed out of nervousness. Sergio slowly opened the crate. He gently guided his hands inside and pulled her out. The first thing I saw was Amaya's huge glowing eyes. Sergio started petting her head to soothe her.

"The money you guys paid for Amaya, put that shaman and his whole family up for a year." "He didn't want to part with her, but he really needed the money. She was his pet, and he used her for her powers as well. Amaya was passed down from generation to generation in his family. So, it was very hard parting with her". He came towards me with the snake. "Here, hold her, get acclimated with her" I backed up a bit, I was a cat person. I had to get use to snakes. "Um, um, ok…I guess,". I placed my purse and cell phone down on the table.

"Oh wait, I need a pair of gloves as well." Sergio smiled. "No, you will be her new owner, hold her bare. Let your skin connect to hers". He stared into my eyes. He handed Amaya out to me. I took a big gulp and a deep breath. I held my hands out. Amaya's skin was a rainbow color. When the light hit it, it sparkled and glowed. She was a mystical creature. I closed my eyes, and I felt her skin upon my hands. Cold and dry, not slimy at all. She moved slowly as if she was soothing me. I got an instant connection with her. I opened my eyes. I griped her softly in my palms. It wasn't that bad holding a snake. She slithered her little tongue and looked into my eyes.

I blinked three times to break her trance. Staring in her eyes made me drowsy. I looked over at Beatrice. "Ok, your turn". Beatrice's eye widened, "I um, I'm kind of afraid. You're the animal person Ty. She seems to like you". I rolled my eyes and sighed. "Whatever Beatrice". Sergio laughed; he held his hands out and reached for Amaya. The truth was, I was getting comfortable holding her. I handed her to him slowly.

Sergio placed her back into the crate. Sergio lifted the crate with the handle and passed her to me. "Hope Gretta and Gisele are ok with Amaya." Beatrice smiled. "I'm sure it will be Ok. If anything, those cats will probably scare her. What are you feeding those things? Steroids? They're huge"!

I rolled my eyes again. "Gretta and Gisele are a special bread. Half domestic and half-wild. They are Bengal breeds". I gripped the handle of the crate. Sergio leads us back to the elevator. We rode back up to the top floor. He led us towards the door. "Well, it is always a pleasure to see you, Beatrice." He hugged her tightly. Again, another awkward moment for Beatrice. Sergio turned and looked at me and extended his hand. "It was a pleasure meeting you as well." I shook his hand, and we both headed out the front door.

As soon as I heard the door close. I looked over at Beatrice. I whispered, "Sooo, how do we know Sergio again"? Beatrice looked embarrassed; we walked towards her car. "Listen, Keith and I broke up for a little bit in college. "While we were broken up, I decided to try one of those sugar daddy sites." My eyes widened. "And you never told me about this"? Beatrice sighed, "I never told you because some people look down upon stuff like that." I licked my lips. "I'm your best friend, Beatrice. I wouldn't have judged you". Beatrice took a deep breath. "To make a long story short. I was struggling to pay some of my tuition. And Sergio was a friend who did that for me. I never lost his number. As I said, he's been a friend. Nothing more, since Keith and I have been married". Beatrice opened her car door.

I got close to her and hugged her. "I wouldn't have judged you." She got inside her car and closed the door. "Let me know how the first night goes with Amaya. I'll call you in the morning. Please get home safe". Beatrice sat in her car. Until I went over and got in mine. I started my car, and she started hers. Beatrice backed out, and I followed. We never drove off and left one another. We always left at the same time. It was our girl code for safety during my drive home. I tried extra hard, not hit any bumps. I didn't want to frazzle Amaya. The good thing was Sergio didn't live far. I pulled smoothly into my parking garage. I looked around to make sure the parking lot was clear. I opened my door. I walked around to the other side and pulled the crate out of the car. I briskly walked towards the elevator. Pressed the button and hoped no one was on it.

I mean, it wasn't a crime for a girl to carry around a crate? I just wanted to avoid those nosy people who like to strike up a conversation. As the elevator went up, my heart pounded. To my surprise, I made it to the eleventh floor, without one single person getting on. I gently but quickly walked to my door. I placed Amaya's crate on the floor and pulled out my key. I put the key in and opened the door. I slowly picked up the crate and moved in quickly. I put the crate down, shut the door. Locked it and peeped out the peephole. No one on sight.

Greta and Giselle ran out to greet me. They both stopped dead in their tracks. They both paused for a moment. Greta started to hiss at the crate. "No, Greta, No". I left the crate on the floor and went over and picked up Greta. Gisele jumped in my other arm. They were both heavy. I carried them into their bedroom and shut the door. I had a two-bedroom condo, so I turned one of the bedrooms into a kitty lounge for them. Of course, cats wouldn't like a snake. They probably smelled her as soon as I brought Amaya to the door. They were also very competitive for my love and affection. Also, very protective of me. I picked Amaya up and carried her into my bedroom.

I placed the crate on top of my dresser. I begin to take off my work clothes. I took a quick shower to refresh. I slipped into something more comfortable. I grabbed a glass of wine and sat on my bed. I stared at the crate. I closed my eyes to try and connect with Amaya. I visualized my heart charka glowing green. I imagined the glowing green light around my heart, become a long tunnel. A beam of light. I sent it into Amaya's crate to connect with her heart. I wanted her to know, and I wouldn't harm her. And, to open her thoughts up to me. So, we could connect and talk to each other telepathically.

You see, a lot of people think telepathic communication is through the mind. And it is, but once you say the words in your mind. Then you transfer the words into your heart. Next, you see the words traveling through the green beam and connecting to the other person's heart. It's hard to explain, but once you master it. You can talk to anyone, any animal, plant, tree, hybrid humans, and beyond.

I waited for a moment after sending the first green wave.
I closed my eyes and listened. Nothing. I sent the green
beam with my message again. Only this time stronger. I
used all my might. I paused, I heard Amaya jump and start
moving around in her crate. I was for sure she received
that one. It probably scared her. Not too many humans
tapped into their telepathic abilities. Amaya belonged to
a shaman. I'm sure he spoke to her, not sure how. Every
time you send a green beam with a message from your heart
to another. It's like a car with a dead battery. And you
connect the battery to the spark plugs. You send the
electrical vaults from one car to the other — the same
thing when sending messages from your heart to someone
else's heart.

I sparked her twice, and the second time it worked. I
sipped my wine some more. I was getting tipsy, and I
glared into Amaya's crate. As I was glaring, I saw a
rainbow mist coming from Amaya's crate. I waft it towards
my nose, and it was intoxicating. I started to get light-
headed. I put down my glass of wine after. The rainbow
mist was doing something to me. It was taking me under. I
must have connected with Amaya, and now she was taking
me.

I tried to shake it off, I looked into the mirror and
slapped myself repeatedly. I needed my Obsidian to block
her. My head was hazy. I tried to call upon my ancestral
spirit guides. "Elta, Iolean, Cisealy," I shouted. I knew
I must say each name three times. But, I couldn't, I
looked into the mirror. My body was fading. She was
taking me under, into another realm. I glanced at the
clock, and it was 10:30 Pm. I fell to the ground, and I
was weak.

   As I lay on the ground. I started to feel this weird
tingling on my scalp. I grabbed my forehead. The tingling
moved from my scalp down to my face. My body started
vibrating. The tingling continued down. Down to my
shoulders, breast, then further down to my waist.
Finally, the tingling moved down to my legs and then down
to my toes. My entire body tingled for several minutes.
And just like that! The tingling stopped. I glanced at
the clock, and it was still ten thirty PM. I felt really
lite, like a feather. I felt like I was floating on a
cloud. The light from the T.V. shined onto the mirror

over my dresser. I saw an object above me. I was floating in thin air.

I glanced at the mirror to see what it was. I grabbed my chest with fright! I looked even closer. To my surprise, the object floating above me was my very own body! I gasped with fear! I was floating, staring up at the ceiling. I turned over onto my stomach. I looked down and saw my lifeless body lying on the floor. I was horrified and scared. I mean, I had out-of-body experiences before but was induced by myself. Amaya was controlling this. I closed my eyes and opened them. I was hoping it was a dream. But it wasn't. I float over my body, lying on the floor. A sound like a soft cyclone filled my ears. It was a sucking noise. It got louder and louder.

My body drifted uncontrollably towards the sound. It was pulling me, and I couldn't stop it. I let out a scream as I gravitated towards it. I was wrapped inside a whirlwind. I begin to spin. I spun and spun and spun. I couldn't stop it. I let out another scream as it sucked me in. I was sucked in at high frequencies and altitudes. All of a sudden, it all stopped. I caught my breath, my eyes were still closed. I had landed in a damp place. I felt around with my hands. I felt rock-like walls. I finally opened my eyes.

I was inside a cave. There were candles on the stones walls that gave off a glimmer of light. There were about twenty people in rags Sitting on a bench with me. We were all lined up, waiting For what, I don't know. I looked around at the unfamiliar faces; everyone looked afraid. I glanced down at my attire. It looked like I was wearing a potato sack that had been ripped to shreds. A very funny looking, pale, a small man with a pointy hat walked in. He was wearing a purple robe. He approached the podium and stood before us. His hair was long and gray. He was holding two crystals balls. One in each hand. He then spoke out to the group.

"Who will be next, to try and defeat the Angel Rapers"? Angel raper? What the hell was going on? Who would be so cruel as to rape an actual angel? I was so confused. The wizard looked around the room. When no one volunteered, he took a deep sigh of disappointment. The little man speaks with anger. "Well, since I have no volunteers, I will appoint people! Let's see how about you, over there"? The wizard pointed to a tall man with olive skin. He had blonde hair and piercing blue eyes. The man was too afraid to look up. He jumped with fright. When he realized the little man was talking to him.

The wizard rose to his feet and started walking around. He spoke in a vexed tone. "Yes, you, over there! Look at me in this instance! And you, over there"! The wizard pointed to a female with very dark hair. Golden skin and extreme almond eyes. She started to panic. She stood up quickly. The wizard looked around the room. His eyes stumbled across mine. I anxiously looked down at my toes. I tried not to give him any more eye contact. He called out again, in a ghastly voice! "YOU! Over there, come forward!" I stood up slowly as I walked over. I notice the other two people were walking behind me. I was afraid. I didn't even know why I was here, in this realm. I looked up, and he stared at the three of us.

"Come with me to my chambers." He pulled his hands in front of his chest with the two crystal balls. He led us down a hallway, using the crystal balls to illuminate the dark path. The hallway reminded me of a walkway in a dungeon. It was very dark, and I couldn't see my feet if I wanted to. He led us to a room that looked like an office. There was a round table inside. He guided us over to the table. He then turns to us and speaks. "You may take your seats now."

We all pulled out a chair and sat down, apprehensively. He placed each crystal balls on a mantle. I looked around the room. There were multiple crystal balls. Each crystal ball had its own mantle. He walked towards us and sat down in a huge purple chair. He sat at the head of the table. He parted his lips to speak. "I have made my selection tonight. Based on my instincts. The powers that be have selected the three of you. To attempt this task. The powers that be have also informed me Only one of you will make it out alive".

My eyes widened as he said that last statement. The wizard continued talking. "Now, I will tell you all the tasks at hand." He spoke to us while pouring a special brew into three teacups, Dispersing them to each one of us. We all looked at each other. Then back down at the tea. "HAVE A SIP!!" I grabbed my chest, and his voice startled me. We all slowly lifted the mystery drink to our mouths and slowly sipped. He continued to talk. The drink had a black liquorish taste to it. He pulled a glass jar out of a black velvet bag. I stared intensely. There inside the jar were little fireflies like things. They looked fascinating. But, the aroma of the little creatures, infused my nostrils. And to my surprise, they smelled like death! I started coughing uncontrollably. The pungent funk was stuck in my throat.

I looked around at the others. They were still under the spell of the fireflies. They couldn't take their eyes off the jar. The olive-skinned man was so intrigued, and he began to speak. "What are those"? The wizard looked at us with excitement. "These are what we call…Angel rapers!! When the lid of the jar comes off. They will fly into the air and latch onto the walls. They will increase into the human size and become beautiful, alluring, glowing angels." The small wizard begins to smile. "They have gorgeous white fluffy wings that spread out wide, like eagle wings. They are completely naked underneath. Some are males, and some are females. Their wings cover them like a cocoon. They will float above you like tamed butterflies, penetrating and tranquilizing your soul.

They are inviting and will keep you in a trance. You will feel warm and fuzzy on the inside. Until you let down your guard." The wizard continued talking with seriousness. "As they lure you over towards them. They will infiltrate your mind. They will want you to touch their wings. At this point, they will grab you and wrap you into a coil, inside their wings. They have flesh-eating slime on the inside of their wings. It is ten times the strength of battery acid.

Once they have you on the inside of their wings, your flesh will be disintegrated. Until nothings left but your bones." He continued to speak in his ghastly tone. "As your soul leaves your body. They will devour it in every sexual way possible. Against your souls will". My heart started to beat rapidly. I called upon my spirit guides inside my head. The wizard continues talking. "The only way to defeat them…is simple". He paused for a minute. "Never…ever… look back!

Keep going until you are at the end of your journey.
If you look back, they are entitled to your soul. Never
give in to them, luring you towards their wings, fight
temptation! Only the strong will survive this task"! That
last sentence, only the strong will survive, played in my
head three times. Like a dreadful echo. I mean, this was
stupid, why were we doing this anyway? The wizard had
already foreseen; only one will make it out alive! Why
would he put our lives at jeopardy, two will die today! I
kept my composure. I closed my eyes and visualized a
shield around my body. A three-dimensional circle. That
no one could break. Not even the angels' rapers.

I felt my energy fields opening and growing strong.
I felt a boost of energy. The wizard got up from his
chair. "Let's go to the halls of doom!" His words gave me
chills. They ran up and down my spine. We all looked at
one another. I took a deep breath as I got up from my
chair. I followed behind the others. The wizard led us
out of the room into a dark hallway. He stopped us at a
pitch-black point. We couldn't see anything. I could hear
the others breathing rapidly; they were afraid. A glimmer
of light begins to shine. The wizard had pulled the jar
out of his black velvet bag.

The glow from the little fireflies lit up the hallway.
The hall was long and deep. So long, we couldn't see the
end to it. The wizard raised the jar slowly and started
to unscrew the top. I took a deep gulp. The wizard popped
the top off. The little fireflies drifted into the air.
Their wings were glowing brightly. With rapturous
enchanting beams of light. They flew higher and higher
and became larger and larger. I didn't realize how high
the ceiling was until the hallway lit up with a gorgeous
white illuminating glow.

I could finally see. I looked all around, from the top of
the ceiling to the floor. The walls and the ground were
made of gold. The walls had carvings of leaves and trees
Made of silver with emerald accents. They were amazingly
breathtaking. I glanced back at the fireflies. They had
grown into human size. They tamely float above us,
wrapped in their winged cocoon, staring. They were
unimaginable beings. Like nothing I've ever seen. How
could something so captivating be so evil? We all stared
at them while they stare back at the same time. The

proclaimed angel rapers all unwrapped themselves. Their cocoons opened. And, their wings stretched out wide. I glanced up; they were completely nude.

Their skin had a soft golden glow. That looked like it would melt, like butter, if you touched them. They were magical; people who were airbrushed in magazines didn't look this good. Their bodies could have been an exhibit on the perfect human specimen tour. The women had perfect hourglass figures. The men were muscular, like athletes. They were like Gods and Goddesses. This was unreal in my eyes. But, it wasn't' a hologram, just a different realm, of some sort. The wizard looked over at our faces and saw how we were gawking. He immediately became upset and yelled. "CONTROL YOURSELVES! THIS IS THE TYPE OF BEHAVIOR THAT WILL GET YOU KILLED!

Once you cross that line, there is no turning back! You must make it to the other side without having that temptation. You must never look back or touch them! Is that understood"? We all nodded our heads and replied, "Yes," at the same time. As we approached the starting line, I took a look at my opponent's face. The female with dark hair was almost in tears. I took a deep breath and decided. I will have no fear. If I had to do this, then I must be strong. This was my only way out.

The wizard raised his hand and spoke out to us. "You will now embark on your journey"! The wizard lowered his hand. We began to take baby steps as we crossed the line and walked slowly. Calm winds whipped through my hair. I felt a warmth on the inside. My nostrils were penetrated with the scent of fresh roses. Lilly's fell from the sky and landed gently in my hair. I walked faster as more lilies fell from the sky, showering my feet. The glow throughout the hall was heavenly and very bright. I glanced at the guy with the blonde hair. He darted out in front of me.

He was attempting to run in order to complete the journey. An angel flew down in front of him and floated above him. He kept walking, resisting the temptation. He did his very best not to look at her. The angel extended her wings and then a voice came to him. A soothing voice seemed to calm his ears. The angel did not move her lips. They were telepathic. "Come with me… come with me where everything is peaceful, and there is harmony in the land of Ever More".

The angel's voice was enchanting. We all somehow could hear the angel. The angel's voice echoed into our minds, body, and souls, Sending vibrations down my spine. The angel extended her other wing out, as she bared her naked, glowing, golden body. The angel stared down at the man with blond hair. He ran faster, but she stayed ahead of him. Floating in the nude, taunting and teasing him. The olive man begins to cry as he opened his eyes. The angel begins to speak telepathically again in her echoing, alluring voice.

"Come with me… come with me, come with me…" The man with blond hair took his eyes off the angel. He kept running as fast as he could. I walked slowly, trying not to bring attention to myself. But, I could feel a presence floating above me. The other female opponent was walking behind me. I couldn't see or hear her. But, I dare not look back. The angel started talking again. "Come with me…Come with me...!" The angel was floating so close to the man with blonde hair. The angel's nose was almost touching his lips.

He stopped running from exhaustion to catch his breath. He walked slowly and began to wipe the sweat from his forehead. The man with the blonde hair started staring at her gold, glowing naked body. When he did so, music filled my ears, and it was a violin. It was peaceful and deranged all at the same time. The man with the blond hair was becoming mesmerized. The angel moved her body seductively to the mellow sounds. He watched every move. Every erotic motion the angel made with her artistic sculptured frame. He was very intrigued. She was glammoring him. He found himself staring into the angel's eyes. Her nose pressed firmly against his lips. At that moment, I heard the footsteps of my female opponent.

Both of us stopped walking. The elegant violin came to a screeching halt! The color in the angle's face turned grayish. The gray started to invade his face. His life glow begins to leave his body. Before I knew it, his skin was totally gray. From head to toe. He stopped breathing, and his weakened body hit the floor. I felt a tear trickle from my right eye. I could hear my opponent whimpering behind me. The other angels detached themselves from the wall. They flew over to the feast that lay before them.

The angels gathered around him. They stood in a circle. They attached and locked their wings together. They all bowed their heads as a mysterious glow filled the circle. His soul begins to leave his lifeless body. It rose from his corpse slowly. A female angel flew in front of his soul. She just kind of fluttered there for a moment. She lifted out her wings. She shoved his soul back down onto the ground. She climbed on top of him. She pinned his soul to his body on the floor.

Her appearance begins to change. Her golden skin and heavenly glow became a dark gray. Her face became demonic. Fangs grew from her mouth. They dripped with salivation. She forcefully inserted his penis into her acidic vagina walls. Here moisture was stronger than battery acid, just like the wizard had foreseen. The olive man let out a horrific roar! "Ahhhhhhhhhhhhhhhhhhhhhhhhh!" The angel's breast bounces up and down as she devoured his soul. She continued riding him like the motion of ocean waves.

The others gathered around and watched her take him. They formed a line. Like a train, and started taking turns on him. The sounds were excruciating. I could hear my other opponent breaking down in tears. I was becoming weak. While the angel rapers were busy. I decided to console my opponent. I whispered to her. "Hey, back there, come closer…walk with me, and lets finish together. Let's be each other's support system. We have to make it out of here alive!" I felt heavy breathing against my neck, and a cold, clammy hand grasped mine. I let out a sigh of relief.

I looked to my side and saw the dark-haired girl. I was relieved, I felt stronger, and blood begins to pump through my veins. The power of human contact was indescribable. We passed the group of angel rapers feasting on the blond-haired man. We walked by quickly separating ourselves from the feasting angels. My opponent leaned in and whispered in my ear. "Let's run; let's just go!" I looked at her and nodded my head in agreement. At that point, we looked at each other. Broke the bond from our hands. We darted down the hall. We ran fast, we ran hard, down the hall for distances. We kept running and running and running to the point of exhaustion. I started to see a small white light shining in the midst of the golden glow. I was coming upon the end of the golden tunnel. I was running out of breath.

The violins started playing again. The glowing enchanting angels appeared before me. One angel got very close to me. She floated between the two of us. She uncoiled her wings. She extended the right one to both of us. I moved my arm so her wing wouldn't touch. My opponent saw the angel's wings come towards her. The angel then began to speak in an echoing voice. "Come with me… Come with me!"

Not wanting the angel's wing to come any closer. My opponent swatted her wings out of fear. She begins to lose her balance. My opponent tripped over her shoe. Her shoulder landed in the center of the angel's chest. My opponent became stuck! The angel smiled, spread both her wings out wide. She then Brought them together down low. She wrapped and coiled my opponent inside her wings. The beautiful golden glow left the angel's body as she became gray in color. I stopped running, and I could barely breathe. I almost passed out, I had to rest. As I slowed down, I watched as the angel disintegrated my opponent's body. Horrible screams filled my ears. As the flesh-eating slim on the inside of the angel's wings melted her flesh.

The angel then opened her wings out wide. Crushed bones came tumbling out and hit the floor. The bones were covered in slim. There was nothing left of her. Her soul rose from the ground into the air. The other angel, rapers, flew over and piled on top of her. They devoured her in a corner. I held in my screams. I caught my breath while doing some deep breathing. I decided to run like hell. My lungs had enough air. I took off running as fast as I could. The soft white light was becoming clearer and brighter. I could visibly see the end of the hall. I heard something floating above me.

I dashed down the hall. I tripped and fail. I slid across the ground. As I lay on my back, I blacked out for a moment out of exhaustion. When my eyes reopened. I realized I already crossed into the white light. I was

exhausted and happy at the same time. I gripped and
hugged the floor. I slowly pulled myself up. An angel was
floating on the golden side. We just stared at each
other, as she couldn't cross. I was looking back, which
was forbidden. I was no longer in the golden tunnel. The
angel spread her wings and flew back into the golden
light. I laid down on my back to catch my breath. I begin
to cry; tears rolled down the sides of my face. The
glowing white light became more dense and brighter. My
head begin to tingle. The whirlwinds came and whisked me
away.

Chapter eight

Guinea Pig

The whirlwind threw me back into my bedroom. I landed on
the floor. I sat up and shook my head to snap myself out
of it. I was still a bit dizzy. As I raised my head, I
glanced at the clock. It was ten-thirty PM. At the same
time, it was when the whirlwinds came and took me away.
While I was in the other realm, time stood still as it
did at times. I quickly remembered how this all happened
in the first place. Amaya!!! I glanced up at her crate. I
could tell she was sleeping. I couldn't hear the rattle
from her tail. I quietly inched up from the floor until I
rose upon my feet.

I tiptoed over to my closet. I opened the door. A small
creek let out. I heard a small rattle from Amaya's tail.
I moved quickly inside. My Nuumite and obsidian necklace
was hanging where I left it. I grabbed it and put it
around my neck. I glanced over at Amaya's crate. She was
waking up. Her red eyes widened. She was surprised I had
made it back. She was trying to take me under again but
she couldn't. My necklace was protecting me. The rainbow
mist came floating out of her crate. I stood there,
staring at her. It wasn't working at all.

I walked over to the vault. Where I was keeping the book
of Nigron. I spun the code into the lock. I opened the
safe and pulled the book out. When Amaya laid her red
twirling eyes on the book, she became afraid. Her tail
started rattling loud and fierce. I looked at the book;

it was glowing. Amaya's red twirling eyes became green. Amaya rolled over in her crate and fell into a deep sleep. I scratched my head out of confusion. The book was controlling Amaya. I grabbed my cell phone and called Beatrice.

Beatrice answered on the first ring. I started hyperventilating. "Beatrice listen, something weird has happened! I need you to get over to the condo now! Beatrice half asleep. "What? Why? What's going on"? I caught my breath. "Listen, Amaya put a spell on me, and somehow pulled me into another realm. Against my will Beatrice. I almost died in there"! Beatrice became quiet. "Listen calm down, Ty. Where is Amaya now?" I calmed down a bit.

"She's in her crate, passed out. I grabbed my protection necklace. Her magic couldn't get through. Then I pulled the book of Nirgon out. She became afraid, and then she passed out…sleep". Beatrice was yawning. "Well, Ty, that means you need to have the book on you at all times. I can't drive over there right now. Keith and I are in bed, sleep. Just keep the book by your side at all times. Just until we can get Amaya to your grandmother's bed and breakfast". I was still afraid. "Easy for you to say, she's not in your house"! I heard Beatrice sigh. "Listen, Ty, just sleep in the living room. Close that door and lock her up just until I can get there.

You shouldn't have to go through this alone. I promise I'll be there in the morning". I let out a yawn. I was exhausted. "Ok, I'll sleep on the couch. Talk to later, call me." I hung up the phone. Grabbed the blankets off my bed. I tiptoed out, with the book of Nigron in my hands. I shut the door quietly, and I locked it and laid on the couch. I was so tired, and I passed out, everything went black.

I awoke that morning to a frantic knock at my door. I grabbed my chest out of fright. I almost jumped out of my skin! I rolled off the couch and ran over to the door. I peeped out of the peephole. It was Beatrice. I unlocked the locks and opened the door. "Why are you knocking like the God damn police or something? You scared the shit out of me. Beatrice walked in with one small bag of luggage. She looked around the living room and glanced at my attire. "Why aren't you dressed?" I scratched my head and thought about it for a moment. It was Saturday morning. I grabbed my forehead. I totally forgot. We were to transport Amaya to Grandmother's bed and breakfast.

"Listen, Beatrice, I totally forgot, I mean… I almost died last night!" Beatrice rolled her eyes. "Ok, ty, take a quick three-minute shower. Grab some clothes and let's go. You know my time is limited. I have to get back to Keith and Cameron around the same time tomorrow." I was still clutching the book of Nigron in my hands. "Oh my God Ty, did you sleep with that book all night?" I rolled my eyes out of embarrassment. "Of course, I did, once I pulled the book out, she became very afraid." Beatrice glanced over at my bedroom door. "Amaya's in your bedroom? She's still asleep, right"?

I shook my head. "I don't know, I haven't been back in since last night. She fell into some kind of deep slumber. "I noticed once I put on my protection necklace, and her powers didn't work anymore. Then I pulled out the book of Nigron, and she became afraid, and fell asleep." Beatrice slowly walked towards my bedroom door. She quietly twisted the knob and popped open the door. Beatrice peeked her head inside. I glanced over, Amaya was still asleep in her crate. Beatrice was about to tiptoe in. "Wait!" I took my nuumite and obsidian necklace from around my neck. I handed it to Beatrice.

Beatrice grabbed it and put it around her neck. She then stepped into the room. She took the dark blanket off my dresser. She threw it over the crate. She picked the crate up by the levers and carried it out of the room. She placed the crate in front of the door. "Go take your shower, get dressed, pack, and let's go!" I ran into my room. Packed a few outfits and my toothbrush. I hopped in the shower, got dressed, and was ready to go.

Beatrice carried the crate down to her car. I help put her inside the trunk. I kept the book of Nigron clutched in my hands. We drove straight through to South Carolina down to the islands. It was always an eerie feeling coming back home. Every time we got close. I would roll the windows down and smell the intoxicating air. Id deeply inhales, and feel the breeze whip through my hair. My scalp tingled, felt like the fingers of the ancestors were stroking my hair, welcoming me home. We finally arrived, and Beatrice pulled into the driveway. She had driven the whole way. She knew I had an awful night. It was only four hours, three and a half with no traffic.

Beatrice always became a little sad. She had nothing left on the islands anymore. Both her parents deceased. Her older brother sold the land to the resort people. Beatrice and I were in college at that time. She had no say in what happened. The property was left to her brother. We got out of the car and carried our things towards the door. I would never sell this place. At that moment, my mind beamed a Hologram of my grandmother. She looked the same, as she did when I was a child. Grandmother She-wolf turned and looked at me "How will the children know of their legacy? If they can just take the land and make condos. The land is sacred; the trees are thousands of years old.

They hold the secrets to our existence. I know the land will be safe with you, Tituba". She smiled at me. A tear ran down my face, from my right eye. I wiped it away quickly and continued to walk towards the door. I opened it and walked in. The smell of cinnamon and white sage came tumbling through my nostrils. That scent of my grandmother never left this house. I took my bags into her bedroom and unpacked. Even though there were eight rooms in the house. Beatrice always stayed in the room with me unless a few of the other girls were here to share a room with.

I was thinking about reopening bed and breakfast on the weekends only. Maybe hire someone to run the place. But, now that Beatrice and I will be running a youth spa, it could be pretty lucrative if things go right with Amaya. Beatrice looked over at me. "Why don't we take Amaya down to the basement and condition her there." I shook my head. "Yeah, you're right; we shouldn't do it in grandmother's room." I sat down on the bed. Beatrice sat next to me. "Hey, I was thinking, we shouldn't try this the first time on each other. Let's go downtown tonight and pick us up a Guinea pig".

I looked at Beatrice, and she was starting to reek of greed again. I thought about it for a minute. Beatrice did have a point. "Well, where would we find one

Tonight?" Beatrice had a smirk on her face. "Well, I figured, we could convince a homeless person to do it for five hundred dollars." I glanced deep into Beatrice's eyes, and this was all premeditated. It was a painful gift to know the truth. But, I played dumb as usual. "We could try Beatrice". She smiled, "Hey, it's cold outside tonight. That's like three nights of hotel stays and groceries for the week." I nodded my head. "Your right Bea, we shouldn't be the ones to go first. But, before we go downtown, let's make sure Amaya is safe. We have to put a spell on her so that she will obey us". Beatrice grabbed her hands. "Yeah, your right, wasn't looking forward to that part. But we have protection. Plus, I know your grandmother is here with us".

Beatrice played the role of cool, calm, and collective. But, I could smell nervousness seeping out of her pores. We were both nervous. But so desperately needed a change. All we talked about in college was going into business together and becoming independently wealthy. I smiled to myself. Those were young girl dreams. Then you get into the real world and those dreams, kind of fade. Beatrice pulled me out of my thought. She tapped my arm. "Hey, let's take Amaya down now, and try." I only got twenty-four hours. Until I go back to my demanding child and over-sexed husband. We both laughed.

We left Amaya sitting in her crate in the hallway. We both got up at the same time and walked over. I kept the book of Nigron tight in my hands. Beatrice grabbed the handle of the crate. She lifted the crate slowly. We both looked inside. Amaya was still asleep. We tiptoed downstairs to the basement. We sat Amaya on a desk. It was a little dusty in the basement. Neither of us sat down. We took the book to a corner, and I opened it up. I fumbled through the book until I found the spell to control the rainbow serpent.

Beatrice pulled the string above us to turn on more light. We both hovered over the book of Nigron. We read at the same time. We had to say her name three times. While stomping our foot three times. This will awaken her again. We read down further. Once she is awake, we can ask her whatever we want. And as long as the book is present, she will do whatever we want. We both looked at each other.

"Well, let's do it together, Bea. On the count of three."
Beatrice nodded her head, yes. We both stomped three
times. We looked at each and gulped. We said her name
three times. "Amaya, Amaya, Amaya!"

We both look over at the crate. Her eyes begin to glow
red. The rainbow mist begins to fill her crate. The
rainbow smoke started drifting outside of the crate. The
smell was sweet and intoxicating. Beatrice and I looked
around. The whole room was filled with the rainbow mist.
We glanced back at the crate. Amaya was increasing in
size! We both stepped back a little. Beatrice grabbed my
arm. Amaya was almost the size of a boa. The top of her
crate came off. She projected into the air. Amaya was now
about six feet tall. Beatrice and I were afraid. I grip
the book of Nigron tighter.

Amaya finally stopped growing. But, the top half of her
body begins to morph into a woman — Amaya shape-shifted
right before our very eyes. From the waist down, she was
still a rainbow serpent. From the top up, she had become
a ravishing being. Amaya had long black hair, deeply
tanned skin. Amaya's face was alluring and youthful. Her
eye lashes were long and thick. She had thick pouty
lips. Above her top lip was a black beauty mark. Her
breast was big and firm, and she was bare. Amaya's Snake
bottom half begins to glow, mostly red, but a rainbow.
Amaya had a red rose on the right side of her hair.

She finally flickered her long black eye lashes. Amaya
opened her eyes wide. She looked like she was in a
trance. She looked at Beatrice and I. She inhaled deeply.
"Hello, I am Amaya, you have summoned me, how can I help
you?" Beatrice fumbled for her words, so I stepped in.
"We read in our book, you hold the power of youth and
immortality?" She smiled and fluttered her lashes. "Yes,
I do, how can I be of service to you?" Beatrice finally
got the balls to speak. "Well…how does it work?" Amaya
bowed her head and began to speak.

"Well, I coil back down to my small size. I must be
placed in the mouth of the one who wants to become
immortal. From there, I will lay my eggs. And the
participant will swallow." Beatrice and I had read all
of this in the book. We just wanted to make sure it was
correct. I scratched my head and asked her a question out

of confusion. "How…how are you able to be in this form?"
Amaya smiled. "Well, firstly, I am a Naga. I am of the
Naga species. I am half women half snake. My kind became
extinct a long time ago. Well here on earth, in the
material. We are no longer able to walk in this world
because of the low vibrational frequency. I can appear
for a short period because one or both of you are in the
eighth dimension.

I only have a short time before I coil back down into a
snake. That is the only way, I can survive right now." I
took a deep breath. "Why…why did you send me into that
other realm." Amaya became quiet and looked me in the
eyes. "I wanted you to feel what it was like to be pulled
out of your home against your will." I looked into her
eyes. "I'm sorry, I apologize. But I almost died." Amaya
chuckled, "And, you think my journey here was easy?
People are quite afraid of snakes. They will do whatever
possible to protect themselves. Even if the snake is calm
and posing no possible threat.

I was poked, beaten, and locked into tight quarters. All
the way here, it was a very long journey". I smiled,
"Once again, I am sorry. You will be a very important
addition to our team." Beatrice stepped in. "Do we have
to worry about being pulled into another realm?" Amaya
smiled, "As long as you have the book of Nigron. I am to
obey. When the book is not present, I can't be sure of
anything. I'm sorry, I'm just honest. I am a serpent."

Beatrice and I looked at one another. "Well, we plan on
getting our first client today for you. Is that ok?"
Amaya flickered her long eyelashes and rattled her tail.
"If the book Of Nigron is present, I will obey." I
cleared my throat. "Is that a yes?" Amaya smiled, "yes,
it is, happy to be a part of the team. I will go back to
my crate and get some rest. Being in Naga form, in this
frequency, is quite draining. I glanced down at the book.
"Yes, of course, will see you in a little while." She
bowed her head and rattled her tail. The rainbow mist and
enchanting scent filled the air. She shrunk back down
into a small snake. She slithered back into her crate. I
walked over and put the lid on top. I placed the lock
back on.

Beatrice looked over at me. She took a deep breath. "Well, you ready to go find our Guinea pig?" I smiled, "I guess! It has to be done before we take the big plunge." We both started laughing. "Um, downtown is probably going to be our best bet. "Yeah, your right Bea". We gathered our things and headed upstairs. I turned and looked at Amaya's crate. "Shouldn't we take her upstairs? It's so dark, dusty, and cold down here." Beatrice sighed, "You are such an animal lover Ty. Grab her and let's go upstairs. At some point, we will make a special procedure room that she will stay in. I went back and grabbed the crate off the table.

We went upstairs, and I placed her crate in one of the vacant rooms. With the money we bring in, I could remodel this whole house. Grandmother kept it nice and up to date. But, it needed a modern touch. Beatrice and I loaded up in the car and headed downtown. We pulled into an area that was known for panhandlers. We parked the car by a gas station And staked out. It was still light out. So, we could see what we were dealing with. Beatrice put the car in park. "Ok, so… what exactly are we looking for, Ty?" I swallowed my coffee. "Well, I would say, a female in her late thirty's. The early forties, Maybe a few bags under the eyes. Someone who will make good before and after picture".

Beatrice reached into her purse. "Well, I got the five hundred in cash on me. You think that's enough to let a snake crawl around in your mouth?" I sipped more of my coffee. "Hey, if it's done right, the outcome is priceless. Unfortunately, there are people around here who would do a whole lot more for a whole lot less. If you catch what I'm saying." Beatrice smiled, "Yeah, you're right." As I made that statement. I thought of my cousin Taylor, and her drug addiction. When I got back to my grandmother's house, I had to call and check up on her. Haven't really spoken to her since I left New Orleans. Just a few checkup texts, here and there.

Beatrice spotted a woman. "Look, her, right there." I glanced over. I saw a woman maybe in her thirties. But aging badly because of the drugs. She had long blonde greasy hair, pale blue eyes. I looked at Beatrice. "She'll work!" I placed my coffee into the cup holder. I opened the door and stepped out. She was standing at a payphone. She was smoking a cigarette. She looked as though she was waiting on someone. I Glanced back at the car. Beatrice shooed me with her hands. For me to get closer. I turned back around and proceeded. I took a deep breath and approached her. The smell of demonic sex burned my nostrils. Sex demons had a burning type odor. She had an attachment. I could see it faintly above her head. I continued to approach her, and attachments didn't' scare me.

She stopped mid smoke and turned around and smiled. "Hey there gorgeous, how can I help you today?" Her accent was deep south, very country. She stared at my breast then took a puff of her cigarette. I swallowed deeply. "How would you like to make a quick five hundred dollars." Her eyes widened. "Well, hot damn!" she clapped her hands. "I haven't made five hundred in one night in a long time. What kind of kinky shit you into?" I scratched my head. "Um no, see, um it's for my friend and me, over there in the car."

She looked over in the car at Beatrice. She smiled and waved. "Heyyyyyy, girlfriend!" She took another puff and licked her lips. "Well, I must admit, I ain't never had me two exotic black girls in one night." She dropped her cigarette to the ground and stomped it out with her foot. "So, is that your girlfriend over there? You two got some type of lesbian love going on over there?" People were starting to stare. We had to move this convo to the car. "Hey let's go talk about it in the car, is that ok?" She smiled "Well shit, for five hundred dollars, we can talk where ever you want?" We walked over to the car. Beatrice's eyes bucked. I opened the back door and guided her into the car. I opened my door upfront and got in.

Beatrice turned around to the back. "Hi, I'm Beatrice." She put her hand out for a shake. The lady took Beatrice's hand and kissed it. "Nice to meet you. I'm Candy." I cleared my throat. "So, um Candy, we aren't really looking for any sex tonight." She popped a piece of gum into her mouth and began to chew and smile. "I see, just a little licky licky, I suppose." We both laughed; I had to explain more to her. "No, Candy, we are both scientists. My friend Beatrice here works in an anti-aging lab. We both create beauty products. We also do procedures to keep people looking younger and feeling better." Candy stopped chewing her gum and licked her lips. "So, no sex huh?"

Beatrice laughed. "No, not from us. But, we do have five hundred dollars cash! If you'd like to be our first participant for a new procedure." Candy started chewing her gum again. "Well, I could use that five hundred dollar regardless. So, the answer is yes!" Beatrice and I smiled at one another. I glanced back at Candy. "Oh, I'm Ty, by the way." Candy smiled, "What's Ty short for? Can't be your full name." I sighed and rolled my eyes. "It's Tituba." Candy's blue piercing eyes lit up. "Tituba, like the witch trials Tituba, in Salem?" I rolled my eyes again. "The name goes back much farther, then the Salem witch trials. It is a historical name". Candy could tell I was annoyed. "Hey, I didn't mean anything bad about it. I like the name, use to be a history major, that's all." I smiled, "Well, thank you."

Beatrice cranked up the car and drove off. It was awkwardly quiet in the car. I turned on the radio. I glanced in the back seat through the rear-view mirror. Candy was smacking her gum and staring out the window. "So, hey guys, where we headed to?" I smiled, "we are going to Low country." Her mouth dropped with excitement. "Down by the water, nice little vacation spot." I smiled, "Yeah, my grandmother has a bed breakfast; it's where I grew up." Candy smiled, "nice, island girl, huh?" Beatrice laughed. "Yeah, we both are." Candy's phone begins to ring; she glanced at it and placed it in her purse. "Damn parasite, always calling for his half. Well, he ain't getting half tonight." Beatrice and I looked at each other. We were close to bed and breakfast and turned onto our block. We pulled into the driveway. We all got out of the car. Candy's eyes lit up. "Wow, I hit five hundred and a vacation spot. I get my room and can stay the night, right?"

I smiled, "Yes, of course, there are no other people here. It hasn't been open to the public in years. But, yes, we'd like you to stay overnight. We need to make sure everything is working properly." Beatrice led us to the door. I popped the key in, and we all went inside. Candy looked around, "Wow, nice place, a little ancient, but it has character. So why isn't it open to the public?" I sighed, discussing my grandmother's death always made me sad. "Well, my grandmother passed when I was still in college, up in Atlanta. So, it's been closed since." Beatrice stepped in. "Were turning this place into a spa retreat. People will come, vacation, and get procedures done."

I decided to show Candy to her room. "Your room is right down here. Get adjusted for a little bit, were going to set up the procedure room." Candy smiled, "Great because I needed to use the bathroom, like an hour ago." She ran into her room. Then stuck her head back out the door. "Love the room!" She went back in and closed the door. I glanced over at the crate in the hallway. I walked over to my purse and grabbed the book of Nigron.

"Hey Beatrice, let's take the crate in my grandmother's office. We can do the procedure there. There's an old school couch where grandmother use to do readings. Like one of those shrink couches. Where you tell your psychologist all your problems." Beatrice laughed, "Great, let's get Amaya in there. And, oh, check these out." Beatrice pulled a folder out of her purse. It looked like a small suitcase. I grabbed the folder and opened it.

It was a consent form for the procedure. I smiled, "Damn it, Bea, you are so good, I totally forgot." She smiled as she pulled the crate into the office. "Hey, that's what partners are for, got it covered, in case anything happens." My smile went away quickly. "I appreciate it, but nothing will happen, ok?" Beatrice sighed, "Ty, it sounds like your trying to convince yourself, I'm fine." At that moment my phone rang. I dug my cell phone out of my purse. It was Kent walker. "Hey, I need to take this call, be right back." I walked into my grandmother's room and answered my phone. I closed the door and sat on the bed.

"Hello, Kent…how are you?" He chuckled, "I'm fine, so you finally answered your phone?" I paused, "Yes, Kent; I'm sorry, just had a lot going on this weekend. How are you?" "I'm good; I just wanted to spend some time with you." I fumbled for my words. "Yeah, I know, hey, let's hook up when I get back on Sunday?" "Sounds good Ty, I look forward to it, talk to you soon." I hung up the phone. I had a connection with Kent. But I had to put my selfish feelings aside. I needed to find out more about my parents and my brother. Who was obviously still alive. And, Kent had some or all of those answers. Or at least his father did. I had already seen most of it in a hologram. Beatrice came and knocked on the opened door. "Earth to Ty, we have a procedure to run here."

I got up from the bed, placed my purse down. Carried the book of Nigron tightly in my hands and headed to the office. I walked inside, and Beatrice was sitting down at the desk. Amaya's crate was sitting on top of the desk. Beatrice looked up at me. "Well, you ready?" I sat in the chair across from her. "As ready as I'll ever be." Beatrice licked her lips. "I'm honestly a bit excited, if this works, this will be our freedom. Freedom from our lab coats." We both started laughing. "Well, let's summons Amaya."

I pulled her crate closer to me. I called out her name three times and stomped my foot three times. The rainbow mist begins to fill the room. That enchanting scent opened my nostrils. Amaya begin growing in her crate. She broke the top of the lid off and popped out. She continued to grow until she was full size.

Her tailed rattled and filled our ear drums with an enticing sound. It was almost unreal. Her long rainbow tail uncoiled onto the floor. She opened big beautiful baby doll eyes. She smiled, "You summons me?" I held the book of Nigron tightly. "I…I did, we have our first client today." Amaya bowed her head. "Bring her in." Beatrice looked concerned. "Hey, why don't we put Amaya behind the white screen we have here.

This way, we move the screen and reveal Amaya. Instead of the client walking into to a big shock. I will have her sign the paperwork. Then have Amaya do her part." I thought for a minute. "Your right Beatrice, I'm sure no one in our lifetime has seen a Naga." Amaya bowed and slithered behind the white screen. You could see her silhouette, but for all candy knew, she could be a statue.

Beatrice got up from the desk and walked down the hall. I put the consent form on a clipboard and grabbed a pen. Beatrice came walking into the room with Candy. I stood up, "Hey, Candy, you ready for the procedure?" Candy smiled, "I'm ready for that five hundred dollars and my night here in paradise." Beatrice smiled.

'Well, have a seat here on the couch. Ty will go over the paperwork with you." Candy walked over and sat on the couch. She glanced at the white screen and made a curious face. I went and sat next to her. "Well, Candy, we will need you to sign this consent form." I headed her the pen and clipboard. She looked it over. "So, this procedure has something to do with snakes?"

I leaned over and looked at the clip board. "Why, yes, that's what I wanted to explain to you. This is an anti-aging procedure, using natural products. You will have to ingest snake eggs." Candy giggles a little. "Well, I've eaten caviar, so it can't be worse than that. Look, I really need that five hundred dollars. I had some quiet time to think in the room. That five hundred dollars will put me right at one thousand dollars when I add it to my other money. You see I need to get an apartment to get my kids back. I'd swallow a donkeys' ass right now, to get my kids back." I looked over at Beatrice; her eyes were big. I held back my laugh. "Well, Candy, I'm glad you have that team spirit. There is one more step before the eggs." Candy signing her consent form.

"We have to put the snake inside your mouth." Candy stopped writing for a minute. "You mean… a live snake?" I used my eyes to calm her. I stared deeply and sent calming vibrations. She took a deep breath. "Well, it's a trained snake, right?" Beatrice stepped in. "Why yes, of course." Would you like to meet her now?" She glanced down at the form and finished off signing her name. "Well, let's get this over with." I smiled, "great before you meet Amaya, I just want to go over a few things." Candy handed me the clipboard and pen.

"O.K spill the beans, I'm listening." I got up and walked the clip board over to Beatrice. I went back and sat down next to Candy. "Well, once the snake is in your mouth, do not move. Let her climb inside and lay her eggs. Since you are the very first, we are not sure how long that part will take. We will be timing it with a stopwatch. But now I get to tell you, the perks of this procedure, other than the money." Her eyes widened. "Oh, wow, I get more than money and the one-night stay." I shook my head. "Yes, when the serpent lays her eggs in your mouth, you will swallow them once the eggs are swallowed if you don't move or talk. You will become youthful again in appearance. All your wrinkles, sagging skin, and boobs, will perk up again." Candy's eyes lit up. "Not only that, your health will change for the better. You will live a very, very, very long time." Beatrice shook her head yes. "Yes, Candy, a very long time."

She looked at Beatrice and looked at me and smiled. "Well, let's get this show on the road." Beatrice grabbed her phone. "OK, if you can just stand up against the wall. I need to get a before pictures." Candy got up from her seat and went and stood up against the wall. Beatrice took close up pictures of her face. "Ok, candy, can you strip down to your panties and bra? I need to get a body shot." Candy pulled off her shirt and jeans and threw them on to the floor. Candy stood back against the wall. Beatrice snapped a few pictures. "Ok, great, these will do. You can have a seat back on the couch."

Candy walked over and sat down. She laid down on the couch. I rubbed my hands together. "Ok, time to meet Amaya!" Candy shook her head, yes. "Ok, I'm as ready as I'll ever be." Beatrice moved the white screen to the side, and Amaya slithered out. She appeared before Candy. Candy's eyes widened. "What…what the hell is that? She's human size! I can't fit her in my mouth!" Beatrice walked over. "No, no, she shrinks back down, will let you know, when to Open Your Mouth." Candy calmed down, I grabbed my phone and went to the stopwatch app. Candy pointed, "Is that thing real?" Amaya's tail begins to rattle loud; she begins to speak.

"I am Amaya, and I am not a thing." Candy's eyes widened more. "It talks, by golly it talks." Amaya's tail begins to rattle loudly again. "I am Amaya, not an, It." Candy became apologetic, "Oh, please forgive me, it's just, I've never seen anything like you before in my life. "I actually think you are quite gorgeous." Amaya smiled, "Thank you." Beatrice came closer, "Ok, its time." Candy relaxed on the couch and laid back. She closed her eyes. I got my stopwatch ready. "Ok, Amaya, do your thing." Amaya bowed and started to shrink back down into a baby snake size.

We watched her transform. Candy opened one eye and watched. When Amaya became super small. Candy closed both eyes again. I walked over and picked up Amaya from the Ground. I looked over at Candy. "Ok. Candy, it's time, Open Your Mouth!" Candy took a deep swallow and opened her mouth. I moved my hand closer to her mouth. Amaya slithered inside. Candy's eyes opened and then closed again. I started my stopwatch, as Beatrice took a few pictures. I shined a light from my phone into Candy's mouth. Beatrice and I leaned in and looked. Amaya swirled around and around. Candy looked as though she was going to gag, but didn't. I watched the time. Finally, Amaya stopped swirling. The pupils of her eyes begin to twirl as if she was under a spell.

My eyes were glued, the room was quiet; you could hear a pin drop. Finally, a green slime came from Amaya's tail. And out plopped the first egg, then the second. Beatrice grabbed Candy's hand. She looked as if she was going to gag. But didn't. Amaya's eyes stop twirling. She paused for a second and slithered out of Candy's mouth. I stopped the stopped watch. I grabbed Amaya as she slithered down Candy's chin. I walked her over to the crate quickly and put her back inside. I walked quickly over to candy. Beatrice said, "Now, swallow!" Candy gulped the eggs down. She took a deep breath. She sat up and opened her eyes. "I need a glass of water, please."

I grabbed her bottled water off the desk. I cracked it open and handed it to her. Beatrice and I kept our eyes glued on Candy. Within seconds, the crow's feet and bags around her eyes disappeared. The fine lines around her mouth smoothed out. The cracks in her forehead disappeared. Candy's face became twenty years younger. I looked at her boobs. They began to perk up and became full. Her stomach flattened. Candy's waist slimmed, her hips became curvy. She looked at her hands. No dents or discoloration. She glanced down at her breast. She smiled, "I need the mirror; where's a mirror?" Beatrice opened the closet door, inside was a full body mirror.

Candy ran and got in front of it. She paused for a minute and touched her face. Candy then touched her breast and hips. She was speechless for about a minute. "Oh, my God! I mean wow! How?" I could tell she was pleased with her results. "The eggs, the eggs that you swallowed, made you youthful and immortal." Candy continued to touch her face in disbelief. "How long will this last?" Beatrice walked over, "Forever!" Beatrice reached in her pocket and pulled out the five hundred in cash. "You held up your end of the bargain, here's your cash." Candy's eyes became electric, looking at the money.

She grabbed the money and began to count it. She stopped and looked in the mirror, mid count. "So, this is the new Candy, forever? My kids probably won't recognize me. But it's ok; I'm gonna be around for a long time." Candy quit counting the money and shoved it into her bra. "With a body and face like this, I can get off the streets. I can go back to working in gentlemen's clubs. Making some serious money for my kids and me." Beatrice pulled her phone back out. "ok, I need to get a few after pictures, and you can relax in your room for the night. Also, we will need to see you back in two weeks for a follow-up. Just to make sure things are going great." Candy posted back up against the wall.

She decided to do model poses for these pictures. She was so happy with her results. And Bea and I were ecstatic. Everything worked out wonderfully. Candy gathered her clothes and put them back on — her pants kind of sagged off her hips. Candy noticed and tugged at them. She looked up with a smile. "Well, time to do some shopping. New body New face, new clothes." She headed for the door and then turned around. "Thank you, guys, so much. This is going to change my life."

She walked out and closed the door. Beatrice and I looked at each other. We both started jumping up and down. We muted our happy screams. It worked! Beatrice bounced over and hugged me. We started jumping up and down together. Beatrice pulled back and looked at me. "Were going to be rich! Filthy rich! Do you know how much people will pay for something like this? I think we should charge 10,000 a pop!" My eyes widened. "OMG, ten people would be 100,000. Split that's fifty grand apiece!" Beatrice licked her lips. "That would include their stay and a brunch." I watched her eyes light up. "I got it all planned out in my head!"

That smell of greed infused my nostrils. I mean, I was excited as well. This was a breakthrough for us. And both of us hated being tied to our jobs. We wanted our freedom. I mean, our salaries weren't bad. But we still couldn't walk away if we wanted to. Beatrice looked at the crate. "Where's Amaya going to sleep tonight?" I looked around, "she can stay here in this room tonight." Beatrice nodded. "Are you going to take her back to your apartment." I rolled my eyes. "Do I have a choice Beatrice, she has to be fed." Beatrice sighed, "Ok, just let me talk to Keith. I think we can swap every other week just until we start making money. Then we can hire someone to feed her and work at the spa."

I thought about it for a minute. "Yeah, your right; I am going to need a break, so please talk to Keith." Beatrice smiled, "I will, I promise, just give me little time." Beatrice started to yawn. "I need to get some z's, gotta travel back early in the morning. Plus, we have to drop Candy off." I sighed, "yeah, your right; let's get to bed."

We walked out and left Amaya in the procedure room. I closed the door behind us. Beatrice followed me to my grandmother's room. I slept on the bed, and Beatrice slept on the couch. The couch let out into a bed. I went into the bathroom, brushed my teeth and washed my face. Beatrice did the same down the hall. I climbed in bed, got cozy, and started to read a book.

I noticed Beatrice was not back from the bathroom yet. All of a sudden, I heard a loud thud! I got up from underneath my covers and jumped up. I threw my book upon the bed. And walked out of the bedroom into the hall. The door to the procedure room was open. The rainbow mist was filling the hallway. I hurried and ran in. Beatrice was on the floor, and her eyes were flickering. Her body was jerking as if she was having a seizure. Amaya was pulling her into another realm. I jumped on the floor and tried to pull Beatrice up. I became dizzy and fell onto the floor. I heard the whirlwinds coming at high speeds. We were both being pulled into the whirlwinds. I looked at the time on the desk clock. It was eleven P.M. I was frozen in time and being pulled into another dimension.

Urban Demonics

Chapter Nine

Beatrice and I were flung into an unknown bedroom. I landed on my butt in a corner. Beatrice landed under a window on her side. She sat up on the floor and grabbed her hip in pain. The room was tight, packed, dark and damp. It reeked of urine. There was one small bed set in the middle of the room. The bed was old with metal sidings. There were two little twin boys with big brown eyes. They had to be about four or five. They had that cute but insane look.

They were sitting in front of the bed on the floor. There was a teenage girl with the same big brown deranged eyes. She was sitting in a chair looking out of a window. She stared out the window. Looking into the sky as tears rolled down her face. She had a look of hopelessness about her. The girl had brown skin and shoulder-length hair. It was pulled back neatly into a pony tail. There was a teenage boy that sat across from her. And a young girl, about ten sat next to him. The stank of despair swirled up in my nasal cavities and slid down my throat. It was hard to pick up on emotional scents because the urine was so rich. But despair seeped through the pissy cracks. I was beginning to feel nauseous.

Beatrice looked over at me, and we locked eyes. She crawled across the floor and sat next to me, in the corner. Beatrice whispered in my ear. "Where the hell are

we, who are these people? Can they see us?" I whispered
back to Beatrice. "I'm pretty sure they can." At that
moment, the brown skin girl got up from her chair. She
had something shiny and metal in her hands. I looked a
little closer and realized it was a gun! I became
frightened. Beatrice must have seen the gun at that same
moment I did. She grabbed my arm as her eyes widened. I
licked my dry lips. The brown skin girl started pacing
the floor. She started crying harder. She stopped pacing
and walked over towards me. She looked into my eyes and
said. "Ieasha… it's time!"

Beatrice and I looked at each other. Who the hell was
Ieasha?" I stared back into her eyes with disbelief. I
didn't know what to say. I sat there, staring at the gun.
Her face became angry. She walked closer to me. "OH COME
ON IEASHA! Don't tell me you're scared. We've talked
about this for months. Today is the day! And there's no
turning back." She got closer to me with the gun. I
scooted back on the floor, away from the gun. "What…what
are you talking about? And who's Ieasha?" Her face became
angry, and she looked at me with disgust. "WHY ARE YOU
DOING THIS? YOU TRYING TO SHOW OFF IN FRONT OF YOUR NEW
FRIEND OVER HERE!" She pointed the gun in Beatrice's
face.

Beatrice backed away. She pulled the gun down to her side
and began to cry again. "Look, you promised us, you
promised us ALL!" The two twins looked over at me and co-
signed. "Yeah, you promised Ieasha." The twins said this
at the same time. I was confused, and my heart started
racing. I started to breathe fast and hard. Beatrice
could tell I was nervous. Beatrice leaned over and
whispered in my ear. "Glamor, her damnit!" I shook my
head, no. My powers were dormant in this realm, this
time. I could tell. I calmed down and decided to gather
information. I looked into the brown skin girl's eyes.
"What…what was it, that I promised to do?" The brown skin
girl took a deep breath. She looked annoyed and responded
sarcastically. "You promised to shoot me in the head,
REMEMBER?"

"You promised to kill me. So, I can be on the other side.
I can't take my own life; it won't work that way. You
promised me Ieasha, please, we need this!" My hands begin
to shake. I gathered my thoughts and I proceeded to ask

more questions. "Why would I do that? Promise to kill you? And What's on the other side?" The brown skin girl stared into my eyes and broke down crying. Her face became angry again.

"WILL YOU PLEASE STOP THIS NONSENSE! We've gone over this a million times! Look around this room! Are the rats and roaches crawling on you at night not enough! Mama's gone again, and there's no food! Jimmy and Jay's sickle cell is acting up again! God forbid we take them to the hospital again. They would take them away from us and put them in foster care. So, they sit here, in pain! Randy is seventeen years old now. He can go to an adult jail for robbing cabs!

Kizzy's ten and still wets the bed. Because of all those terrible things uncle, Leroy use to do to her! There's no help for us, Ieasha! NO ONE WILL HELP! Not even that rich boyfriend of yours who you lie to about where you live. Stealing clothes out of expensive department stores to look uppity and rich! He's Not STUPID IEASHA, and HE KNOWS YOU LIVE IN THE SLUMS! And even if he doesn't know. He will know soon enough. And trust me, he will dump you! Just like all the others! There's no help for us, Ieasha, this is the only way out! The brown skin girl grabbed my hand. Everything went silent. It was like that moment was in slow motion. I saw the gun come down in slow motion. She slammed the gun inside my sweaty palm. The sound of the slap it created, boomed in my ears. And echoed over and over again.

I was now holding the gun. My body started to shake. Beatrice looked over at me, with fear in her eyes. My bottom lip begins to tremble. She just stared at me with her big brown piercing eyes. She begins to cry and got down on her knees, in front of me, begging.
"Please…please just think about it if I was on the other side. I could make momma win the lottery! I could help Dr's find a cure for sickle cell anemia. I could make Randy win a basketball scholarship. I can finally get help for Kizzy. Maybe a counselor to help with her depression! I could float above us and be the family's guardian angel.

We'd be rich and happy! Of course, I won't be here in the flesh. But I'd be here in spirit. I'd float above you, all day and all night. I'd make things right for us! I can make things happen on the other side, just like in our favorite movie, Ghost. You know Ghost Ieasha, it's our favorite movie. Remember how he helped her?" I looked at Beatrice and then up at the Brown skin girl's face. Tears were pouring from her eyes. "And what if it doesn't happen that way? What if you cross over, and you're not able to contact us or help? Then what?"

The brown skin girl became angry. She rose to her feet. She got close in my face again. But, this time, closer. I backed up more and more until she finally had me cornered. "WHAT IF… WHAT IF… WHAT IF…! You and your doubts! I'm sick of it! I told you I'd be fine! This is the ONLY WAY! THE ONLY WAY OUT! This pain and suffering have gone on long enough! What am I supposed to do? Stay here on earth and let my family suffer! I can't take the pain anymore! Now, this has gone on long enough!

STOP thinking of your self Ieasha! You know what? You are so fucking selfish! SOOOO FUCKING SELFISH! You always have been, "You and mama run the streets putting that shit up your nose! Just look at Jimmy and Jay! Isn't it bad enough that they live with the pain of sickle cell daily! Plus, they haven't eaten in two days, now they have hunger pains! I MEAN…WHAT DO YOU WANT US TO DO? I heard a scampering noise across the floor. I turned to look; a huge rat darted out in front of us! The brown skin girl quickly flips out a switchblade. She quickly sinks it deep into the rat's back!

Blood spatters on her face. A few drops hit my forehead. I gasped when I felt the wetness. The twins screamed with fright and began to cry. The brown skin girl lifted the rat in the air, as it hung from her blade. She raised it to my face. Tears streamed down her face. "IS THIS what you want us to eat tonight? Huh, is it!" She stared at me with rage in her eyes! "DO IT IEASHA! DO IT! JUST GO ON AND DO IT! I was confused. My heart started pounding fast! Tears erupted from the eyes. I looked over at Beatrice, and she was crying and afraid. From being in the other realm. I learned one thing. The only way out was to finish the task at hand! I wrapped my pointer finger around the trigger tightly!

I had to get Beatrice out of here. I looked over at
Beatrice. Her eyes widened, she started shaking her head,
no. She didn't understand, and this wasn't real! Or maybe
it was, just in another realm or timeline. But we had to
get out of here. I closed my eyes. I gripped the trigger
tighter. Beatrice reached over and tried to pull the gun
away. I shoved Beatrice off! And squeezed the trigger!
Blood erupted all Beatrice's face. I could feel a few
more drops splattered onto mine. The odor of despair
disappeared. The brown skin girl's body hit the floor
with a loud thud.

The brown skin girl's soul rose up towards the ceiling.
She floated above us. The room was quiet. Everyone just
stared at the soul. I noticed she had a great big smile
on her face. I dropped the gun and grabbed my forehead.
The tingling was starting back again. I glanced over at
Beatrice. She was lying on the floor. She looked as if
she was having a seizure. The tingling moved down my
body. The sounds of the whirlwinds filled my ears.

Chapter 10

The unknown Realm

The wind tunnels whisked us away. But only this time, the
whirlwind was frozen in time. It stopped spinning, but we
were still inside. I glanced around, Beatrice was on the
floor of the tunnel. It looked like an elevator on the
inside. Only no doors! I dropped to the ground and helped
Beatrice up. She was quite faint but came too. I held her
up until she felt stable. Her eyes were wide open.

Beatrice turned to look at me. She was holding her chest
like she was having difficulty breathing. "Why doesn't
this affect you, the way it's affecting me?" I licked my
chapped lips. "I really don't know Beatrice, I feel
tingles, from my head to my toes. But, that's about it,
and then I can feel my soul leaving my body. But, against
my will, not like an outer-body experience. I'm being
sucked in for some reason.

Well, I know the reason; it's Amaya." Beatrice stared out
of the whirlwind into deep space. "You killed that girl!
Why did you kill her, Ty?" I turned and looked at her
face. She was confused and afraid. Afraid of me, I felt

it. "Beatrice, of all people, you should understand why I killed that girl. We were in a different realm, different time zone. She's not really gone; there is no such thing as death. Look, you don't understand ok when I got pulled into that other realm. I did what I had to do to get out. I was released after that. That's how it goes; it's the only way out of these realms."

Beatrice sighed, "So you killed someone in that realm? You also killed a man in real life with your magic Ty! The man in New Orleans, he was in the same realm we lived in! How many people have you killed Ty?" I turned around and stared into her eyes. "What would you know? You gave all this up, remember? To live a normal life. To have a husband and a child to fit in just like everybody else! Just like in high school. You're not in touch with this site anymore; you gave it up to be regular! You should be happy you have a choice. I don't! I can't turn this shit off and on, like you!"

The whirlwind capsule became silent. Why were we still frozen here? Why couldn't it just whisk us back to my grandmother's house? The whirlwind tunnel begins to shift. I almost lost my balance. I grabbed onto the side rail. It was almost as if it was stuck and trying to get free. Beatrice became afraid of the movement.

She ran over close to me and grabbed my arm. She was frightened out of the corner of my eye. I saw through the capsule glass. A silver looking space ship. Beatrice saw that something had my attention, and she looked into that direction. She gasped and covered her mouth. This space ship looked familiar. The doors opened, and out walked Elta.

My tall dreaded, blue-skinned spirit guide. She stared at me through the glass. She telepathically told me to step away from the window. I grabbed Beatrice's hand and pulled her to the other side of the whirlwind capsule. Elta telepathically told me to cover my ears. I turned and looked at Beatrice. "Cover your ears now"! I covered my ears as well. Elta let out a loud pitch. It shattered the capsules glass into nothing. We were left standing on a metal sphere-shaped floor. I looked all around. All I saw was a dark matter. The big beautiful stars lit up the dark skies like glitter. Beatrice stood there with her mouth dropped open.

The metal circle Sphere we stood upon, begin to wobble, and tilt. The dark matter no longer supported it. I grabbed Beatrice's hand. I looked up at Elta, and she screamed telepathically. "NOW"! I ran as fast as I could, dragging Beatrice behind me. The sphere-shaped metal ground begins to fall, right under our feet! When I felt the hard surface leave from under me. I jumped hard and high.

I was in the subconscious realms. My powers were strong and fierce. I felt the dark matter of the universe become one with my skin. I looked at my hands. The glittery black goo was becoming a part of me. It tingled and gave me even more power. It felt like I was moving in slow motion. I was still flying in the air, from my jump. I finally landed hard! Right on the ship's stairs. Beatrice and I fell, but we were on the stairs. We were safe, and the stairs pulled us into the space ship. I breathed deeply, catching my breath. Beatrice rose up slowly. She sat up and grabbed her back. As if she was in pain. I pushed my self up from the ground. "You ok, Beatrice"?

Beatrice was looking around. "Yes, I think! Where the hell are we?" I looked around for Elta, there she was, in her chambers. I didn't recognize the ship from the outside. Usually, when I go inside my subconscious mind to speak to my ancestors. Everything would go black, and I'd wake up inside the ship. I extended my hand out to Beatrice and pulled her up off the ground. I turned to her, "Follow me." Her eyes bucked wide, but she followed.

I walked into Elta's chamber. She was viewing something on a hologram. She held up her hand, like she throwing up a high five. She then pulled all her fingers together, to close her hand. And the hologram closed. She smiled at me when I walked through her door. She opened her arms out wide. "My child, come here". I walked quickly into her arms and embraced her. I hugged her deeply and tightly. I pulled back for a minute. "Thank you so much for rescuing us." She smiled and released her grip. "You are welcome, my child." She glanced over at Beatrice. Beatrice still looked frightened. Elta was super tall. About 7 feet, she had blue skin, with long black dreadlocks. Her facial features resembled a feline appearance.

"Oh, I'm sorry, let me introduce the two of you, Elta; this is Beatrice. Beatrice, this is one of my spirit guides, Elta". Beatrice's eyes seem to stay glued wide open. Beatrice speaks in a low voice. "Please to meet you". Elta picked up on her fear. "No need to fear me, child. I am a gatekeeper, I come with peace in my heart". Beatrice lightened up a bit and relaxed. Elta smiled, "What type of mess have you gotten yourself into now Ty?" I was caught off guard by her question. Elta turned around and walked to a table. I picked up a tray and turned back around and walked over towards us.

"Tea, anyone?" Elta placed the tray in front of Beatrice. Beatrice grabbed a cup and sat down on one of the cyber couches. The color of the couch went from blue to red. Beatrice noticed the color change, as she sipped her tea. Elta glanced over, "You don't have to be afraid my child. No one is going to hurt you". Beatrice stopped drinking mid-sip. "I just, I…never been on space ship before. Nor have I ever seen an alien before." Elta begins to laugh. "What if I told you, most humans are hybrids. Hybrids who can't remember who they are. Well, a small percentage still remembers. And as the earth upgrades with different shifts, so does the human. And more and more people will awaken. They will soon remember. The dormant DNA that holds these memories of who they are. The star children have always known. Hybrids like Ty, have always known the truth.

When they come back to earth, they know from birth. Or an accident is created when they are children. We pull the subconscious back up. Download the information and send them back to earth." Beatrice nods her head and sips her tea. Elta continues, "Only a small percentage are selected for this mission. Unfortunately, the resistance has created a species called clones. The more hybrids and humans copulate with these creations. The more the human race will self-destruct. Human offspring will become extinct, at some point." I grabbed a cup of tea and sat down next to Beatrice. Elta sat down in the grand chair, which looked like a chair made for a queen. It was made of Moldavite crystal, it looked like vines and leaves, very mosaic.

Elta smiled at me. "My dear child, you have not answered my question? What kind of trouble have you gotten yourself into, at this time? What are you doing up here in the ethers? You didn't beam up, and I didn't pull you in. You're here against your will child." I sipped my tea and looked up at Elta. I sighed, "Well, Beatrice and I have started a new business. I found a book in my grandmother's room, with a holistic remedy for immortality. Elta almost spits out her tea. "Immortality?" she laughed, "In the human body?" I put my tea down. "Yes, but more, youthful, renewal regeneration, never becoming old, no more aging. No more cycles of dying, becoming another form of energy, and moving into the next body." Beatrice budded in, "Why do we reincarnate? I mean, I hear people say all the time. It's so we can remember who we are and learn different lessons. But why would it keep going and going and going?"

Elta was intrigued by her question. "Some are sent back repeatedly on missions, to bring about change. Others don't go back to earth, and they are assigned jobs here in the ethers. Of course, that's after about ten cycles of a lifetime, equal to 1000 years. And the rest are just trapped, souls. You see, the earth, my dear, is a prison planet. Humans should be able to transcend to different realms, in their physical body. Not just through the subconscious mind. Like you guys are right now." Beatrice looked confused. "So, where are our bodies now?" Elta laughed. "Right Where you left them, in Ty's grandmother's house, lying on the floor. Unharmed, of course, and time is standing still. When you return, time will be the same as you left it." Beatrice puts her cup down. "Great, it feels like I've been trapped here for days."

Elta smiled and looked over at me. "So, finish up, my dear child." I smiled back. "Well, we kind of an issue with Amaya, a rainbow serpent. Sometimes, I don't know. She gets angry or vindictive and sends us into other realms. We are unable to control what's going on. As long as we have my grandmother's spellbook, the book of Nigron, we are safe. But when the book is not in my hands or the room. "She can overpower us and send us into different realms."

"We really need to find a spell in the book. Which there is one. We need to move forward and just put a spell on her. So that she can not keep retaliating against us. At this point, we would be able to control the outcome better. And, not be sent into other dimensions, against our will." Elta stared at me for a second. Elta begins to speak. "And why are you doing this? For money?" I took a deep breath, and I felt a lecture coming on. So, I tried to explain. "Yes, Elta, for money. When we are on the material plane, we need money to live."

Neither one of us is passionate about our jobs. Not Beatrice, not myself, we work them to maintain our bills. Beatrice has a son and a husband. All I have is me, but we work these jobs to take care of ourselves. We are not in love with what we're doing right now. And we would love to have our own business and make our own money. Do something we're passionate about. We are passionate about regeneration, youthfulness, making women feel good about being fresh and young again.

Elta looks at me and sips her tea. "You know, I'll never understand why in the world you would want to pay to live on your planet. Your kind is always waiting for the New World Order to begin. Little do they know, it already has. It's called money, why do you think it says, in God, we trust on each bill? Unfortunately, on your planet. Money is God, and you worship it." Elta begins to laugh. "And nobody even realizes it.

I have always been an andromite from andromeda. So, we have never paid a dime to live on our planet. I've never experienced being a human before, living on earth. So, you see my child; I just don't understand. I am your alien ancestor, your grandmother, and other humans, from your lineage. I Can relate to those things better. I've always been in space or other realms.

I've always lived on another planet. So, I don't understand. Humans are making other humans pay. To live in a place they inhabit, a place where they were born. I've never understood this concept. But, I do have your back about wanting to do something passionately for a living. And not just working a job to pay bills, I understand that. So, if you are going to continue to do this. To get financial gain, to earn your freedom. Then, yes, I would suggest you find the spell and cast it upon the rainbow serpent.

Because, if you don't do something, you are going to get hurt. I stared off into space and then back at Elta. I sipped on my tea. There was silence in the room, so I began to speak. "Well, I'm glad we have your blessings, Elta." Elta laughed out loud and sipped more of her tea. "Now, I'm not one hundred percent ok with this. But, I understand wanting freedom. I understand what you have to do, to live on the planet Earth, to survive. It saddens me, but at the same time, I understand. So, what that being said, I just wanted to say this, I understand. And if you and Beatrice want to continue, to be apart of this, then I think that's fine."

I also wanted to say that you were about to be pulled into an extremely dangerous realm. When you're in-trouble Ty, we have a radar here, that alerts us. When you're going into your highest peak of danger, the radar goes off. I always know when you're in trouble, in the subconscious and material planes. The world that you and Beatrice were about to be sucked into could have possibly killed you both. On that note, I had to rescue you guys.

I had to get you out of the whirlwind. You were about to be pulled into territories I can't even explain. You must put a stop to what this rainbow serpent is doing. Or both of you are going to find yourselves in extreme danger, trying to make money. To be free and live on earth. So, the first thing you guys want to do when I send you back to your grandmother's house. Is to get up immediately when the consciousness comes back into your body. Immediately run to your grandmother's room. Grab the book of Nigron. Find the spell that is in the book. Quickly, put it on the rainbow serpent. So, you're not pulled into any more realms.

I don't need my radar hitting the roof when you're in trouble. I can't always come, but I was here, and you have your other guides. You have your dragon Ciseley, and you have IOleon Who is your ancestor, your spirit guide. Your safe at all times." Elta put her cup down and glanced over at Beatrice. "Beatrice?" Beatrice startled a bit, puts her teacup down. Elta finishes speaking. "Beatrice, do you ever talk to your spirit guides, sweetie?" Beatrice takes a deep breath. "I use to when I was a little girl. That's what I was taught, growing up on the island. To always speak to your ancestors. So, I spoke to my ancestors. Somewhere down the line, things just got complicated. My mom and my dad became a little religious with Christianity.

My ancestors would respond when I spoke to them. Not through words, but signs. But, it's been so many years. Since I actually talked to them. Or connected to them. I don't know, and I think they may be upset with me." Elta stared at Beatrice. "What makes you think they would be upset with you, my child?" Beatrice glances back up at Elta. "It's just been so many years that I have not called upon them. I haven't been in deep meditative states. I do miss them, and I do miss their guidance.

They protected me when I was a little girl." Elta smiled, "What makes you think, they are not still over you, protecting you?" Beatrice paused for a minute. "I don't know, I just figured they would be angry with me. Basically for, forgetting about them." Elta smiles again. "My dear child, please contact your ancestors. Call upon them verbally, go into deep meditative states and meet them in the subconscious realms, for they are your keepers, your watcher, your protection. Your magic, your everything. It is so important." Beatrice smiled; she almost teared up. Listening to Elta, telling her to contact her spirit guides.

Elta looked over at me, "Whenever you guys are ready to go back home, I will send you." I looked over at Beatrice, from the look on her face, I could tell she was ready to go. I smiled at Elta. "We are ready". Elta smiled and snapped her fingers. Everything went black. We woke at my Grandmother's house in the office. I got up from the ground immediately. I pulled Beatrice up fast, and we ran out of the room.

Amaya was still in there. and I couldn't risk us being pulled into a different realm again. We fled down the hall quickly and into my grandmother's bedroom. I glanced at the time. Over at the tick-tock clock, on the wall. It was made of onyx. It hung above my grandmother's bed. It was the same time it was when we were sucked into another realm. I glanced over at Beatrice. She collapsed on the bed from exhaustion. It was night time and still dark out. "Ty, how long have we been gone? Keith is going to kill me!" I smiled at her. "Time stood still, its Saturday night. Tomorrow is Sunday, and you can return home at your usual time."

Beatrice stood up and walked over to her purse. She scrambled around for a minute and pulled out her cell phone. She checked the date and time. "Oh my God, your right, Elta was right, no time lost." I immediately dropped to my knees and opened the hidden door on the floor. I pulled out the book of Nigron. I looked at Beatrice, "According to Elta, I have to cast a spell. So, when we don't have the book of Nigron. Amaya can't pull us into different realms." Beatrice shook her head. "I don't know, Ty. I'm really exhausted, and I just want to sleep tonight. And go home in the morning."

I smiled annoyingly. "Amaya still has to be fed and taken care of in my apartment. This spell is important! We just can't leave her here and go home. She will die, and so will everything we worked for. We just immortalized a woman. Leaving her more youthful in appearance and the ability to live as long as she wants. This is groundbreaking, Beatrice! I need your help. We need to cast this spell. I stood there, holding the book of Nigron close to my chest. Beatrice became quiet for a moment and looked up at me.

Beatrice sighed, "Ok, let's get this over with." I smiled, "great!" I sat on the bed and began to flip pages through the book of Nigron. I found the spell, I read through it. I cleared my throat. "According to this passage, we will need a flute." At that exact moment, the hidden door on the floor begins to glow. Beatrice looked over at me. She got down on the floor. Beatrice opened the door. A bright green glow filled the room. Beatrice looked inside. She stuck her hand down inside the hole.

Beatrice looked over at me. "I feel something metal." She looked inside again, and the green glow was so bright, it blinded her. She looked away but continued to pull the metal object out. The green glow disappeared. To my surprise, it was a golden flute. My eyes lit up. Beatrice smiled, "Wow, that was quick; what else do we need?" I continued to read. "A glass jar, according to the book.

We will need the glass jar to put her soul in." Beatrice looked over at me. "Her soul?"

I nodded my head, yes. "Yes, the flute playing will put Amaya in a trance. I say these three words; her soul will levitate from her body. I will lure her inside the jar and put the lid over it. According to the book, she will be easily controlled and at our command." Beatrice's eyes bucked, "Wow, this is some Illuminati shit. Stealing souls!" I rolled my eyes. "We are not stealing it, and we are borrowing it. We will give it back when we've stacked enough money and can retire.

We will keep it safe inside the jar". Beatrice sighed, "Let's just get this shit over with. I got a man and a child to go home to in the morning." I continued reading. "According to the book, we will keep our distance. Three feet away and play the flute for two minutes. Then we will enter the room. I will say the magic words and the soul will leave the body. I will capture it in the jar. So, Beatrice, you will play the flute. According to the book, it's already tuned. Just below, and she will fall into a trance."

We both took a deep breath, "let's get this over with." I grabbed an empty jar from my grandmother's shelf. She had a ton of empty jars lying around. I unscrewed the top. Beatrice picked up the flute. We headed outside my grandmother's room. I brought my cell phone to keep the two-minute count. We walked down the hall. We got about three feet away from the office door and stopped. I nodded my head to Beatrice. She put the flute in her mouth and blew.

The sound was enticing and alluring. The tones filled my ears, and the notes danced on my earlobes as the sound entered my eardrums. It was lovely and haunting, all at the same time. I started to fill this throbbing in my forehead. And tingles in my eyes. I shook my head to snap out of it. I looked down at my phone, thirty more seconds until the alarm would go off.

I cleared my mind and focused on the process. I had my jar inside my hands, ready. I looked over at Beatrice. She was playing like an experienced flute player. Her eyes looked tranced. I snapped my fingers, and Beatrice came to. I got close and whispered in her ear. "Focus,"!

I checked my cell phone. In five, four, three, two one! I nodded my head at Beatrice, and we entered the room.

Slowly, we tiptoed in. To my surprise, Amaya was floating in the air above her crate. Amaya's eyes were tranced. Beatrice continued playing the flute. I took a deep breath and swallowed. "Amrita Bharata, come to me!" I snapped my fingers. Amaya's soul begins to leave her body. I lined up my jar, with Amaya's soul. As if I was a child with a net, trying to catch a butterfly. I swayed slowly and guided her into my glass. I covered it quickly and screwed the lid on top tightly. I was feeling a bit guilty inside. But I knew that we wouldn't hurt her, or her soul.

And once we made our riches, we would give her soul back. It was just a matter of time. Beatrice starred into the jar. Amaya's soul looked like a sparkly, glittery, rainbow, fireball. I glanced over in her crate. Amaya's physical body was awake but calm. I looked over at Beatrice. "Let's put her on my grandmother's shelf." We walked out of the room and down the hall. We entered my grandmother's room. I walked over and placed her on the shelf. I wanted to keep an eye on her. Beatrice looked at the jar and then looked at me. "We're going to sleep with her in the room?"

I sighed, "Amaya's soul is in the jar; it will be fine. I need to keep her here, just to keep an eye on her". Beatrice sighed, "Ok, I'm beat anyway." I walked over to my grandmother's bed, I was so exhausted, I plopped down on the bed, and passed out cold.

A brother is a gift to the hea

After a long successful weekend of immortality with Beatrice. I was back at my desk, Sipping my coffee in front of my computer. I was insanely tired. I glanced down at my watch. It was just about lunchtime. I needed to perk up. As I was packing my things up in my purse, That scent of confidence, mixed with a little Jean-Paul Gaultier, entered the room. Before I even turned my head, I knew it was Kent Walker.

The allure of this man was imbedded in my nostrils. Plus, my short-term memory. It caught me off guard. I decided to take a deep breath and turn around. He was standing right behind me. He had a big smile on his face. He was holding a file. He stretched his arms out wide. I stood up and walked right into his arms. Not caring who was watching or who was around. We hugged each other simultaneously. I felt endorphins pop, chemicals, tingles in my brain. I only had this feeling once before. And it was in high school, with Tony Wells. The same feel, it was enticing and real.

I finally decided to let go. I wanted to look at him and see his smile. I unhooked my arms gently and looked into his eyes. Kent's eyes interlocked with mine. He begins to kiss me, not caring who would see us. I didn't care either. This was so odd. I mean, I was never caught off guard when it came to a lover. I had to be careful with this energy as much as I hated to think about it. He could be a handler as I pulled myself from under his spell. I pulled my head back once again to look at him.

Kent was smiling, he pulled back a little and smiled. He took the file he was holding. He placed it inside my hands. I glanced up and smiled at him. "What's this"? He looked confused. "You were very inquisitive about the lost boy. I found a file on him, top-secret". My mouth dropped. He put his finger over his lips. "Shhhh, I can get in a ton of trouble for this." I was lost for words; I began to stutter. "What…what do I owe you for this?" He smiled, "Another date, you seem to be so busy, especially on the weekends." I smiled, "No, not really, just exploring a side business with my best friend."

He smiled, "I think that's awesome. I'd like to see you soon." I smiled, "Of course, I'm available this weekend. Next weekend is another business adventure." Kent Smiled again, "Wonderful, so, I'll see you this weekend." He pecked my lips, loosened his grip. He walked away slowly. I glanced down at the file. I decided to walk over to Starbucks. I ordered my favorite. I sat down alone in a corner. My heart was beating a mile a minute. I looked around; no one was watching.

I took a few deep breaths. I closed my eyes and slowly opened the file. I flipped through a few pages. There were pictures of him and different name changes. He had my mom's eyes and my dad's grin. He looked just like a masculine version of myself, almost like twins. I peered deeply into the information. It looks like he had been fostered around repeatedly. And he was eventually adopted by a family, right here in Atlanta. My eyes begin to grow as big as apples. He was approximately four years older than me. He resided right here in Atlanta. His name was now Butch Diamond. His occupation was a Steam Cell Researcher at the CDC.

I bit my finger. I was nervous. I never even knew I had a brother. Until the Hologram revealed it to me. They killed my mom and my dad. They took my brother because of his powers. He was only a child. How could they do this to him to us? My grandmother knew all about this. I wanted to be mad at her. But I got intel from my spirit guides. They told me she did it to protect me. Because they would have taken me as well. And they had already killed my mom and dad. My poor brother had just disappeared. And now, here I was with his information right in my hands.

I took a deep breath. I decided that I would make an appointment to meet with him. I had to do more research. I gathered my things and headed back to work. I would do more research once I got home. I kept myself busy at work with tasks. I didn't want to think about the information until I got home. That was the longest half a day, and I had at work. It seems it lasted a lifetime. I was anxious, and I wanted to get home quickly and research my brother online. I wasn't stupid enough to use a computer at work.

I sped home as quickly as I could. I ran upstairs to my apartment door. I opened the door and ran to my bedroom. I knew my laptop was on the bed. I was out of breath. I plopped down on the bed to catch my breath. I stared up at the ceiling. I decided to get comfortable. I laid the file on the bed. I went into the bathroom and took off my work clothes. I got into the shower. I let the stress of the day melt away. I put on some comfortable sweat pants and a t-shirt.

I proceeded to lay on the bed. I grabbed the file. I opened my laptop and signed on. I searched for his name and position. An article came up about him. I clicked on it — a picture of him and a guy in a wheelchair. I read the article thoroughly. It was about my brother being the first Dr. to have a patient walk again after he severed his C7 spinal cord injury completely, he healed his injury with stem cells. The man was now able to walk. According to the article, this was groundbreaking material.

I wrote down the address. I glanced at the time, and it was 4:30 pm. I grabbed my cell phone and called the number in the article. I didn't even know what I would, I say. I just needed to make an appointment to see him. I did some deep breathing to calm myself down. I heard a lady pick up the phone. "Dr. Diamonds office, how can I help you?" I took a deep breath. "Hi, I um, I would like to make an appointment with Dr. Diamond please?" The phone became silent for a minute. "Are you a regular patient of Mr. Diamonds?" I paused, "Um no. I'm not, and I would be a new patient."

I heard a deep swallow. "Oh, I see, I'm sorry, dear. Dr. Diamond does not take new patients. Most of his clients are research only, at the moment." I scratched my neck. "Oh, I see, well, is there any way to contact him? To see if he would take on a new client for research?" She sighed, "Honestly, No, his clients are picked for him by the board. But if you're someone who'd like to persuade him. He eats lunch every day at the Camel Black restaurant at twelve noon. Don't tell him I gave you that information." I brightened up a bit. "I won't, and thank you for the information. You've been very helpful".

I wrote down the information she gave me. And decided I would meet him tomorrow for lunch. Hopefully, he'll be eating alone. At that moment, I got a text from Candy. She was confirming her follow up appointment. She said she had great news for us. I was so caught up with the information Kent had given me. I had forgotten all about Candy and how she was doing. I sent her a quick text to confirm the appointment. I had to move fast with this new information about my brother. I'll worry about Candy next weekend.

I decided to grab some red wine from the kitchen. I drank a few glasses. I Continued to search online. Not much information, but of course, his name had been changed so many times. I stayed up late and decided I needed to rest. The wine had me relaxed in good mental space. I stop fighting and let the powers of the wine take me under.

I woke up frantically to my alarm clock ringing. I hit it twice and rolled over. I was really knocked out in deep space. Must have been traveling to different realms. I dragged myself out of bed and into the bathroom. I took off all my clothes and got into the shower. I let the water wash the drowsiness away. I perked up, threw on my work clothes. I made up my face, fixed my hair, and headed out the door. I'd pick up breakfast on the way. I was notorious for not making time for breakfast.

I got to my office. It was always quiet very early in the morning. Until everyone started rolling in, around 9 am. I always got there early. I wanted to receive the results from the labs that went in late. Get them into the computer and start the next batch. I tried to keep my mind off my brother. And just focus on the day. I went over to the coffee station, poured myself a cup. I decided I would drown myself in files. This way, my brain had to focus on something else.

By the time I finally looked up at the clock. It was 11 am. I got enough work done to take a three-hour lunch break. That was my plan, just in case, I needed extra time. I packed up my things and decided to leave early. I had to find the place and set up, like a stakeout. I grabbed my purse and locked up my drawer. I didn't make eye contact with anyone. No time for small talk. I breeze through all the crowds without getting stopped. I placed a mental shield around me for protection. I made it to my car. Put the name of the restaurant into the GPS.

The restaurant wasn't far at all. It was 11:15. I beat the lunch rush. I found a park and pulled in. I caught my breath from panicking in the car. I walked through the parking lot and into the restaurant. A hostess greeted me. "Table for one, thank you." I looked all around, and the place was small. I spotted a corner all the way in the back. From that angle, I could watch everyone walk through the door. And watch to see where they would be seated.

I sat down with the file. I ordered a drink from the waitress. I was too nervous to eat. I looked at the time on my cell phone. It was 11:45 am. I could feel my forehead moisten up. I was starting to sweat. I started fanning myself with the file. I sipped more of my ice-cold drink. I imagined myself on the island, with cool breezes whipping threw my hair. I took a deep breath, held it, then released slowly. I did a cycle of breathing three times. And I was calm. My drink also helped calmed me as well. I was drinking a raspberry Sangria.

It was working well. I was in a deeply calm state. Not drunk or high, just calm. I looked around, and some lady was staring at me like I was a nut. I didn't care, and I had to take a deep breath. Plus, I was wearing shades to cover my eyes. Great protection and disguise. I took another deep breath. I glanced towards the door. And there he was Talking to the hostess. I knew it was him immediately. I felt this heaviness come over my heart chakra. And my third eye started tingling. As if I felt a spirit.

He was walking my way. At that moment, I took my shades off. I wanted him to see. I wanted him to see…me. The eyes were very powerful. I often didn't glamor people unless I needed to. But I decided to use my magic. To pull him my way. Although he wasn't looking in my direction, yet. I pierced deep into his soul, with my eyes. He finally felt my eyes on him. He looked over in my direction. Now that our eyes locked. I delve even deeper. I lured him towards me. I kept my eyes on the prize. I reeled him in. Until he was right there standing in front of me.

He finally pulled a chair out and sat down. He looked confused. "Excuse me, do I know you?" He didn't even know it. But he was under my spell, in a trance. This wasn't a good sign. This trick worked on most people who have been brainwashed or MK Ultra. I finally broke eye contact and released him. I smiled, "No, you don't, I um…I mean, you do… but you don't." He looked even more disoriented. The waitress walked over. She asked for his order. He shook his head and wiped his forehead.

"Oh, Hi Cindy, I'll have my usual." The waitress smiled, "Coming right up." He sighed, "Ok, let's go over this again. How do you know me"? I sipped more of my sangria and licked my lips. He looked so much like my mom. Well, the pictures I saw at my grandmother's house. His face, his whole being was so haunting. I swallowed, "I'm an old family friend, I recognized you immediately." He looked bewildered. He picked up a menu and glanced at it, out of discomfort. He started shaking his head. "No, that's not possible. I don't have any family friends. Or any childhood friends for that matter."

He placed the menu down back down on the table. He looked perplexed. "Although, I noticed right away. I noticed that you have my eyes. Now how is that possible?" I almost teared up. I had to keep together. I looked into his eyes again. "I don't know how to put this, and I know it sounds crazy." The tears exploded from the seams and trickled down my face. I tried to wipe them away quickly. But, before I had the chance. He grabbed a napkin and handed it to me. His gesture of kindness permitted me to release.

"I am your sister," I smiled. He stared vacantly for a moment. I got nervous, but then. He smiled; he opened his mouth to speak. He stuttered out of nervousness. "How, how did you find me?" A tear fell from his reddened right eye. He wiped immediately. The waitress walked over with his food. She looked at both us with a perky smile. She could tell the conversation was heavy. Both our eyes were slightly red from tears. Her smile went from perky to concern. She put the plate in front of Bruce. She paused for a second and did a double-take at both our faces. "Oh, I see, a family reunion? Right? Are you guys twins?"

We both started laughing. I looked at her, "No, um, sister and brother." She smiled at Bruce. "Mr. Diamond has been coming in here for years. I never knew you had a sister." She seemed to be creeped out; her energy changed. "Well here's, your meal, if I can get you guys anything else. Please let me know." She became a bit cold. I looked at him as she walked away. "What was that all about." He went deep into thought for a minute.

"Look, our meeting may not be safe for you. I believe you when you say, you are my sister. I look at you, and I instantly see my grandmother, my mother, and my father." He started to tear up again. "Look, we need to go somewhere else. I have a few more patients to see today, but I can cancel. Do you know of any secluded areas?" It was a warm day, and my mind took me to a safe place. My guides pointed me in the right direction.

"I do, I know a safe place. Neither of us have on the right shoes. But I know we will be safe there." He wiped his face and looked around. He hadn't touched his food. He pulled out his wallet and reached in. He took a hundred-dollar bill out. He laid it on the table. He looked over at me; he was afraid. I could smell it. It reeked from his body. "I'll follow you, walk to your car first. Wait until you see me in the parking lot. Pull off, I'll follow." I shook my head yes. I got up from the table.

I briskly walked to my car. I waited for him to come out. He looked around the parking lot. He saw me inside my car. He nodded his head. Walked over to his car and got in. I cranked my car up and drove off. He followed behind me. I drove slowly, I knew of a magical place where nobody would find us. The ancestors protected it. I felt it, the first day, I stumbled across it. It was about 15 minutes from downtown. Deep, in the old Atlanta neighborhood. Right in the city. Only the majestic knew this place existed.

It came to me, in a dream one night. I did some research on the web and found it. I called my job and put them on speaker while I was driving. "Hello, Kacy, hey, its Ty, um… kind of had an emergency, won't be able to make it back in. But I finish all my work. Half is already done for tomorrow. So, this emergency actually came at a good time." A small moment of silence came over the phone. "Well, I guess that's fine. Were all the results downloaded into the computer? Were they sent to the proper people?"

I kept my eyes on the road. "Yes, of course, all done." I could hear the commotion in the background. "Ok, then I'll see you in the morning, Ty. Take care of your emergency." I sighed, "Thanks, goodbye." The phone hung up. I continued to drive slowly. Often checking my rear-view mirror. I had to make sure Bruce was still behind me. He was keeping up pretty good. I turned into the waterfall preserve. Hidden deep in the city of Atlanta. I pulled into the parking lot. He pulled in behind me.

I got out of my car. The energy changed; the air became soft and pure. My eyesight became 20/20. This place always reeked of divine energy. Every time I stepped out of my car. I was definitely in another dimension. The majestic could feel it right away. He parked next to me. He stepped out of the car. He walked over to me. "What is this place?" I smiled. "It's a waterfall with different trails. We will be safe here, it's protected." I started walking towards the preserve out of the parking lot. He followed, he still looked distraught.

We walked down the boardwalk that led into the magical forest. I could tell Bruce was admiring the greenery. The enticing breeze fell upon my skin. It whisked through my hair. He kept starring at me and looking away. There was silence; I smiled. "Once we get to the waterfall, we can talk." He shook his head yes. We continued to walk deep into the forest. Aluminous birds flew by. A wild, colorful, blue and yellow, big butterfly, zoomed by us. And then circled and came back. She spread her wings wide and was frozen in time. Right in front of Bruce's face. She fluttered slowly above him.

He looked at me with disbelief. "Is that a butterfly?" I shrugged my shoulders. "Could be a hybrid, looks mixed to me." He gave a bewildered look. Then, he smiled. We finally approached the waterfall. Bruce's eyes lit up with wonder. The pure water flowed through the green moss. There were several falls. Some high above inside a cave and some near our feet, down below. "How did you find this place?" I started to take off my shoes. "Came to me, in a dream one night. The ancestors wanted me to find it. It's where I come to gain back my energy. Being in the matrix for long periods can drain you."

He grinned, "Are we not still in the matrix?" I turned to look at him. "No, not here, this is a portal. Like most natural preserves on earth, not human-made. They are either portals or higher dimensions. This hidden gem is both, and I'll show you. Take your shoes off. We will climb up into the cave." Usually, this place was full of people. But, at certain times of the day, I could always find myself alone. Not a person on sight. Just me and my brother.

He rolled up his scrub pants and took off his lab coat. He laid it on some nearby rocks. I was in business casual attire. I didn't care if my pants got ripped. We climbed all the way up to the cave. The water splashed from he the falls. We got slightly wet. We found a dry spot inside the cave. I sat down and crossed my legs. As if I was meditating. He watched and followed suit. He looked nervous. "Relax, we're safe here." He loosened his shoulders. I laughed.

"What was so distressing that we had to leave the restaurant?" He sat across from me with his legs crossed. I couldn't believe I found him. I couldn't believe he was accepting of the truth. He looked into my eyes. "look, I'm not who, you think I am. I mean, I am your brother, I know that for sure. I'm starting to have a memory of my past again." I looked into his eyes. "What do you mean, again?"

He sighed, "how do I say this, without making you afraid." I touched his knee. "Nothing you say could ever make me afraid. I am already aware of somethings." He smiled, "your like grandmother…magical. I was about five when I realized what she was." He scratched his head. "What I was, what we are." He stared into one of the smaller falls. He then looked back at me. "I'm starting to remember again. When I start to remember, they find me and fix it." I licked my lips.

"Who are these people?" His eyes started to tear up again. "The same people who took me as a child. They took me away from mom and dad. When my teacher found out what I could do she…she." His eyes watered up more. I gently touched his other leg. "Listen, I know what they did. I saw it in a hologram." Bruce grabbed his mouth with his hand. He ran his hand down to his chin. "I watched the news after they took me from my home. They lied to the public. Like it was some drug bust gone wrong. It was a lie, and it was all a lie! Mama and daddy died because they wanted me!" Tears erupted from his eyes. I crawled over and sat next to him.

I hugged him deeply. Something strange was going on in my body. I felt tingles, I felt dormant DNA in my body starting to reactivate. I had heard about this before. A star seed I once met Told me when she met her biological father. Closed condones in her body begin to open up. Almost like a key was entered into her body. And what was unlocked, made her more powerful. More conscious, more awake, almost immortal. She told me how money issues disappeared. And how she quickly got rid of unworthy men in her life. I remembered that conversation, as I hugged him.

I felt missing pieces come together like a puzzle. I got a surge of information and unknown emotions. It was overwhelming. He hugged me back tightly. He loosened his grip and looked up at me. "I've lived a lonely life. They kept us inside glass cages in the lab. They were afraid of us. But they wanted our powers. They ran experiments on us. They used us. We weren't apart of society. We didn't go to school. We worked for them. Once I turned thirteen. I became a psychic bodyguard for them. I rode around in their limousines. If danger was near, I would tell them. I would provide them with a safer route.

I did that for some years. They forced me to protect some very bad people. Once I turned eighteen, they sent me out in space. I was a fighter pilot on the planet Saturn. And also, Mars. Once again, protecting some very bad people and beings not quite humans. It wasn't until I did something for them. They decided to set me free under a different name and Identity, of course. But only I wasn't free. They would still pop back up. They wanted me for missions. One day, I ran away. I changed my name again. I moved to another state. Everywhere I went, they found me.

Because I wouldn't play by their rules, they blackballed me. I couldn't find a job. No one would hire me. I became homeless, and I lived on the streets. I had met a few friends in a yoga class while working for them. They were loyal good friends. They would wire me money from time to time. I'd get a hotel, and I would eat for a few days. Then, back on the streets. They never knew my real identity; no one has ever known. That I was that missing child. Who was taken during a drug bust gone bad." He wiped the tears from his face. I kept my arm around him. "Well, when did they send you to school to become a Doctor?" He started laughing and shaking his head.

"I'm not a real Doctor! I got tired of being homeless. So now I'm back working for them." My eyes grew intensely. Bruce noticed, he teared up again. "Please…please don't judge me. I…I…" He lost his words and began crying again. I squeezed him tighter. "It's ok; I'm not judging you at all, brother." I lifted his chin. "You're doing what you have to do to stay alive. And I don't fault you for that. I'm no angel in this world. I've had to do what I've had to do, in the past, as well." He cleared his throat. "Even killing a man?"

Tears rolled down his face. I looked into his eyes. "Yes, Yes, I've killed a man. A man who deserved it. A man, I'm not quite sure, was one hundred percent human." I stared into the waters of the waterfall. He looked up at me with discerning eyes. "Did they come for you too? I actually thought you were dead. You were just a small baby. Mama had just brought you home. I use to stare into your eyes when you were in your crib.

From the moment I looked into your eyes, at the restaurant. I knew who you were." Tears were streaming down my face. "They never got me, because mama hid me. When they came and kicked the door down. Grandmother had a vision. And she came and found me. She took me into hiding to protect me. She never told me I had a brother. And, as far as mom and dad, I thought they abandoned me. A while ago, I had a lucid dream. During the hologram, I was shown everything that happened to you. Well, up until the point of your disappearance." He wiped his face again. "I'm starting to remember; they will come for me soon."

I cleared my throat. "And what will they do?" He sighed. "Clear my memory, and program me with things they want me to know. I'll dress how they want me to dress. And speak how they want me to speak. I will continue their mission and research. I have to break this cycle! Somehow, someway!" I rubbed his back. "Well, it's not a coincidence that we are meeting right now. This is divine timing, Most likely the powers of grandmother. Speaking of grandmother. I can take you somewhere safe. They won't find you, and it's where I was raised. Where grandmother took me, to keep me safe. The islands of South Carolina. Where us Gullah people are from. Back on our land, where we are protected. And our magic is strong. They know the land is powerful. That's why they want to destroy it. Destroy the land, and you destroy the power. They offered grandmother lots of money to sale. But she wouldn't. Of course, they've tried to buy me out. But I'm reopening bed and breakfast. And adding a spa, My own business. The area has become so popular, lots of tourists. We can live off the land. It's just as much my home, as it is yours."

I looked into his eyes; I saw a bit of hope. "If I don't finish out this research, they'll come after me for sure." He was afraid I could see it in his eyes. "Listen to me; the land is sacred. Whatever power they have, it won't work there. Grandmother knew this, and they never came for us. Trust me; I'll drive you out there tonight if you want. What other options do you have? You go back to them, and they'll slave you out. Doing evil until the day you die!"

He looked into my eyes. "Are you sure it's safe?" I grabbed his arms and looked into his eyes. "I know it is. Our loved ones and magic protect the house." He swallowed deeply, "We'll have to get rid of my car."

I shook my head. "Ok, but first, I want to take you through one of the trials. I want to show you something. There are plenty on Gullah island. But I found one, right here in Atlanta." I stood up and held my hand out. He looked up and put his hand inside mine. We climbed back down the waterfall. We put our shoes back on as I led him towards the Spring trial. He followed in silence. I looked over at him. He was mesmerized by the enchantment of the forest. "Tranquilizing, isn't it?"

He smiled, "Yes, just doesn't seem real." I smiled, "It is, one of the earth's real natural forests. Not some matrix, human-made forest." As we walked through the forest towards our destination. I deeply inhaled the fresh forest air. I buried the invisible healer in my lungs. This kind of air was hard to fine. It nourished my body. Oxygenated and awakened my cells. My heart became encased with it. During every inhalation. I held it as long as I could. I had a thing for getting high off nature.

I brought my mind back to the trail. "We'll take a turn Left here, onto Ridge trail." We walked a little longer until we approached our destination. I stopped walking. My brother noticed I stopped walking. He came to a halt as well. "look," I said to him, as I pointed. As he looked ahead, he saw what I was staring at. His face lit up with a smile. He walked closer towards it. The sun was shining directly down upon it. Like it was the only attraction in the forest. White butterflies danced seductively in its presence. I walked closer as well. His eyes lit up. He started touching the outside of the alluring brown portal tree. It was one of those trees with a hollow inside. Made by only by nature. When I was a little girl, grandmother would put me inside a portal tree. And I would travel to different dimensions.

He smiled at me, as tears of joy streamed down his face. "How'd you know?" I licked my lips. "I didn't know, I just figured. If you spent time with grandmother, as a child, Then, she most likely put you inside a portal tree." He smiled as he touched the outside of the tree. He stuck his hand inside the opening of the tree. He closed his eyes. "I can feel it, just like when I was a kid.

Where does this one go?" I walked over and touched the tree — several different dimensions. Grandmother always told me, if you stumble across a portal tree. You are no longer in a 3-dimensional world. You have either leveled up in your dimensions. Or you've just crossed into another one. But not everyone will find or experience a portal tree. We should be honored; the forest chooses us." He looked at me, then back at the tree. Looked at me and then looked at the tree.

"Let's get inside and see where it takes us." He extended his hand out to me. I placed my hand inside of his. He climbed in first. His hand guided me in. I maneuvered my body through a very thin opening. He sat down, and I sat next to my brother. I inhaled the inside of the tree, and It smelled delightful. I was holding my bother's hand. We were so connected. We looked at each other and smiled. We both closed our eyes as we felt the heaviness of the darkness approach. We were almost intoxicated with the smell. We felt our bodies and subconscious minds take off.

Like a rocket launching from its pad. I opened my eyes as we looked out of the opening of the tree. We were moving at the speed of light, bypassing the stars and smaller planets. Bruce opened his eyes. He was surprised to see what I saw. We were floating above the stars in the darkness of the universe. We bypassed unknown planets and dimensions. We rocketed higher and higher until we were suspended in the unknown.

We looked at each other. We both moved forward and looked outside of the hole of the portal tree. I looked down, and so did Bruce. We were suspended beyond the stars in the darkness of the multiverse. The portal tree was suspended in space. Bruce looked out, as well. His eyes lit up. "I haven't seen this site since I was a kid. I always thought it was a dream." I smiled, "Yeah, it's not; it's always been real." As we both admire the dark matter in which we were created. A glowing white light came projecting through.

A vision of my grandmother's silhouette was starting to form. I hadn't seen my grandmother in ages. I mean, I felt her in the house. She would often drop messages. But, actually seeing her. It had been years. The vision became clearer and clearer. Grandmother was being pulled closer to us by the white light. She appeared in the opening of the tree. She climbed inside, my heart dropped. I grabbed my chest, and tears welted up in my eyes. Before she sat down, she reached over and hugged us both. She sat down after, with a big gorgeous smile on her face.

She begins to talk. "I am so proud of both of you. I've been working on each of you in the ethers. I've been waiting for this day for so long." I looked over at her and teared up. "Why didn't you tell me, I had a brother." She started to stroke my hair. "You already know my child, protection. I knew if I told you to soon. You would go looking for him. Those people who stole your brother were very bad people. I took you back to the islands on the scared land. Where I knew we'd be safe." My brother looked over at her. A tear streamed from his eye. "How come you never came for me?"

She let out a big sigh. "I couldn't, and I tried several times. But I knew one day, you would be set free." He glanced over at her. "Free? I'm not free. Every time I run, they find me and fix me. That's not free." Grandmother reached over and touched his hand. "You are free now, go back to the sacred lands with Tituba. They can't harm you there. Their time is almost over. It's a new wave of energy on the planet. Their time is up, and they know it. So, unfortunately, things may get a little worse for the people and the planet. But there are safe grounds. Many know of them. But they keep it a secret from the general public.

The same lands they aim to destroy, with buildings and resorts. Are the same lands, that will protect the people. Mother earth and the ancestors control these lands. There are many all over the earth. But they will never disclose the locations. You go back with your sister, and you will be safe there." I smiled and gave her a big tight hug. She smelled the same as when she was in the material plane, just like cinnamon and white sage. Grandmother reached over and pulled Bruce's head towards her. She hugged us both. "Your portal tree will go back soon. Don't worry, and I'm around. I've become an elder here in the realms. My life cycles on earth are over. I get busy sometimes out here. But I'm always around for my grandbabies. So, is your mom and dad. They will come to you shortly." She smiled and stood up. The white glowing light shined inside the portal tree.

The glowing light slowly sucked my grandmother back into the darkness and disappeared. The portal tree whisked back down. Felt like a rocket ship going backward. Before we knew it, we landed with a big thud. Dirt puffs filled the air. I begin to crawl out of the portal tree. Bruce followed directly behind me. I stood up and dusted off my knees. He stood up as well. He looked at me. "Well, I guess I'm going back with you." I smiled and gave him a great big hug. I pulled back and looked at him. "Great, let's go hide the car."

As we made our way back down through the trails and past the waterfalls. I felt the protection of the ancestors with us. It always felt a little eerie. The lite brisk winds make the hair on the back of your neck stand up. The captivating sounds of the forest put you in a trance. You begin to see things you've only read about in books. Like fairies, but then you convince yourself it was just a large butterfly. You see a little elf darts out by your feet. But it seems unreal. So, you trick your mind into believing it was a squirrel. Not anymore, now I embrace what I know to be true. And I know that these fairy tales I see with my own eyes are real.

Chapter twelve

Unknown forces

That night my brother and I drove both cars 2 hours deep into Georgia. I knew of a place with lots of water, that was secluded. He drove behind me as I guided him. We stripped the car of its plates And drove it off a cliff into a bank of the water. We both watched it sink. We climbed into my car, and I drove him back to my grandmother's resort on Gullah Island. It was a quiet drive. I guess we both had a bunch on our minds. We finally arrived at our destination. It was very dark outside. I forgot Amaya was still here in her cage. I had left her plenty of food and water for the weekend.

I pulled into the driveway. He looked around and then looked at me. "Is it an abandoned resort?" I smiled, "Not abandoned, just closed for right now. My best friend and I are opening up a special spa/ rejuvenation center. It's going to be awesome. We've created treatments that no one on this planet has discovered…yet". I opened the car door and got out. He followed. I walked up the steps and unlocked the door. I opened the door wide and invited him in. "Welcome home brother". He smiled as I held back tears.

He stopped and stood for a moment. It seems like he was taking in all the energy. He walked in and looked around. He glanced over at me. "May I?" I looked at him, "Sure, it's your home just as much as it is mine." He walked around. He looked at all the pictures on the wall. He touched the different crystals displayed as décor. He walked down the halls and opened the doors to different rooms. He walked back over towards me. "Where is grandmother's room"? I walked him over and opened the door. He walked in slowly. I walked in after him.

He looked around and then looked at me. "I always heard of this place as a kid how our family owned a resort. Grandmother hadn't inherited it yet when I was a kid. She lived in an old house not too far from here. It's beautiful." I smiled, "yes, it is. This place is ancient; grandmother did some upgrades. But I'm going to do more. Once the spa opens, which will be soon, hey, let me take you to one of the VIP suites. You can shower and rest up. I led him down the hall, to the grandest room we had. He smiled as we walked in.

"I'll shower up and relax, come back in an hour, ok?" I nodded yes, I closed the door. I went to check on Amaya. I opened the door to the office. She was inside her cage. She was asleep, as she was most times until we awakened her. Her food bowl and water were empty. I refilled them both. Amaya had been tamed since we separated her soul, from her. I straightened up the office a bit. Just trying to pass a little time. After the hour, I went back to the VIP room. I knocked on the door. "Come in." I opened the door. He was lying in bed under the covers, in his undershirt. He smiled, "I totally forgot, I have no clothes or anything here. I left it all behind."

I smiled and sat on the bed. "Don't worry; I'll run to the mall tomorrow and get you somethings. We can build up your wardrobe by buying some clothes online." He smiled, "yeah, there's no way I can go back to my apartment. They have me on lockdown, they probably already figured out, I'm missing." I became concerned about the people after my brother. I sighed, "What was your name before it was Bruce Diamond?" His eyes rolled back into his head. "Um, let's see, I think I was Bobby Jenkins. I've had well over a dozen names. Since they took me from mom and dad." My eyes bucked, "Wow, I'm so sorry that happened to you."

I licked my dry lips. "You said earlier that you weren't really a Dr? How is that even possible?"

He started laughing. "These people can do pretty much whatever they want. It's all a quick process, really. They wipe my memory clean. Then program my brain, with what they want me to know. For instance, they have a chip that's programmed with all the knowledge I need to know as a DR. They insert it in my legs or arms. It takes about 24 hours to upgrade into my body. The next day, I am fully programmed. I know what to do and what to say as a research Dr.

No real schooling or degree needed." My eyes bucked, "Wow"! He shook his head. "Nothing is what it seems out here in the matrix. This whole world is a façade." I looked deep into his eyes. I started to smell that foul odor. I coughed a few times and swallowed deeply. "There's nothing to fear, my brother; you're safe now." He started laughing, and then tears rolled down his face. He looked at me. "You know, I use to believe that.

Everyone on this earth is in danger. When I was sent to Saturn and the moon as a fighter pilot. I learned some valuable information. It just came back to my memory last night. When I was asleep in my apartment." He took a deep sigh. "Basically, Beings have taken over humanity. We're like batteries, and they feed off our energy for different reasons, of course. We use to have two suns in our binary system. One was taken away; they killed it. I can't remember why. But Saturn is the dead sun as our energy feeds and resurrects the dead sun/son or both. The earth, the people, the planet, will be no more.

His eyes looked tearful. Also, when they sent me to the moon for a mission. I discovered that they harvest souls there. They keep them there until a body is available on earth. Then they are sent down to nourish the beings all over again. It's a vicious cycle that keeps repeating its self. Over and Over again! When we die, they trick us. They tell us to go towards the white light. They send a being appearing to look like a loved one. Once we step into that white light. Your soul goes to the moon until a body is available."

I thought deeply for a minute. "You mean when a baby is born?" He looked into my eyes. "Yes, that is exactly how it happens." He wipes the tear from his eye. "I've seen the evils of the world since I was a child. Having my memory wiped clean over and over again. But somehow, when the vibrations of the earth elevate. My memories always come back to me. It's in the DNA, and it just lies dormant. You can also unlock memory codes from your past lives. You can remember who you were and what you did. And bring those old thoughts into your new life. Your consciousness, which is energy, it never dies. The body does, but even that's been altered. A long time ago, when we transcended, we could take our bodies with us. Now we can't, just our consciousness.

But they have found ways to shut down those strands of DNA. We are all genetically modified. It's like an endless trap, an endless cycle." I touched his hand. "Sleep now bother, you look tired." He looked into my eyes. I starred back and pierced through his. I begin to glamour him with a calming energy. There was silence for a moment. I took a deep breath. "You're right; I need some sleep. I haven't been able to sleep well lately. Not with the thoughts racing through my head." I smiled at him and squeezed his hand tighter. "You'll be able to sleep well tonight, brother." I let go of his hand. He laid back slowly onto his pillow. I covered him up a bit and turned out the lamplight. He fell fast asleep.

I had the gift of healing others i Got it from my grandmother. But us healers had a bad habit of not healing ourselves. To busy healing others. That's why I always wore my prehnite and epidote necklace. It heals the healer. I could feel the stone at times. Becoming very warm around my heart chakra. Sometimes really hot! I quietly got up and headed into my grandmother's bedroom. It was time for me to rest. Candy would be here in the morning for her follow up. And so would Beatrice. I took off my clothes and got under the blanket. I held my crystals around my neck and fell fast asleep.

Chapter 13

Living the Dream

I woke up to loud banging at the door. I almost jumped out of my skin. I checked my phone. I had about 100 missed calls from Beatrice. I dragged my body out of bed and threw on a t-shirt and sweat pants. I rushed to the front door. Bruce beat me to it. He was already standing there talking to Beatrice. I walked over, Beatrice had a big smile on her face. "Soooo, who is this handsome gentleman?" I laughed as I flipped my hair out of my face.

"It's not what you think, Bea." Bruce smiled. "I'm sorry, allow me to introduce myself. I am Bruce, Ty's brother." Beatrice paused for a minute. She stared deep into his eyes. "Oh my God, ty, how come you never...said a word?" She looked over at him. She shakes his hand. "Pleased to met you". I smiled at Beatrice. "I never told you because I didn't know. I mean, I knew because of a hologram. That came to me one day. But, I didn't know he was alive. He has to stay here on the island. He's in danger."

Beatrice smiled. "Yes, the land is quite protective." The three of us stood for a moment of awkward silence. Beatrice scratched her neck. "Well, have you introduced him to Amaya yet?" I smiled, "No, I was getting around to that." Bruce looked at me, "Who's Amaya"? I turned and started walking. "Follow me".
Beatrice dragged her suitcase, and Bruce followed. I opened the office door. I walked in slowly. Bruce and Beatrice followed.

They walked in, and I closed the door. I had a blanket thrown over Amaya's crate. I walked over slowly and pulled it off. Bruce walked over and looked into the crate. "Wow, so you like exotic reptiles?" I laughed, "have a seat; I'll tell you all about Amaya." Bruce sat down on the couch in front of the desk. Beatrice looked over at me. "I'm going to run my luggage to one of the suites and get ready for today's follow up." I nodded my head. Bruce looked confused. "Follow up?"

I smiled, "remember I told you, I was turning this place into a spa?" He nodded his head, yes. "Well, were a different kind of spa. We've actually been experimenting. We think we have found the fountain of youth." He nodded his head, yes again. "Ok, how is that?" I walked over and pulled the crate top off. I looked inside, Amaya was sleeping. I gently picked her up and pulled her out of the crate. I pet her slowly as I walked Amaya over. I stood in front of my brother. This is Amaya. He starred strangely for a moment.

"What does a snake have to do with running a spa?" I swallowed, "Well, she's a special rainbow serpent. Her eggs can make any person youthful again. Ingesting her eggs takes about twenty years off your life. And, you'll stay that way forever." Bruce looked at the snake and then back at me. He scratched his head. "Forever? How is that possible?" I continue to pet Amaya while she slept. "Well, we did our first experiment two weeks ago. The subject is coming in for a follow-up today."

We need to make sure everything is ok with her. Then we will move on to our next subject. Beatrice has volunteered if everything is good with Candy. We will move forward with Beatrice." He started shaking his head again. "Wow, if everything goes well, and what your saying is true. Then you guys are going to be rich." We both started laughing. Bruce's face became serious for a minute. "Wait, you said ingest? So, the eggs have to be eaten?" I walked over and placed Amaya back in her crate. "Well, swallowed, not eaten. It's a whole process if everything is good with Candy. You'll see how the procedure works with Beatrice." I smiled, "Take it easy while you're here. Just rest brother, you are home. Explore the land if you like. Everything around here is magic." He smiled, stood up from the couch, and hugged me. "Any magical food around here, because I'm starving." We both laughed. "Well, let me shower up. I'll get dressed, and I'll be happy to make you something to eat. We have lots of fruit and veggies. Some hibiscus or lemonade to drink. Fresh muffins or bagels. Continental style breakfast.

I watched grandmother for years run this place. I still have a lot of her muffin recipes." Bruce smiled, "great; I'll go explore the kitchen and fix my plate. You get ready for your follow up." He walked out of the office. I placed the blanket back over Amaya. I walked into grandmother's room. I showered and got dressed. Candy's appointment was at 2 pm. I sat in front of the mirror and began to brush my hair. My face begins to change. Visions of my grandmother appeared. Her face intertwined with mine. It was quite freaky and often happened for some reason, although it hadn't happened in a while.

The doorbell rang. I glanced at the clock. It was only eleven A.M. I got up from my chair and put my brush down. I headed out of the bedroom and towards the front door. Beatrice was down the hall. Making her way towards the front door as well. I decided to stop and wait for her. "Beatrice, are you expecting anyone"? Beatrice shook her head. "No…no, that's why I was alarmed." We both turned and looked at the door. The doorbell rang again. I put my finger to my lips. "Shhhh," I tiptoed to the door. I pulled the curtain back and peaked out.

My eyes widened. It was Lilly and the crew. I turned and whispered to Beatrice. "Omg, it's Lilly and the girls." Beatrice rolled her eyes and whispered. "Oh my God". She glanced down at her phone. She rolled her eyes again. "Ty today is the 15th. Earth to Ty, our monthly girls retreat!" Beatrice scratched her head. "You forgot to cancel it?" I took a deep breath. A loud bang came from the door. Bruce came out of his room. He walked towards the door. I put my finger to my lips. "Shhhh". He begins to whisper. "Is everything ok"? I smiled, "Yes, just some unexpected friends." He shook his head and whispered. "Ok, I'm going to go grab some more coffee."

At that moment, another loud thud. Beatrice's eyes bucked. "Ty, our cars are outside, we have to let them in." I sighed deeply. I turned back to the door and slowly opened it. I produced a fake smile. If Lilly wasn't brown, her face would be red. She was angered. "What the hell took you guys so long?" Beatrice stumbled for words. "We forgot about our girl's retreat." Lilly looked confused. "Well, if that's the case. Then what the hell are you two doing here this weekend"?

Beatrice and I looked at each other. I opened the door wide and all the girls poured in. We greeted each other with hugs. The girls took their suitcases and headed to empty rooms. Lilly stood and waited with Beatrice and I. She stared at us both. "You two are up to something, I can tell." She smiled and dragged her luggage down the hall. Beatrice and I looked at each other. I whispered to Beatrice. "Please control your sister." Beatrice rolled her eyes. "I didn't know that was possible." I licked my lips. "What are we going to do about Candy? She'll be here at 2 Pm." Beatrice rolled her eyes.

"Look, Ty, the show must go on. I mean between work and other things we got going on. There's no way I'm pushing this back. We need to move into stage two and get things rolling. Taking real clients, making real money Ty. We might have to let Lilly in on what's going on." My eyes widened with anger. "NO, way Beatrice. You know how she is. First of all, she is a gossip queen. She will tell everyone what we're doing. Second of all, she will try and take over. Third of all, she is a plastic surgery queen." Beatrice shook her head. "Your right, just text Candy and tell her to park her car around back. We will sneak her into the office through the back door."

Beatrice shook her head. "I'll keep the girls entertained while you do the follow-up." I looked down at my watch. "ok, I need to go get dressed, we don't have much time until Candy arrives. I went into my grandmother's room and put on something relaxing but casual. I looked in the mirror and brushed my hair. I felt and looked tired. I started to remember what my grandmother told me about mirrors. They are portals, so when you're looking in one. You better like what you see. Or the mirror will continue to give you what you look and feel like. So, I perked up and put a smile on my face. I didn't want to look or feel tired of the rest of my life.

I repeated these words and said them out loud. "I am strength, and I am a beauty." I stared directly into the mirror and repeated the statement over and over. Until I looked beautiful and felt the energy. I put a smile on my face and came back to reality. I put on a little makeup. I looked at the clock it was almost 2 pm. I texted Candy and requested she parked around back. She responded, "Yes, sure." I walked down the hall and knocked on my brother's door. The door was halfway open, so I walked in. He was sitting on the bed with his eyes closed. "Sorry, I didn't mean to interrupt." He opened his eyes. "It's ok; I was finishing up. Just a little meditation, just looking to receive some answers." I smiled, "I do the same thing when I need answers. I go within. I wish I would have known this technique as a teenager." We both started laughing.

"Well, I was just going to let you know. It may be a little loud around here for a few days. I totally forgot it's our monthly girls' weekend. My friends and I come here every month just to get away from everyday life. Once we turn this place into a Healing retreat, you will have to find somewhere else." He nodded his head. "It's cool, no worries." I smiled, "Well, this is your home now. So, I want you to be comfortable." He picked his cup up from the nightstand and sipped more coffee. "Don't worry, I am. I think I'm going to go out by the waters today and just relax on the island." His face transformed from a smile to concern. "You know Ty, and it has been a long time since I could just relax." I shook my head. "I'm so sorry, brother. I promise to do my best to give you some respite time. I know you have been through a lot."

He nodded his head. "Yes, I have." He smiled again. "It's going to be ok, and I feel a sense of relief here." I smiled again, "Well, my client is going to be here soon. Rest up, relax, I'm happy you're here." I smiled and walked out. I closed the door behind me. I called him brother because Bruce was not his real name. Not the name my mother gave him. One day I will find his real name. But for now, I had to greet Candy around back. I walked towards the back of the house. I went outside the back door. I sat on the back steps and waited for Candy.

I took a really deep breath, held it as long as I could. And released, I did this often to nourish my brain and body. Something about the Gullah Island air, it was healing. I looked at the time on my cell phone. Any minute now, Candy would be pulling in just as that thought entered my brain. A Black Mercedes Benz pulled into the back of the house. I glanced in the driver's seat, and it was Candy. She saw me sitting on the back steps. She rolled her window down and yelled. "Hey Girl," I looked around to make sure no one heard her. She turned the car off. I walked over and hushed her. Candy opened the door. Her blond hair was full, thick, and long. She had on a pair of movie star sunglasses.

She smelled of confidence with a hint of rebirth. Candy got out of the car and hugged me tightly. I hugged her back. She stepped back and did a spin to show off her new look. Her clothes and handbag were quite expensive. She pulled her huge shades off. "Look at me! I have you to thank for this". I smiled, grabbed her arm. Quietly escorted her into the house.

"You are so very welcome, Candy," I said in a low voice. Before I opened the back door, I peeked down the hallway to see if anyone was coming. The coast was clear. I rushed her in, and she gave me a concerning look. She begins to open her mouth. I shushed her and walked vigorously down the hall. I got to the office door. Opened it up and Guided her in. I closed the door behind us and locked it. Candy looked over at me with concern. "Are you ok"?

I walked over to the desk and sat down. "I'm so sorry we got some unexpected guests. They can't know about the process. We're still in stage one. No one can know right now. Have a seat, let's talk, it's safe now." Candy sat down on the couch. She placed her purse down and smiled. "Well, I got my kids back! Now that I look fabulous. I was able to get myself off the streets, hooking. I am now working in an upscale strip club, making big money! Before, I couldn't get into clubs like this. They only want the young busty type, with no wrinkles.

I look and feel amazing! I no longer have cravings. You know, for that little habit I had. When I was out on the streets, which is crazy." I grabbed my notebook and pen.

"So, your saying, you had a drug issue? But the rejuvenation cured you of your addiction? Candy shrugged, "Well, I guess. I mean, I've been to rehab. But I've never been able to kick it. When I swallowed those eggs. I felt my tired, drug-addicted body become new. It was a refreshing feeling. Like, when you're thirsty as hell. And you get that first sip of water. That's what it felt like to me. Throughout my whole body. From my scalp, all the way down to my toes."

I wrote everything down Candy was saying. I stopped writing for a moment. I put the end of the pen into my mouth. "Any negative side effects or complaints?" Candy thought about it for a minute. "Well, I don't have any negative side effects. But my dreams seem to be more vivid, and I can remember them. Even several days after I've had them. For a long time, I couldn't remember my dreams. But now I can. And I had a few creepy out of body experiences, which I've never had before. It's almost like, it opened a door inside my brain." I took more notes.

"Anything else you can think of." She swallowed deeply. The look of concern came over her face. "Well, yes, I wasn't going to say anything about it. My partner and I got into a fight the other night. I'm sorry to say I'm in a domestic violence relationship. I'm working hard on getting out of it. But, he choked me until I was blue in the face. I couldn't breathe at all. I felt myself blackout. I felt my soul leave my body." My eyes widened as Candy continued. "I was floating above my body. I could see him still choking me. I felt disconnected from my body. I know this sounds crazy. But I was dead, and I knew it."

I swallowed. "What happened after he choked you?" Candy Continued. "Well, when he saw my body was limp and no longer moving. He stopped choking me. He went and grabbed a stack of money. I had it inside my top drawer. He ran out of the house. My soul then traveled back to my body. And I became alive again. I woke up inside my fabulous body." I wrote everything she said down, word for word. At that moment, there was a knock at the door.

My eyes widened, I looked at Candy. I put my finger to my lips. "Who is it?" I said aloud. "It's Beatrice, let me in." I got up from my desk. I walked over and let Beatrice in. I pulled her inside quickly and closed the door. Beatrice glanced over at Candy. "So, how's the follow up going?" I smiled and got my notebook off the desk. "Here, I took some notes." Candy smiled and began to speak. She stood up and hugged Beatrice. She let go of Beatrice and did a spin. "I'm looking good and feeling fabulous. Thanks to the two of you."

Candy sat back down. Beatrice begins to read. Beatrice's eye bucked at the information. Beatrice looks over at Candy. "So, no negative side effects, huh? Awesome!" Candy smiled, "Well, just the enhancements in my brain. They're not negative, just different." Beatrice glanced back at the note pad. "I see, any headaches or migraines?" Candy shook her head, no. Beatrice glanced back down at the notes. She looked at Candy. "So, you believe your boyfriend, choked you to death. But you didn't die?" Candy shook her head, yes?

"I'm a hundred percent positive. I felt the life being sucked out of me. But as soon as he left, I became alive again." Beatrice smiled, "Well, the legend has it, that immortality will follow. Because it's like having the fountain of youth. You're young, and you never die. Anything else you want to report?" Candy shook her head no. "Great, this means we can move into stage two." Beatrice was starting to reek of greed again.

She turned and looked at me. She walked over to my desk. She placed the file back into my hands. Beatrice rubbed her chin. "Guess who's next for the procedure?" I was alarmed at her question. "Who"? Beatrice smiled, "Myself." I sat back in my chair. Candy smiled, "Well, you already look great. You have a little sagging in the boob area — some fine lines around your eyes. But the procedure is going to fix all of that. I mean, just look at me." Beatrice's smile turned into a disappointing frown. Candy noticed, "Oh… no offense, just telling you areas you can improve, that's all."

Beatrice smiled, "No offense taken, I know I need some work done." Candy got up from her seat and smiled. "Well, the energy is what you're going to love the most. I feel twenty years younger." I smiled, "I would love to feel twenty years younger right now." Candy grabbed her purse.

"Well, I can't stay long. Gotta get to the grocery store, before work tonight. I'm fine, and this procedure has saved my life." I stood up as well. "Great, once we get the website and social media stuff going. If you could leave a five-star review, we will be very appreciative. Plus, before you go, we need to give you another follow-up date. For the next two weeks." I grabbed a card off my desk and wrote down a time and date. I handed it to her. "We need to see you back again. After this appointment, we will scale down to once a month. Until about six months, and you'll be free to go. It's a new procedure. We have to make sure there are no negative side effects."

Candy smiled, "oh, of course, glad I did it. It's changed my life." Candy walked over and hugged me. Then Beatrice and begin to head for the door. Candy twisted the knob. At that moment, there was a knock at the door. My heart dropped into my stomach. Candy proceeded to leave out as Lilly popped in. Candy looked at Lilly. "Hi, you must be here for the procedure?" Lilly's eye's widened. "Procedure, what procedure"? At that moment, Candy realized she said to much. She turned and looked at us. "Well, I'll see you guys in a few weeks."

Candy walked out of the office. Lilly walked in and closed the door. Lilly had a smirk on her face. She started to reek of curiosity. "Sooo, what kind of procedures are guys doing in here? And how come nobody told me about it?" The room was silent. I sat back down in my seat and stared at Beatrice. It was her sister, and she should deal with her. Lilly got impatient. "So, no one's going to tell me what's going on"? Beatrice sighed and rolled her eyes. "Look, we started our youth rejuvenation spa. Candy is a client of ours. She was having her follow up."

Lilly walked all the way in. Closed the door and sat on the couch. I didn't like the look in her eyes. All she saw was green. Greed started to infiltrate the room. Lilly glanced over at Amaya's crate on the table. "What's in the crate? Isn't that the kind of crate for wild animals?" Beatrice sighed again. "It's a snake; you want to meet her?" My eyes bucked at Beatrice. She was trying to scare Lilly off. But this wasn't the way of doing it. I looked over at Lilly. "Look, we're experimenting. It's still in the first few stages. But so far it's going well. We just didn't want to tell anyone until we got things up and going."

Lilly crossed her legs. "I get it, I understand…So why do you guys need a snake?" I sighed, "She's apart of the process; we need her eggs." Lilly looked confused. "So, you're putting snake egg yolks on people's faces to make them look younger? Does it work? If so, I'd like to try. Let me be your guinea pig. I'm so tired of paying for plastic surgery. My credit cards are maxed." Beatrice took a deep breath. She grabbed the folder off the desk and handed them to Lilly. "What's this?" I rubbed my forehead. "Just have a look at the pictures, Lilly." Lilly looked inside the folder. She pulled out the before and after pictures. Her eyes widened even more.

"Wait, this isn't just her face. It's her entire body and face. She looks like a fifty-year-old hag. Her boobs, obviously fake, needed a lift. And she had sagging skin on her arms and neck." Lilly started shaking her head. "There's no way egg yolk did all of this. This woman looks twenty years younger." Lilly looked at my face and then at Beatrice. "There's more, isn't there? You guys are hiding something. Are you both back into that magic stuff again? Like in high school?" Beatrice swallowed deeply. "The only magic is within the serpent eggs." Lilly was staring at the pictures more. "Ok, I'm listening, what exactly do you have to do with the eggs?"

I remembered I had the footage on my phone. I filmed the whole thing. I pulled up the clip and handed Lilly my phone. Beatrice and I looked at each other. Lilly started watching the video. After a few moments, her eyes enlarged. "Wait a minute, you're putting the snake inside her mouth? What the hell! Why? Why put the snake inside her mouth?" Beatrice walked over and sat down next to her. "Just keep watching".

Lilly continued to stare at the phone. Her eyes bucked again. She covered her mouth. "Oh my God, the snake laid the eggs in her mouth, and she swallowed them. Yuk! You mean that's what you have to do?" We both shook our heads, yes. "Wow, it's disgusting and gross. But if that's what it takes to look like this, then I'm down!" Beatrice and I looked at each other again. I shrugged my shoulders. Lilly was smiling, "I want it done, I want it done tonight." Beatrice and I looked at each other. I cleared my voice, "ok, tonight it is." Beatrice was not happy; I could tell. She wanted the procedure for herself done tonight.

I had to step in and give the dangerous details. "Listen, Lilly; it's not as easy as just swallowing the eggs. Amaya is very dangerous. If you gag, bite down or swallow before the eggs are laid. Death can encounter." Lilly became silent for a moment. "Why would death happen?" I sighed deeply. "It's just one of the stipulations using the rainbow serpent snake. You can't move, but it only takes one whole minute for Amaya to get inside your mouth. Find a comfortable spot and lay the eggs. We've timed it perfectly."

Lilly rubbed her chin. "Well, how do you that will even happen?" Beatrice rolled her eyes. "We don't, but from what we've researched, it will happen. So, you must follow the rules. Candy was our first participant. We are still in the trial stage. Lilly took a deep breath. "Well, I'm sure I can do this. Like I said, my credit cards are maxed. And two of my co-workers have started going to Mexico for cheap procedures. Both have horror stories. I'm willing to try." Beatrice and I looked at each other. I sighed.

"Ok, Lilly, but you can't mention this to the others. Of course, I will have to film it, but just for our records and marketing once the business takes off. We will need video and pictures of before and after. I plan on building a website soon for services." Beatrice smiled, "Well, we got another guinea pig to try the procedure on." I laughed, "Well, I think we should wait until everyone falls asleep. Don't get wasted today. Let them drank and party. You just chill. Once they are smashed and fall asleep, we will start the procedure. It really is quick, and the trick is, just don't move. Don't chump down or swallow before time. Please, we don't want to lose you."

Lilly smiled, "look, I don't plan on going anywhere soon. I got a husband and four kids who need me. I'm not checking out anytime soon. I'm sure I can do one minute of just holding still. Besides, I've had several procedures done." Beatrice laughed, "Yeah, but you were under anesthesia, so you didn't feel anything." Lilly started laughing, "You still have to recovery after surgery, and that's no fun. Nor is it painless." I sighed, "well, if you're set on doing this. We have to do it tonight. We all have to return to Atlanta Sunday morning."

At that moment, there was a knock at the door. "Who is it?" I walked over to the door quickly. I slowly opened it, just a crack, it was Bruce. I smiled and welcomed him in. He walked in and looked at Beatrice and Lilly. He waved, "Hi, sorry to interrupt. But I was in grandmother's room. Going through some old photo albums. I saw something sparkling high up on Grandmother's shelf." I frantically looked down at his hands. One was behind his back. He continued, "Well, I grabbed a jar down off the shelf. It's kind of strange but. I know I heard a voice call me by my name. A name I haven't been called since I was a child."

I tried not to panic; I stayed calm. "Did you open the jar?" Beatrice looked over at me with wide eyes. Bruce proceeded to pull the jar from behind his back. The top was off. My heart almost jumped out of my chest. Bruce looked into my eyes. He could tell I was frightened. "I um, did I do something wrong?" I remembered Amaya being in the room with us. I slowly walked over to the crate. I pulled the cover from over it. I glanced down, and Amaya's eyes were glowing red. My eyes widened again. I grabbed my chest. At that moment, I heard the whirlwinds. I felt the winds whip through my hair.

I looked over at Beatrice and Lilly. Beatrice was on the floor, covering her ears. Lilly dropped down to help Beatrice But fell to the floor herself. Due to the strong whirlwinds. Bruce ran over towards me, covering his ears. The whirlwinds were so strong. Papers were flying all over the office. This was my fault. I forgot to inform my brother. If the whirlwinds had to take anyone away, it would be me and only me! I quickly used my mind. I closed my eyes. I saw my brother, Beatrice, and Lilly. Inside a protection bubble. I saw the bubble, big and strong, unbreakable. I harnessed the three of them inside safely.

The whirlwinds became louder. I grabbed my ears. I have quickly swept away as I spun out of the dimension. I looked down and saw my brother. Lilly and Beatrice were looking up at me. My brother screamed, "NOOOOOOOO!" I have whisked away into the Cosmo's. It was out of my control. But, at least I spared them from a potentially dangerous journey.

Chapter 14

Vampires Realm

I was thrown into what felt like a tree. Branchlike objects hit my face. I opened my eyes and looked down. I was in a tree very high up. My eyes widened as I lost my grip. I fell, I started screaming as I free fall. I reached out my arms. I was able to grab a strong branch. I stopped falling. I gripped the branch with both hands. I was now suspended in midair. I looked down, and the bottom was still far reached.

I looked back up and gripped tighter. I saw a tree ledge. I decided to swing back and forth, back and forth. Until I got high. I swung fast at high speeds. When my feet were touching the ledge, I jumped and let go of the branch. I fell right onto the tree ledge. It hurt a little, but I was now, secure and safe.

I caught my breath and sat down for a moment. I looked around, and it was very dark. There was a pink glow. I turned to look at it. A huge pink full moon lit up my area. I looked around; I was in a forest. The pink moon lit up the whole forest. I gripped the tree bark and looked around a little more. I was afraid; I was in unknown lands. It looked like a magical forest. For some reason, it was comforting. There were millions of trees all around, with illuminating multi-colored dragonflies.

I continued to hold the branch. I scanned the forest again with my eyes. I also took a deep inhale. I smelled the ocean. My eyes cascaded to an alluring sandy beach. There were big boats nearby. They floated on top of a charming pink sea. I glanced down at my attire. I was half-naked. I was wearing a bra made of golden beads. With lustrous pearl accents and matching half mini skirt. Each wrist had a beautiful gold bracelet with a huge moldavite in the center. I glanced down, and I was wearing matching anklets. My feet were bare, and there were markings all over my body.

I looked like a tribal princess. I had a machete tied to the side of my hip. I looked and felt like a radiant warrior. I heard voices approaching. I clung to the branch as I looked down. I heard footsteps that seem to be getting closer and closer. Screams pierced my ears. I looked closer, two men with rifles were dragging people inside of a huge net made for animals. A man and a woman with a small child were inside the net. The two men commanded them to stay quiet and stop moving.

They pointed rifles at them. An overwhelming feeling came over me. A feeling I couldn't control — a feeling I had never encountered before. My body became hot. I started salivating, and I felt a throbbing pain in my gums. Something sharp was busting through them. I touched my mouth. I noticed two teeth were extremely longer than the others. I became thirsty and thirstier. The taste for blood was on my tongue. The feeling overwhelmed me. I had to have it. I had to decide whether I wanted to taste the blood of the innocent family. Or the blood of the evil men. All of a sudden, I could smell something. The scent of testosterone was alarmingly like braised short ribs. It had to be the teeth and the jungle. I decided if I would take blood. It would be the blood of the two men, harming the family.

I prepared myself, I looked down, finding the perfect ambush point. I gripped my machete. I bent my knees. I was breathing heavily as I prepared to jump. I took another deep breath. I pushed off the tree with great force. I flew down and landed in front of the two men. They were frightened and caught off guard. I grabbed one of their rifles and kicked the other man in the chest. He hit the ground, slamming his head on a rock. His rifle flew from his hands under a bush. I pulled my machete out and held it to his throat. I hissed as I went in for his neck.

Digging my teeth inside his flesh and ripping open his jugular. I drank his blood. I sucked and sucked until he was dry. I then removed the machete from his neck. I pounced on the other guy, lying on the ground. I sucked his blood fiercely until his corpse lay dormant. I wiped the remaining blood from my mouth. I was embarrassed by my behavior. I felt like a wild, untamed animal. I didn't know what had come over me. I immediately turned around. The family stuck inside the nets, were standing behind me.

They had freed themselves. The unknown man stepped forward. He had amazement in his eyes. "Asasa Suku"! he called out to me with a West African accent. The unknown man smiled again. "Asasa Suku…it is you"! I assumed he thought I was someone else. I was the only person standing in the direction he was looking at. He smiled again. "It is you! The guardian over our precious diamonds, crystals, and gold. You protect it; you are a great warrior. You defend our people who are defenseless against the slave capturers."

The three of them got on their knees. They bowed down, continuously. The woman stood up and spoke with excitement. "Asasa Suku! We have heard of your greatness. We are honored that you saved our lives. You're just as beautiful as they say you were in old ancestry times. Please, the men on those boats will come looking for these two soon. We must go, but before we leave. We will make sure you are safe. The Douens will lead you through the forest safely.

I was a bit confused, who were the Douens? So I asked, surprisingly, I spoke in the same tongue. "I'm sorry, but who are the Douens?" The woman stepped forward. "Don't be an afraid child. The Douens are magical creatures who live in the forest. They are the spirits of children who died before they became adults. They roam the forest, and they take the form of naked children. They are small in height, two to three feet tall. Their faces are featureless, except for a small mouth. They wear straw hats. Their feet are turned backward.

They can be malicious little creatures. But they are good-natured. They will guide you to safety. Don't be afraid; we must go now! We will lead you to them." I followed the three of them through the magical jungle. We approached a bright orange glow deep in the jungle. It was a fire-like glow. I followed as they led me to a bunch of small children. They were almost transparent. But I could see them. I saw them very well. The family left me with the Douens and took off fast. Fast into the trees and disappeared. The Douens sat in a circle as they held hands while chanting.

The bonfire was blazed high. All of a sudden, they stopped and raised their heads. It was true; they had no features. Just a small slit for a mouth. They had straw hats that covered most of their faces. As they stood up, I noticed their feet were turned backward. They were completely bare. I couldn't help it, I felt compelled by them. They were like small children. One Douen stepped forward, extending his hand to me. The Douen started speaking. The voice was reminiscent of a child. "Follow us, and we will lead you to your destination."

They all got into a single file. Lined up and then dispersed quickly into the forest. They had a little giggle that echoed enchantments throughout the forest as they led the way. Their straw hats begin to glow green. They lit up the forest. They escorted me to a boat down by the riverside. One of the Douens extended his hand to help me into the boat. He spoke, "This is as far as we go. This boat will take you to your destination." The boat lay upon the pink-colored river as a red moon illuminated the forest. "My destination?" I said, "Where is my destination?" I asked. The Douens just giggled. "Our destination was to get you to this boat safely. Where you go from here, no one knows. But you must go now, it is not safe."

I climbed into the boat. The Douens pushed the boat off the sand, into the pink sea. I begin to drift away. They all said "Goodbye". They threw their hats up into the sky. I begin to row the boat; I had no clue where I was going. I rowed and rowed. My arms were beginning to feel heavy. I was getting tired. I stopped rowing to take a rest. To my surprise, the boat was being pulled by some supernatural force. I was exhausted from rowing. I laid down in the boat and fell asleep. As I slowly awakened, I felt a wet sponge rubbing my torso. I opened my eyes up. I was staring at a ceiling. I felt wetness all around my body. I felt scrubbing on my legs, and I glanced down. I was sitting in a pool of blood. I screamed! I was frightened. Four beautiful women came running; they busted into the room. One was wearing a mask.

The tall, pale one started speaking with a Transylvanian accent. She had a look of concern in her eyes. "What have you done to her? You, stupid girl!" The servant girl looked frightened. She looked at the women with the Transylvanian accent. "Nothing madame, she woke up screaming." The tall, pale women begin to walk over towards me. She looked very concerned. She bowed down to me. "Asasa Suku, it is my pleasure to introduce myself. I am Neferata of Transylvania". Neferata had long blonde hair. She was pale, tall, and skinny. She wore a tight-fitting light blue, satin dress. It had embellished blue gemstones on the front.

The women with the mask stepped forward. So, did the other two women. They all bowed. The women with the mask continued. "I am Churel from India." Churel had a hazel colored skin tone, pale of course. Long jet-black hair, past her butt. Big bright tiger eyes, with long eyelashes. She was medium height. Churel donned a long flowy black dress. Another stepped forward. "I am Ada from Italy." Ada had the skin of a porcelain doll. She was the shortest in the bunch. Long wavy chocolate tresses. She wore a long red robe looking dress. Another came forward and bowed. "I am Malaysia, from Malaysia." Malaysia was tall and curvy. She had sandy brown hair. Blue eyes and coco kissed skin. She wore a form-fitted crush velvet purple dress — lots of exotic jewelry. Neferata walked closer and looked down at me. "You do not enjoy Bathory?"

I realized I was naked. I begin to cover my breast with my arms and hands. "Bathory? I've never had Bathory before." Neferata looked amazed and retorted. "But you are a great queen. Bathory is when you drain blood from a servant girl. You bath in her blood. It keeps your skin healthy and youthful. Not that you need it. You are as beautiful as your legend says you are. Asasa Suku, Vamptress of West Africa. The guardian of your countries precious diamonds and gold. Protector of your people. It was once said you freed thousands of your people.

Before they were taken onto those horrible ships, those ships lead them across the sea into slavery. It is said that you, Asasa Suku. Snuck onto one of those boats and sailed off to faraway lands. For over three hundred years, you have turned thousands of them into our kind.

Thank you, Asasa Suku." Ada, the masked women, cut in. "There is a myth in my country that you hide in the trees at night that you have long legs made of hooks. When a passer comes by, you hook them with your feet and pull them into the trees and suck their blood."

Neferata looked annoyed, and she turned to the slave girls. "Now, ladies, Let her dry off and get into some comfortable clothes. We will talk later over a wonderful dinner. It has been prepared for your arrival, Asasa Suku. Servant girl, please dry her off and robe her. Then take her downstairs to the chambers." The servant girls bowed and replied, "Yes, madame." The four mysterious women walked out of the room. The servant girl rinsed me off with fresh water. She dressed me in a satin long red robe. She pulled my long dark hair up into a tight bun. I looked at myself in the mirror. I looked exquisite.

The servant girl led me down a long hall. The castle had a classically futuristic look. It was an elegant old castle with flat-screen TVs. The TVs were interesting; they just kind of floated in front of the walls. The Chrome appliances looked modern. Led lighting lit up the hallways. The floors were marble-like. The patterns just seem to jump off the floor. They looked very three dimensional. The castle was fit for a queen. The servant girl led me down another flight of stairs. Then into the dining area. They were all sitting around a divine table.

There was a grand feast spread out in front of them. There was one space available. The servant girl led me to that seat. The servant girl pulled out my chair, and I sat down. I was nervous and still wondering what kind of trouble I would get into here. I was really hoping I wouldn't have to kill anyone. Neferata began to speak. "Welcome, Asasa Suku. Let us all greet her to the group with a warm welcome. Neferata, Churel, Ada, and Malaysia said "Welcome" all at the same time. Neferata picked up her empty glass to get the servant girl's attention. "Now, the circle is complete. That is, if you'll be a part of our circle, Asasa Suku?"

The servant girl walked over. She filled all the wine glasses full of blood. I became extremely hot again. The animal-like feeling came over me. A feeling I couldn't control. I looked around, and they were all salivating as well. Neferata noticed I was looking around. She comforted me with her words. "Drink Asasa; it is the best. Purified, organic blood from a vegan human. We only drink the best." I picked up my glass. I gulped it down quickly. I was embarrassed once again of my behavior. I wiped my mouth with a napkin. I swallowed the last drop. I looked up at Neferata. "That was very tasty. Did you say a vegan human? Wow, I have to have more of that. It's very crisp and lite." Churel smiled and gave her two cents. "Yes, it is…it's very hard to find, most humans are meat-eaters, carnivores."

Neferata looked at me, nervously. She led the conversation in another direction. "Asasa, let's get acquainted with one another. We know so much about you. Let me give you some information. About who we really are. Then I will explain why you are the chosen one for our circle." The room went silent, and Malaysia cleared her throat. She spoke first. "Asasa Suku, it is my honor to introduce myself. I am Malaysia, my name means, made beautifully by magic. I once had everything a woman could desire and more. I came from a family of wealth, prestige, power, and honor.

When the time was right, I was paired with my prince. He was everything you could ever want in a husband. No concubines, just me. Which was unheard of for a man with his power. He loved me, unconditionally. He was obsessed with my beauty. No other women in the land possessed beauty like mine. One day we married. Soon after, I was confronted with a disaster. My husband went out one day. He knew how much I loved fresh strawberries. So, he went to an unknown land alone. He sent servants serval days before to get berries. But, he didn't like the berries they brought back. They were bruised and out of season. Not fit for his queen. He had heard rumors from the servants. They told him about the village. This village supposedly had the ripest strawberries in all the lands. So, he traveled there alone. He found the stunning fresh meadow of strawberries. He picked plenty for me. While he was picking, something tragic happened. A snake bit him. He immediately became ill from the bite. Although he was very weak, he climbed onto his horse and carriage and made it back home.

When he walked through that door, I knew something was wrong — just looking at his face, Made chills run down my spine. He was pale and weak. I rushed to his side. I had a few servant girls help me take him to the bedroom. I laid him down on the bed. That's when I noticed the bite marks on his neck. Where I'm from if a snake has bitten someone. We use our mouths to suck the poison out. I spit it out quickly. So, the poison would not enter my body. But, I sucked and sucked and sucked. As I was sucking, I knew something was wrong. An odd feeling came over me.

I couldn't stop sucking, and unfortunately. I sucked him completely dry. When I finished, I glanced into the mirror? I opened my mouth and saw fangs. The snake in the garden wasn't a snake. It was a vampire. He was attacked that evening. When he came home to me, he couldn't speak. I saw the bites, and I figured they were snake bites. After sucking him dry, I became a vampire. So was he, but he crossed over. He wasn't the same anymore. He became a soulless beast. He'd bit me several times. Sometimes there was no more blood in my body.

Then one day, he disappeared, and I was all alone. Once my family and my kingdom found out what we both were. They banished us from the land. I was alone for many, many years. Until I found Neferata, she accepted me and loved me for who I am a soulless vampire." Tears started to protrude from Malaysia's eyes. I tried not to stare. Neferata took her napkin and gave it to Malaysia. She wiped her tears. Churel looked around, and she noticed the silence was uncomfortable. She gulped deeply and began to speak. "Well, as I mentioned before, my name is Churel. I am from India, and I began my journey many years ago. I was unwed and became pregnant by a king. A very powerful king. I was a concubine — only one of so many. I was only a number to him. He never knew my real name. I doubt if he would even remember my face.

After I became pregnant with his child, I was sent to live in a special chamber. With all the other pregnant concubines. The living conditions were horrible. He made sure we were fed and gave us a place to sleep. But, it was unfit for a pregnant woman. When the time came. Two of the chambermaids help me deliver my baby. I gave birth to my child. He was born cold and blue — no signs of life. I bore a stillborn child. After the king found out, he made me leave. He said having a dead baby was evil. He said I should go immediately. I became distraught and angry. I had nowhere else to go. I begged him to stay. He had me carried off by two men. Who threw me outside of the castle. They locked the doors. I felt hopeless.

I ran to the woods. It was the only place I could go. I climbed high up in a tree. I stayed there for shelter. The tree was my safety net. It kept me away from the terrible creatures on land. They would come at night and hunt me for food. I was terrified and frightened. I found a safe spot high up with a flat surface to sleep. I needed rest. One night I fell asleep. I woke up to a foul smell. Something was breathing on my neck. I slowly opened my eyes. I saw fangs coming at me at full speed. He was to fast. Too quick, and he bit me. Draining my blood until I was dry. He vanished in the middle of the night. I crossed over that evening. I was bitter and angry. I hid in that tree, and I started attacking pregnant women; I wanted their babies to die like mine. No one showed me mercy. And I didn't show them mercy either. I decided to be a soulless beast. I would act like one going forward. Taking no pity and doing as I felt. It wasn't until I met Malaysia and Neferata. I realized I could be civil again someday even though we feed off blood. We don't have to conduct ourselves like animals. Or some soulless beast."

Ada, the masked woman, took a deep breath. She took over the conversation. "I am princess Ada from Italy. My story is quite different from the others. I was a princess. I received gifts from people all the time from all over the world. People have been very generous towards me and very kind. It was my eighteenth birthday. Mother and father threw me a huge birthday party. The entire kingdom was invited. Many people brought me wonderful gifts. There were so many presents to unwrap. After the party, I had servants that delivered them to my bedroom.

It was one particular package that stood out from all the rest. It was a stunning big box. I opened it and inside was a gorgeous small mask. It was made of porcelain and lined with gold. I immediately looked into the mirror. I placed it on my face to try it on. I looked exquisite with it on. I admired myself for a few minutes. Then I instantly felt excruciating pain. The mask became alive, and spikes injected into my face. I frantically tried to remove the mask. It dug deeper into my face and sank into my soul.

There was blood everywhere. The mask left me completely dry. That's when I crossed over. From that day, I've never been able to remove this mask.

Unfortunately, it is now apart of me. Till this day, I never found out who sent the mask or why. Of course, I tried to hide the fact I was a vampire. My mother and father found out eventually. They found it odd that I never took the mask off. I never slept or ate food. My skin was as pale as a ghost. And the smell of my parents drove me Insane. One night I found myself hanging upside down. Over my mother while she slept.

My fangs activated, and a drop of saliva dripped from them. One single drop struck her forehead. She woke and looked above her. She screamed like someone was killing her. She woke my father. They gave me that look of disgust. I ran out of the palace and out of the kingdom. I spent my days and nights. Luring handsome young men into the forest. I was a virgin when I crossed over. I would seduce the men and make them have sex with me. It hurt every time. I became angry with the pain. Not realizing that when I crossed over. I would be a virgin forever. No matter how many times I had sex.

This infuriated me, and I began to bite the men and drink their blood. It wasn't until I met these ladies. That I realized attacking the innocent was not always a good thing. We, as vampires, can use our gifts for good. And, only attack bad or evil people. The room went silent. Neferata took a sip from her glass. She begins to speak in an eloquent tone. "Once again, I am Neferata of Transylvania. I lived in a land of Vampires and Goddesses. I know that sounds like a weird mix.

Everyone in the land was either a vampire or a Goddess. I wasn't a very kind vampire. I was evil, and I fought a lot. I won respect, well I should say fear of many, in the land. They didn't respect me but absolutely feared me. At the time, I confused their fear with respect. I was the antagonist of the land. I was the town villain. I would do anything to anyone to get what I wanted. I was

cruel and selfish. One day I met my match. Which is
funny, because I never thought I had one.

She was a beautiful Goddess named Vega. She was married
to a handsome, powerful count. I wanted him, and I wanted
him so badly, I could taste it. The rules of the land
stated That if a vampire and Goddess is married. You do
not interfere. But I was a badass. I didn't care, and I
had to have him. I was powerful and beautiful myself. I
knew he couldn't resist me. We had a passionate love
affair for some time. Vega soon found out, and she became
vexed.

So, she decided we would battle it out in front of all
the land. We fought a good fight — myself being a vampire
with my speed and strength. I overpowered Vega at some
points during the battle. But Goddesses have magical
powers as well. Vega threw some vaults out of her palms,
which froze me. While I was frozen, she showed no mercy.
But, I was way to fast. I used my ability to tap into her
mind. I could visualize her moves before she could
execute them. I was able to get to her neck. I bit her.

I nearly drained her dry with my fangs still in her neck.
A higher Goddesses stepped in and used her powers to
freeze me. I couldn't move. She took Vega from underneath
me. She placed her hand upon Vega's forehead. She closed
her eyes and began to speak over Vega. The color started
to come back to Vega's skin. She refilled Vega's body
with blood. Vega opened her eyes. She soon became strong
enough to stand on her feet.

The Goddess called out to me. Neferata, you are in the
wrong. You slept with a woman's husband. Is your intent
to now kill this woman? She unfroze me. I came to my
defense. I shouted out to the Goddess. Vega is married to
a count, a vampire. She is a Goddess. She should be
married to her own kind! The Goddess became very angry.
She pierced deeply into my eyes and said. This is the
same attitude that killed off the humans! I will not have
this in my land! That day, the Goddess banished me from
the land. The rules of the land state: That a vampire may
marry a Goddess/God. And when a vampire and Goddess
marry. No one is to interfere. For that, love is more
powerful than any, when combined. I laughed to myself. It

couldn't have been that powerful. I got the count to sleep with me.

But, anyway, I have learned from my evil ways. That's why I decided to create a pack of vampires. Who use to kill for sport or revenge. You see, Asasa, we only drink blood from the bad and evil. That's how we survive — no more preying on the weak or innocent humans. We are better than that. You are like us, and you prey on the bad. You already fit our circle; you do not need rehabilitation. After a fifth member enters our pack, the five powers together will double. We will become unstoppable." Ada cleared her throat. "Have you ever been a part of a hunting pack Asasa?"

I was a bit confused. I cleared my throat and responded. "Why no, I haven't". Ada put her drink down. "Well, let me explain Asasa, a pack is usually four vampires since we cannot reproduce. We create our own families. A unit, so our lives will feel more meaningful. The number four can be altered depending on the hunter's strength if there are too many weak members in a pack. One member will not eat. It is usually the newbie to the group. The alpha vampire will always eat first. The order continues until the newbie feeds if they have leftovers. The pros of joining our pack. We offer you security along with access to an unlimited blood supply."

I was quite overwhelmed. I just wanted to go back home. I sank my fork into my meal. I took a big savory bite. I looked up and met eyes with Chureal. I swallowed and then spoke. "What exactly is an alpha?" Chureal sipped her wine. "The alpha vampire is the strongest. Fastest, smartest, and most beautiful vampire ever created. You see, Asasa, we are all alpha vampires. Including yourself, that's why we can afford a fifth member to the pack. More than four usually means, one vampire will not eat. But, we are clever, intelligent, and quick on our toes. We have plenty to share. No one has to eat last. We can all eat together. We are hybrids, with five combined, there's no telling what we can conquer!"

I was becoming confused again. I put down my fork and swallowed. "Well, how did I become an alpha vampire?" Maylasia looked at me and put her fork down. She had a devilish grin. "An alpha vampire is not elected. We are meritocracies, you are chosen, and that's that! You have been chosen Asasa Suku. Many wonders if vampires can love and be loyal. Well, we do, and that's why we form these packs." Neferata wiped her mouth with a napkin. She had excitement in her eyes. "Asasa, when you finish your meal, we want to give you a tour. We want to show you a project we are working on." I became quite curious and dropped my napkin in my lap.

I looked around the table. All eyes were on me. I spoke up. "Well, I'm done with my food." Neferata looked pleased, she smiled. "Great, we will escort you to the fledgling lab." We all stood up from the table. Neferata leads the way. She steered us down a long dark hall. Around the corner was a huge door made of crystal quartz. Neferata placed her pointer finger onto a pad. It was near the door. The pad read her finger. "No soul," it was what the device said out loud.

The doors slid open. Violins filled my ears. Whimsical music played in the background. We walked into the room. Everything was made of glass. There were individual cells. Six cells with one person inside each one. One cell had a child inside of it. All of them were floating, frozen in mid-air, motionless. Neferata swayed her hand to the right. "This door only allows vampires to enter the room. Humans are not allowed. By placing your finger on the pad. It will detect if you have a soul or not. If you have a soul, that means you are not a vampire. The room will then begin to lockdown, almost immediately. This will cause the alarms to go off. This is the fledgling lab, Asasa. A fledgling is a recently transformed vampire. We are working on an experiment.

We have taken these seven ex humans. Who we believe will be alphas. We take them under our wings and teach them our ways since they've just transformed into vampires. We have a higher chance of converting them." I was a little concerned about the cells. I needed to know more. "Neferata, why are they locked inside the cells?" Ada stepped forward. "It is for our own protection Asasa. They have just crossed over, and their impulses may overpower them.

They have no self-control at this point and time. That comes with maturity or conditioning. Its what we do here in the lab." Once again, I needed some clarity. "So, conditioning, what does that include"? Neferata walked towards one of the cells and explained. "When a vampire is recently transformed. They have what's called an unconditioned stimulus to human blood. It causes the vampire to activate its fangs. Salvation begins; it is an automatic reflex to the sight and smell of blood. So here in the fledgling lab, we condition them. With conditioning, they learn first before they respond.

It's an acquired power to change something. Being a vampire is an incurable disease! But we can treat the symptoms." Chureal pointed to a device. "This is our technology, the motherboard. There are seven buttons for each cell. Each button is connected to each vampire. Once you hit cell one. The vampire in cell one becomes unfrozen. Inside each cell, directly in front of the vampire, is a plate. A dropper hangs over the plate. Blood drips from the dropper onto the plate. The vampire reacts to the blood. A small shock is sent through his or her system. It doesn't hurt the vampire; it's just enough to make them think before reacting. We're vampires; we are always going to want blood as it keeps us alive. We'd die without blood. But if we have vampires out there like us. We can live longer. A vampire has a lifespan of five to ten years before he or she is killed. Of course, the alpha's have a higher mortality rate.

But, creating many, many vampires like us. We can change those statistics." I walked around the room and looked into each cell. There was a male vampire labeled, Jake. I couldn't take my eyes off of him. I was mesmerized by his beauty. Jake looked young and handsome. He was tall, he had long dark hair and was very muscular, Newly bitten of course. But he also looked debonair and smart. I assumed he had been a lady's man in his past life. He also looked gentle and kind. Neferata noticed me gawking. "He was a great warrior. A very, very powerful God in his land before he was bitten." Neferata started smiling. "So, you like what you see, huh?" I started to blush. "Well, he is quite the looker." Neferata walked over and said. "Yes, he is, his name is Jake. He will make a great alpha for our team. He is in the last stage of the program.

He is almost fully conditioned, only one day left. We usually keep them for 21 days until they are rehabilitated. Some vampires, which is rare, finish early. But it is very rare." I wanted to know more, so I asked. "What happens after rehabilitation. What will they do then?" Neferata looked at me and then back into Jake's cell. "Some will stay here in the castle. Others will become hunters. They will go out and capture fledglings for the lab. Others will go off and start their own packs. We don't hold them, hostage, here. They are free to go. We want them out in the world doing good, not evil. Every now and then, we get a bad apple in the bunch. They just can't be conditioned. It is also very rare. But it has happened before."

Interesting, I thought to myself. "How many have been transformed? How do you keep track?" I asked. Neferata had a proud smile come over her face. "We have transformed over two hundred fledglings. We keep a logbook for them all. When each fledgling is done with the program. We brand them with our special mark. It is placed on the back of their necks. It is our Kindred Klan mark. It is similar to a bar code. It is very hard to duplicate. This way, out in the world, we can identify one another. As far as we know, we have the only fledgling lab. No one else cares about making vampires good. A lot of vampires are good. But, the thirst for blood drives them wild. Fucks up their minds. It drives them insane!" Neferata face went cold. I vacantly looked at her for a moment. Then i broke the silence. "How often do you condition them in a day?" Neferata's face became nervous, and she told me. "Ten times a day, every day for twenty-one days. We want to teach you the lab, Asasa. Show you the ropes, would you like that?"

I was kind of excited but kept calm. "Sure, I'd be delighted to learn the lab." Excitement rose in Malaysia's eyes. "So, does this mean you will join the pack?" I was delighted and confused at the same time. I saw the excitement in all their eyes. "Yes…yes, I will!" I realized I answered, "yes" on impulse. My heart was bleeding to belong and have a family. But I could be swept back home into my realm at any time. I was starting to miss my brother and Beatrice.

This mission was weird. I had no clue why I was here yet. I just have to play along. Until I could figure it out, the whirlwinds could come and take me away at any time.

It saddened me a bit, and I was confused. Ada seemed very excited. "Great! We will have the ceremony in twenty-four hours. This way, we can welcome the new fledglings. Plus, our new pack member. All of the kindred clans will attend." Neferata gave me a big hug and whispered. "Wonderful, we welcome you into the pack in twenty-four hours in the ceremony room. I am sure you are tired from your journey. I'll show you to your room. so you can get some rest."

Chureal, Ada, and Maylasia all looked at me and said, "goodnight". Neferata walked me to my room. While the others retired to their chambers. My room was elegantly decorated with gold antiques and mirrors. The bed had a gorgeous gold frame, and music played softly in the background. Neferata led me to the bed. She smiled softly. "Well, we all know vampires don't sleep. But it's nice to relax sometimes. Rest Asasa, and the servant girl will come get you in the morning. You will help us in the fledgling lab tomorrow morning. Tomorrow night we will welcome you. And the new fledglings into our kindred clan. No Bathory in the morning this time. I promise." I was so relieved to hear that. I smiled, "Thank you, Neferata." Neferata smiled and walked out of the room and closed the door. I sat on the bed and stared at the wall. I was still very confused.

A part of me wanted to stay at the castle. But, I had to get back to the spa. My brother, Beatrice, my life. Although while in the ethers. Time kind of stood still. But, I had never stayed somewhere this long. I laid on the bed and stared up at the ceiling. Thoughts of Jake filled my brain. I didn't even know him, but he compelled me by four a.m. I was antsy to rest. So, I snuck downstairs to the fledgling room. I watched my back down every hallway. I didn't want to get caught. I made it safely to the lab. I placed my finger on the pad, and it spoke. "No Soul". Immediately the doors opened and allowed me to enter. I tiptoed in quietly, and I reached Jake's cell. I stared at him in disbelief. Wanting to know more. I walked over to the controls. My heart was beating rapidly! I put my hand on button number seven. I took a deep breath, closed my eyes and pressed it.

Jake became unfrozen. I gently walked over to his cell, and his eyes opened. As his body lowered, his feet touched the ground. He stared at me. We stared at each other. Jake places his hand on the glass. I placed my hand on top of his, over the glass. Both of us closed our eyes. We read each other's minds. Jake spoke telepathically. "Who are you, creature?" I mentally replied. "I am Asasa Suku, an alpha vampire. Can we talk verbally"? Jake smiled. "This glass restricts any form of communication. Only telepathy. It's the only form of communication in the fledgling laboratory. They don't want us communicating with humans." I looked at him. "Makes sense, so your crossing over tomorrow?" Jake paused and stared into my eyes. "Yes…it will be my cross over day, how did you know that?" I smiled. "Neferata told me." My mind was starting to drift to other things. I didn't want him to continue reading my thoughts. "Well, I gotta go now. I'll see you at the ceremony tomorrow." Jake smiled "I'd like that." I removed my hand from the glass. I walked over to the buttons. I pressed seven and Jake floated back into the air and froze. I snuck out of the lab and back upstairs to my room. A few hours later, the servant girl walked in and greeted me. "Good day madam, are you ready to be bathed and dressed?"

I sat up straight, "Yes, I am ready, um, Neferata said I could be washed with water." The servant girl looked at me. She smiled, "yes, madame, Neferata has already informed me." I undressed. I felt very strange. Getting naked in front of someone I didn't know. The servant girl bathed me in warm water with rose petals instead of blood. The servant girl started to wash me gently with a sponge and soap. She looked down at me and said. "Your ceremony is today. You will become a part of the alpha pack now." I looked up at her while she scrubbed my chest and spoke. "Yes…I will, are you human? I'm sorry I didn't catch your name?" The servant girl laughed under her breath.

I'm sorry, madame, we're not allowed to give our names. I am a special breed, a vamp H, half-vampire, and half-human. Or so I've been told. But, you can call me number three." The thought of her not being able to have a name saddened me. "Well, number three it is." The servant girl helped me out of the tub. She dried me off and donned me with a beautiful dress. I glanced in the mirror. "This is a lovely dress!" The servant girl smiled. "Why yes, it is, I picked it out. I thought the color violet would look great on your skin. Violet is a royal color. Your ceremony will begin in twenty minutes. Are you ready to go downstairs? I will escort you down of course.

There will be a lot of people waiting." I was starting to get nervous. The servant girl was very polite. She made me feel comfortable. Number three led me downstairs. She walked slowly, and I followed. We stopped at the door before entering. She stared at me strangely and whispered. "You're different, not like the others." I unlocked my eyes from her. How did she know? I took a deep breath and entered the room. It was decorated with purple and gold. There were so many people in the ballroom. So many unfamiliar faces. I became nervous again. My stomach tied in enormous knots.

My heart raced as the unfamiliar eyes fell upon me. I looked around the room. I was in utter disbelief. I noticed the fledglings were at the party. I continued to scan the room until my eyes locked in on Jake. He was dressed in a black tuxedo with a white shirt and purple accents on his bowtie. We naturally gravitated towards one another. Jake gazed deeply into my eyes as he spoke to me.

"Asasa, you look gorgeous!" I could feel my face overflowing with heat. I was flushed; I knew I was blushing. I was a bit embarrassed, but I smiled brightly like I had found a long-lost crystal. "You look wonderful, also, Jake," I said looking down at my shoes. Jake smiled at my awkwardness. "Asasa, the other day, I asked you what type of creature you were. you didn't ask in return." I smiled, "I just figured if you were in the fledgling lab, you were a vampire." Jake smiled as he parted his perfectly pouty lips. "I am half, and I am a vamp G." I shook my head. "A vamp G, that sounds interesting, what is your genetic make-up?"

Jake takes a sip from his glass. He licked his lips slowly and seductively as he swallowed. "I was born a God in the old world, and a vampire attacked me. He was jealous of my popularity with the ladies. A woman he was very fond of was not interested in him. She only wanted me. He figured if he got rid of me, He could have her all to himself. You see Asasa, once a God or Goddess, always a God or Goddess. After I was attacked and bitten. I was able to have my God powers. Also, I have inherited the powers of a vampire. So, I am a Vamp G, half-vampire, half-God." I took a deep breath, that was a lot to grasp.

"Very well explained Jake." I smiled as I Observed his long eyelashes flirt with me. Jake then asked, "Asasa, are you fully vampire? I'm feeling something so different about you. Something extraordinary and rare." I was a bit surprised at his question. I was a little uneasy. I inhaled and exhaled. "As far as I know, I am a full vampire." Jake looked alarmed. "As far as you know? When did you cross over as a vampire Asasa?" I stumbled for my words and replied. "I um…I don't remember Jake."

Jake gazed into my eyes. "You don't remember Asasa… amazing." At that moment, Neferata, Churel, Ada and Maylasia walked into the room. Everyone turned around and applauded. I was relieved, the attention was off of me. I exhaled with a sigh of relief. I joined in clapping with the crowd. They walked to the front of the room and stood at the podium. Nefertata gracefully stepped forward. "Welcome, everyone, and I am so glad you could make it out tonight. It is a very special day. We are welcoming seven new fledglings into the kindred klan. We are also welcoming one new vampire into the alpha pack." The crowd clapped as they cleared a path to the podium. Neferata continued. I will call each fledgling one by one. As I do so, please walk to the podium and receive your mark. Jake walked down first. Everyone in the room clapped, as Jake walks towards the podium. He kneeled down in front of Nerferata. She took out a metal branding stick. She branded him on the back of his neck. The six others were called one by one, including the child.

They each received their mark. I started to panic. Even though the others showed no fear of pain, I thought to myself, maybe it would hurt. Neferata walks back to the center. She began to speak again. "And now, the moment we've all been waiting for. Our newest member of the Alpha pack Asasa Suku!" the crowd cheered as I walked down the aisle. I walked slowly approaching the podium. I took a long deep breath. I kneeled down before Neferata. I nervously anticipated the pain. I closed my eyes as I bowed lower. I clenched my eyes tighter. I felt the invigorating metal hit my skin.

Tingles crawled up to the top of my crown chakra. More tingles shot down to my feet. It actually felt amazing. No pain! The tingling stopped. I opened my eyes slowly, rising to my feet. Neferata smiled at me. With a proud look on her face. "You are now the newest member of the alpha pack. Welcome, Asasa Suku!! The crowd applauded and said together. "Welcome, Asasa Suku!" The crowd cheered as I walked over and stood with my pack. I felt warmth come over me. The music played whimsically. Everyone took place on the dance floor. They began to waltz to the music. Very sultry jazz type music was playing. I was still standing alone as Jake approached me. Jake extended his right hand to me. "May I have the honors of this dance?" I smiled and responded. "Yes silly." As I put my hand inside his palm. He pulled my body closely to his. Our eyes locked as we swayed to the music. Jake began to part his lips. He stared deep into my soul.

"Asasa, I feel like I know you." I begin to feel nervous. I glanced down at his chest. I immediately looked back up into his eyes. "Really…well, I don't know what to say, Jake." Jake grinned and replied. "You know exactly what to say. You're just too afraid to say it." He was right, which made me a little embarrassed. "Oh, really," I smiled. "How do you know that Jake"? Jake grinned with confidence and said. "Asasa, I can read your mind, remember?"

My face felt flushed. I must have been blushing. My mind telepathically blurted out. "Oh yes, Jake, your right, I forgot." Jake stared, then he asked. "So, where are you really from Asasa?" I glanced down at my toes and fumbled for my words. I started to stutter a bit. "I really can't remember Jake. I don't know who I am. Or where I'm from." Jake clutched my hand and pulled me closer. He whispered into my ear. "Asasa you must not fear me. I will not hurt you. I am a God of peace and serenity. I know you are not who they think you are. I know that you've been on many journeys, and you're confused."

My eyes widened with disbelief. I became lost for words. "Jake…I don't know what to say. Um, can we go somewhere private and talk about this?" Jake looked concerned and replied. "Sure, where would you like to go?" I grabbed his hand and looked around. I spoke to him telepathically, once again. "Let's go upstairs, come on, let's go." I used telepathy in case anyone was eavesdropping. If Jake knew I wasn't really Asasa Suku. Then others would follow. I just really wanted to go back home. I had to pretend until I could leave this realm. The only way was to figure out what mission had to be completed.

We ducked out of the party. We scanned the room, making sure others were not watching. We dashed upstairs into my suite. I opened the door and led Jake inside. I peeked my head down the hall to make sure no one was watching. I closed the door and locked it behind us. I turned around to find Jake comfortably positioned on the bed. I cleared my throat, walked over, and sat next to him. I looked down at the ground. I felt Jake's soft hand touch my chin. He lifted my chin up and asked. "You never look me in the eyes; why? Is it because we are sitting on a bed, all alone?"

I peered up into his eyes and said. "No, not at all." Jake moved in for a kiss. I had been waiting for this moment. Since the day I laid eyes on him. I accepted his invite. One kiss leads to two; two kisses lead to three. And then…I lost count. We kissed intensely as I laid back onto the bed. Jake climbed on top of me and kissed my lips. Followed by my neck and nipples. Over and over again. I indulged in his sweet abyss. As I lay there, I enjoyed every minute of it. His taunting, kissing, touching and caressing.

Jake massaged my back and unbuttoned my dress. He peeled down the front of my gown. Revealing my bare breast. He quickly paused to take off his shirt. Then he pressed his bare chest up against mine. I moaned with delight. I grabbed the back of his hair. In a wild, turbulent rage. He lifted the bottom of my dress up around my waist. He thrusted his body inside of mine. I moaned more and more with great delight.

We continued to feast on one another until we both became exhausted. I rested on top of Jake's bare chest. I beamed into his eyes. He played gently with my hair as he gazed back into my eyes. We simply were in a trance. I could tell Jake was enjoying my private thoughts. At that moment, something felt odd. I started to feel a tingle at the tip of my scalp. I stopped and sat up. I grabbed my forehead. I knew what this meant. I was very confused. All this time, I just wanted to go home.

And now that it was here. I wanted to stay. The tingling continued to move down towards my forehead. I felt hazy. Jake sat up. "Asasa, what's wrong?" I felt the tingles run down to the bottom of my feet. I panicked! I was started to levitate and float. The whirlwinds were pulling me in. I was floating. I glanced down at Jake. "Jake! Please help me,"! Jake looked at the whirlwinds sucking me. His eyes were in disbelief. Jake jumped up from the bed.

He lifted his right hand and shot out a beam of light. It struck the whirlwind. The force shifted the whirlwind in another direction. I fell unto the bed. The whirlwinds went around and around, Building up more speed and power. The whirlwinds headed my way again. I begin to feel tingles again. My body begin to gravitate towards the whirlwinds. Jake, now using both hands, sent out two bolts of light. The whirlwinds were stunned and held still. Jake closed his eyes and kept his beams going. His body became weak, but his beams were strong. As he begins to exhaust, he fell to his knees. He kept up his endurance with the bolts of light holding strong. I dropped back down onto the bed. I shook off my dizziness and ran over to help Jake. I was so afraid, and I begin to call his name. "Jake, Jake!" Jake's bolts of light disappeared as he collapsed onto the floor. The whirlwinds disappeared. I ran over to him. I turned him over and placed his head in my lap. I started to panic. "Jake! Are you Ok?" Jake began to move his head. He flickered his eyes a little bit. He then opened them gently.

He his energy was zapped. His breathing was labored. He looked up at me. "I'm ok; I just need to catch my breath. Asasa, what was that horrible thing? Why is it after you?" My heart begins to feel heavy, and I started to tear up. "Jake, I was going to tell you… I didn't think it would come back so soon." Jake started to lift slowly. "Asasa, what is it?"

I wiped the tears from my eyes and told him. "I don't know what it is. But, I do know that I was born a human in a time where vampires and Gods just don't exist. I paused and decided to tell him everything. "Look, back in my realm. I live my life daily as a DNA lab specialist. Although I am human, I have powers. Like most humans, but most humans cannot access their powers. Most DNA stands are still locked. They don't remember who they are. I have a best friend and two cats. I just recently found my long-lost brother.

This being pulled in and out realms started when I purchased a snake. But not just any kind of snake. A Naga, a very powerful rainbow serpent. I wanted so badly to go back home until I met you. Jake looked confused. "This Naga, this snake, why is she doing this to you?" I took a deep breath. "My friend and I opened a spa.

A rejuvenation spa to help women look young and stay young. Forever…Immortality. The Naga's eggs are what we use. It makes our clients immortal and youthful forever. Jake took a deep breath. "This realm sounds crazy to me. You can live forever here. In kindred, an immortal…if you'd like." While glancing at Jake, I remembered something very important. "Listen, you can't tell the girls. Who I am or what I am. I don't know how they would react. They might be angry with me. "I am not Asasa Suku. I…I don't even know who she is." Jake reaches out and touches my hand. "Your secret is safe with me." He kissed my hand gently.

Jake's thoughts seem to drift. "Will this thing come back for you?" I nodded my head yes. "I'm sure it will. But it always comes after I've completed some kind of mission. I was very surprised to see it come for me so soon. Even though this is the longest, I have been trapped in another realm." Jake stood up. "I won't let it, have you! I'll fight it, with all my power." I smiled slowly. Jake grinned. Surprisingly there was a knock at the door.

It startled me, and I jumped a bit. I pulled my dress up from around my waist. And fastened it quickly. I immediately grabbed Jake's clothes off the floor. I tossed them to him. I quickly but quietly pushed him into the closet. I fixed my hair fast in the mirror. I walked towards the door. I tried to sound calm. "Yes, who is it?" I heard a voice clear. "It's me churel." I maintained my composure and slowly opened the door. "Hi,"

Churel walked in and looked around. She closed the door behind her.

"Asasa, I thought I saw you run off with Jake?" I gathered my thoughts quickly in my head before responding. "I did, for a minute, into the hallway for a chat. Why? Is there something wrong?" Churel sighed, "I take it he finds an interest in you?" I swallowed deeply. "I believe he may, once again, why?" Churel's demeanor saddened. "Asasa, I'm for sure he does. I see the way he looks at you. I don't know if he shared with you, how he became a vampire?" I nervously glanced down at my toes. "Why, yes, he did. He mentioned a jealous warrior vampire."

Churel sat down on my bed. She became fixated on the wall. I decided to walk over and sit on the other side of the bed. Churel looked up at me. "Yes, that jealous vampire warrior was my husband. I married him, not realizing what type of man he was. He was charming in the beginning. So passionate and caring. One day he became evil and cruel. Jake was a friend of his. He would come by to eat dinner with us. Well, from time to time. I admired Jake, and he was so suave and sweet. He was very handsome and always so heroic.

One day Jake came over to see my husband. My husband wasn't at home. So, I sat down at the table with Jake. I begin to cry. I told him all the awful things my husband did to me. Jake, being the kind, loving man that he was. Consoled me and hugged me. I knew my husband was coming home soon. I wanted him to see another man showing me affection. I knew it was wrong. I just wanted to be loved again. We were in a warm embrace when my husband walked in.

There was no time to explain anything. He immediately he became outraged. I demanded that my husband and Jake dual it out in the land. And whoever won could have me. Jake tried to explain several times. That he was just consoling me. So, you see Asasa. It is no mistake that Jake is here. Out of my selfishness. It is my fault he became a fledgling. I had the hunters capture him and bring him back to the lab." Churel sighed. "But now I see, he only has eyes for you." Churel's face became flushed. I looked over at her.

"I'm sorry, I…I didn't know." Churel stood up and walked towards the door. "No, it's fine, you are now apart of the alpha pack. We don't bicker amongst one another. There's way too much evil in the world to fight. You should be with Jake. He'll take care of you." Churel smiled as she walked out the door. I followed slowly behind her and locked the door.

I turned and looked at the closet. Jake slowly came out. Jake had nervousness in his eyes. "Asasa, I had no clue. She planned the whole fight between her husband and I. I never wanted Churel. She was my friend's wife. I can't believe she did this to me. I can't believe a woman scorned could cost me my life! I could have died!" I took a deep breath. "Well, you could have informed me that the women you fought over was Churel." Jake sighed, "Asasa, I was going to tell you. I didn't know the truth. They captured me and brought me here — no explanation as to why. I thought Kindred really needed me for the team. I now see I am here over some jealous rage.

I was going to tell you about churel." Jake walked over to me slowly. He gently kissed me on the lips. "Asasa, let's go back down to the party. People will start to wonder where we've been." I agreed, Jake fixed his clothes and quietly snuck out. I fixed my hair up a bit. I went down a separate walkway. We both entered the grand room, from different entrances. I saw Neferata and begin to walk towards her.

I stood next to her. She smiled and embraced me. She was talking to a group of people. I glanced around the room. I saw Jake mingling with the crowd. One of the servant girls poured me a glass of vegan blood. The crowd grew thicker. More and more people continued to enter. I glanced over at the door. Glittery type dust filled the doorway. The path to the podium begins to clear out. Five enchanting women with wings flew through the door. A couple of them were super tiny. A few were human size.

I looked over at Neferata. She could tell by my face I was inquisitive. Neferata leaned into my ear. "Those five beings are Air, Fire, Earth, Water, and Spirit. They are a pack of mischievous annoying fairies. Air is the leader of the pack." Air had light blue hair. Pouty lips, big eyes with long eyelashes. She had a smooth coffee complexion. She wore a glittery light blue romper. Neferata continued. "She is the strongest, and she's half-vampire, half fairy. Her kind is known as vamp F. She's beautiful, cunning, smart, and a bit on the bitchy side of evil." I laughed as she continued. "Fire is a full fairy, she's pretty, and she knows it. Fire is small in size and is a natural-born follower. She hides behind Air's power.

Air is truly a trouble maker." Fire looked like a large firefly. She was the size of my fist — very pretty kind of pale. Her piercing blue eyes seem to glow. Neferata continued. "Water is also a vamp F. She is of full human size. She has just as much power as Air. But doesn't have as much heart. She is very unsure of herself and awkward at times. She also is not nearly as pretty as the other fairies. I'm sure you've noticed." Water had jet black hair, chin-length. She wore tight black pants. Black boots and a blacktop. She looked very gothic. Neferata continues. "She hides behind her pack for protection and respect. Earth is drop-dead gorgeous. A full fairy that may be small in size. But she has a big appetite. She feeds off anger, and she's both conniving and jealous hearted.

Spirit is a full fairy and wants to be good. But doesn't want to upset her pack. She is a follower. Unlike the others in the group, she is kind and caring.
Spirit could be considered the peacemaker in the group." Neferata was starting to look annoyed. She paused for a second and continued talking. "They are fairies, supernatural humanoids. Mischievous little devils, they are. They can travel into heaven, earth, and the underworld. They live in Dunvegan castle, which is not far from Kindred. I'm wondering what the purpose of this appearance is? They were not Invited."

The word Earth echoed in my brain. I looked at Neferata, and I swallowed deeply. "Did you say Earth?" Neferata glared at me. "Yes, Earth." I was curious as to why some were small, and some were human size. I turned to Neferata. "Why are some tiny and some human sizes?" Neferata swallowed the last sip of her wine. "Asasa, my dear, some are one hundred percent fairy, and others are half. Once bitten by a vampire, they grow into human size." I glanced over at them as they mingled and made their way to the podium. One fairy stepped forward. Before she could begin to speak, Neferata cut her off.

"What can do for you, Air?" Air made a strange face. "Neferata, I am pleased to see you as well." Air's voice was very high pitched. Neferata smiled. "I couldn't be better Air, and yourself?" Air looked annoyed. "I'm great as always…you know me Neferata! We fairies have a strong sense of smell for humans." Neferata's face cringed with confusion. "Are you insinuating that I'm harboring a human here at Kindred castle?" Air walked over towards me. I tried not to look nervous. I kept my cool!

Air glared back into Neferata eyes. "Is this your new alpha, Neferata?" Neferata was becoming angry. I could smell it. That hadn't happened in a while. Usually, my gifts didn't work in other realms. Neferata smiled and looked Air deep into her eyes. "Yes, she is. And what business is it of yours?" Fire noticed the intenseness of the conversation. She walked over and stood behind Air. Neferata becomes even more angered. "Well, Air, what business do you have with my new alpha!" Air grinned, "She Stinks!!" Neferata moved closer to Air. She now reeked of the strongest anger ever imagined. It was foreign to my nostrils. "Air, now you know those are fighting words." Air became even angrier. "She is human, Neferata, and you know it.!"

Neferata face turned red! "Nonsense!" Neferata turned to me. "Asasa, show them your pearls!" I quickly lifted my glass of vegan blood to my lips. I took a sip. I felt a burning sensation come over me. I felt supercharged hot flashes. I started to feel pain forcing through my gums. I started to salivate and hiss. My fangs appeared! Air, Fire, and Earth stepped back with fright. Neferata smiled. "You see, obviously you have made a mistake. And next time you come into my kingdom unannounced, we won't be so kind!"

Air looked confused. "I…I don't understand. I know the smell of a human. I was just on earth the other day. Trying to lure humans into Tiranong. Our land of eternal youth. I know her scent, maybe I encountered her on earth." Neferatta cut her off. "I think I've heard quite enough. How could you have possible encountered her on earth? I think you and the rest of your pathetic fairies should be leaving now." Ada, Churel, and Maylasia walked over as they noticed Neferata's anger. The five fairies begin to back away.

Earth turned and looked at Neferatta. "We were just leaving. But, I must say, this is not over! There is something fishy going on with your new alpha. We will find out what's going on." The fairies begin to laugh as they walked through the crowd and out the door. I turned to look at the pack. "I don't understand". Ada looked concerned. She smiled at me. "Don't worry about them, Asasa. They are known, troublemakers. They are always looking for trouble." I smiled as I could feel they wanted to protect me. I felt like a fraud. I had to go. I decided I would leave when the next whirlwind came. I wouldn't resist it. Jake was great, but I have things to finish, back home.

Maylasia walked over towards me. "Keep your guard up at all times. The fairies cast spells." I was thinking to myself, so did I. I went deep in thought for a minute. Why were they so upset that I was a human? I touched Ada's arm. "Are humans not allowed here?" Ada looked over at me. "Not in this land Asasa, a full human is not allowed. Half-human and any other pieces of bread are used as servants. They are allowed on the land." I was slightly confused. "But, Ada, all vampires, were once humans."

Neferata walked forward. "The humans are the ones who decided that we were soulless. They saw us as a threat. There are groups of humans that form packs. They try to capture and kill us. They think we are evil. That we are filthy animals, they believe we will kill and destroy. We indeed feed off of them. But, with our pack, we only kill the bad ones. Our pack is doing them a tremendous favor." I took a deep breath. "So, what do the fairies want with humans?"

Ada looked concerned with my question. "They use humans in their spells. Fairies can make them into an external elixir. They eat it, drink it. And pour it into their eternal river. They also bathe in it. They do this to stay young forever. For this to work. The human has to be pure, one hundred percent." Churel chimed in. "That's why they wanted you so bad Asasa. They thought you were human. I don't know why. They are trouble makers, so who knows." Neferata smiled. "Well, they are gone now. So, I wouldn't worry about them. They're always looking for trouble. I'm sure they will find some soon enough."

The girls walked towards the crowd and started mingling. I decided to go upstairs to my bedroom. I opened the door and walked over to my bed and sat down. I started to take off my shoes. When I heard a knock at the door. I got up and quickly walked over. "Who is it?" There was silence for a moment. "It's me, Jake". I unlocked the door. Jake walked in; he was hiding something behind his back. He closed the door and continued to walk towards me.

As he got closer. He presented to me what was behind his back. It was a beautiful black Orchid. My face lit up. It had been a long time. Since I actually received a flower of any kind. I put it to my nose and inhaled the sweet essence of the flower. It was mesmerizing. I forgot Jake was even standing in the room. "Thank you so much, and I love the color black." I leaned in and kissed him on the lips. Jake came closer and caressed my face with his hand. He smiled down at me. "I knew only someone as special as you would find beauty in a black flower."

I smiled, "We are vampires, Jake. Anything can become black in our world. At any point and time. But, it doesn't always have to be scary. Black can be calming. Without black, babies wouldn't sleep. The stars wouldn't have a home. The seeds we burry need darkness to grow. Jake's eyes were glued to me. "I wish everyone could see the beauty in everything, just like you do, Asasa. I smiled, "Well, I try." Jake moved in closer and put his arms around my waist. He kissed me gently. He stopped, "Asasa, I have something I want to show you."

I became inquisitive to know. "Really, Jake?" Jake took me by the hand and led me out the door. "Jake, where are we going?" He smiled and pulled me faster. "It's a surprise, Asasa." Jake led me out of the castle into the backyard. Through a field with high grass and lots of trees. Jake took my other hand and twirled me around as we ran through the fields. We ran until we couldn't run any longer. I was completely out of breath. I stopped for a rest.

"Jake, I can't run anymore. We have run for about 3 miles now." Jake took his hands and covered my eyes. He turned me around. A felt a light mist, splashing my face. He released his hands slowly. There before my eyes was the most breathtaking waterfall. We were standing on top of one as well. I looked down over the cliff. The scents of oak, water, and magic entered my nostrils. This was the most alluring scenery I had ever seen in my whole life.

Jake saw how my eyes were lit up and majestic. "This is not the end, Asasa, and this is just the beginning. We need to go inside the waterfall. We must jump, Asasa!" I looked down; there was no visible bottom. I clenched up. "Jake, jump? Down there? You…want me to jump? Down there?" Jake begins to laugh. "Asasa, you won't die." My face felt a little flushed from embarrassment. I forgot I was a vampire, for now, in this realm. I looked into his eyes. "Oh yeah, you're right, Jake, were already dead. I forget sometimes."

Jake smiled. His smile sent a warm, calming sensation throughout my entire body. I couldn't believe how attached I was to this man. I missed my ride with the whirlwind to go home. This was all so confusing to me. Why couldn't I just find a man in my realm to fall in love with? I broke away from his spell and came back to the waterfall. I looked into Jake's eyes. "Stay calm, Asasa, take my hand, and we will jump together." Gentle breezes flew through my hair as I looked at Jake and stared at his essence. From the frame of his face down to his toes. I could find no imperfections. I was secure with him. I took his hand and took a deep breath. Jake gazed deep into my eyes. "Are you ready Asasa?" I took a deep gulp, "Yes, Jake, I'm ready." He smiled again. "Close your eyes, Asasa, and let your body fall into the wind."

I slowly stepped closer to the edge of the cliff. Jake followed. We stayed attached to holding each other's hands. We looked into each other's eyes. Inhaled, exhaled, relaxed, and dove…right off the cliff! Everything immediately became peaceful. I relaxed as the soft winds caressed and carried my body into a sweet abyss. It didn't feel like falling at all, and it actually felt like we were flying. We fell for what seemed to be like minutes. We met a cool refreshing splash. As our bodies hit the water, it rippled and flowed.

We were the catalyst moving everything around us. We delve deep underneath the surface of the waters. Jake turned and looked at me. He spoke to me telepathically. I could hear him loud and clear in my mind. "Asasa, climb on my back. I will swim to our destination." I climbed onto his back and gripped my arms across his chest. As I lay on his back, he glided through the water like a dolphin. The beautiful sea creatures were enchanting and swam all around us.

We were magically floating against the backdrop. A glowing sea highlighted with shades of fluorescent pink and purple. Jake glided forward as our bodies embraced the warm water. Jake finally swam upwards, leading up to the surface. I took a deep breath and smiled. I inhaled the sweet mist that filled my nostrils. The smells landed playfully on my palate. It tastes like cotton candy. I was so mesmerized with the smell and taste. I looked at Jake with excitement in my eyes. "Do you smell that Jake?" You can taste the sweet air on your tongue.

Jake smiled, "It's called rouge, Asasa." I had never heard of this before. "Rouge? Please explain Jake?" Jake chuckled. "Yes, it's the morning dew from the trees, here in Tiranog. It fills the air, and if you inhale, it will taste like my favorite sweet persimmons." Jake swam us to the edge, and I was comfortable enough to let go. He swam towards a cliff and pulled his body out of the water. I followed. Jake extended his hand to help pull me out of the water as I climbed out of the water. I realize that Jake had mentioned the word Tirnanog.

I know that's the place Neferata said the fairies lived. "Jake, did you say Tirnanog? This is the land of the fairies, correct?" Jake pulled himself into the grass area. "There's nothing to fear. They only come here when they lure humans in Which is rare, and this is their land. But, they don't live here, they in Dunveggan castle. Not far from kindred." Jake and I sat down on edge with our feet hanging in the water. Our clothes were drenched from our journey. I was so nervous even though the realm was peaceful. I looked all around the forest. The waterfalls changed its hue from pink to purple.

The forest lit up with a neon golden glow. I turned to look at Jake. I noticed he changed a bit. There was the color to his cheeks. I grabbed his hand. The pale grayish color was lifted from him. His body was full of color, and he looked human. I was bewildered. I touched his face. "Jake…you look alive!" Jake chuckled, "Asasa look at your reflection in the water." I glanced down into the water. I was hypnotized by the mortal I saw. I touched my face in astonishment. I wasn't pale anymore. My cheeks had a rose-colored glow that I hadn't seen in a while.

My lips were thick and juicy. They had their natural glow back. Jake noticed I was shocked. "Asasa, this is the land of eternal youth. No one dies here, and everyone has a soul." I was still staring at myself in the water. I touched my reflection as it rippled up and flowed away. I wanted this to last forever. I looked up at Jake's face. "How long will we be human Jake?" Jake sighed, "Until we leave Tiranog." Jake embraced me with a hug, followed up by a gentle kiss.

Jake's soft lips landed onto mine. At that very moment, it began to rain. The orange droplets cascaded over our bodies. With each drop, there was an intensifying pleasure. My eyes widened as I noticed the sensation. The droplets made my body tremble. I couldn't control it. It was so intense. It was electric! I laid down in the grass. Jake laid on top of me. We were both felt hot and euphoric. Jake entered my body, and I moaned with great delight.

As each droplet hit my bare skin. My body went in and out of convulsions. The rain finally stopped. I opened my eyes. I looked at Jake and caught my breath. Jake's body was still trembling from the last splashes of rain. The rain cleared as butterflies appeared. We both gawked into the sky. We both lay on our backs and looked at the magical formations that appeared right before our eyes. I looked over at Jake. "What kind of rain was that?" Jake smiled, "it was pleasure rain. When the forest encounters true soul mates, the skies will shower pleasure rains." Wow, did he say soul mates? This was odd, and I become even more confused. What was the mission here? I felt like; I'd been gone, away from my home for so long. I wanted to leave, but I wanted Jake! "Soul mates? So, you think we are soul mates, Jake?" Jake chuckled, "That's

the legend of the pleasure rains, Asasa." I smiled,
"Sooo, how many women have you brought to Tiranog, Jake?"
Jake begins to laugh charmingly. "None Asasa, you are the
first...I come here to get away and relax, that's all. This
isn't my make-out spot.

It's just very stunning and invigorating. I wanted to
share it with a creature as ravishing as the land. Jake
sat up from the ground. "We must leave Asasa". I sat up
and fixed my clothes. "I know Jake, and I wouldn't want
the fairies to come back." Jake slipped his clothes back
on. We both slide back into the water. I embraced Jake
back. I squeeze tightly as we glide back under the water
and disappeared back to Kindred.

I arose the next morning feeling refreshed. The room was
dark. I walked to the bathroom to routinely brush my hair
in the mirror as I was brushing my hair. I instantly
begin to feel sick. I ran over to the toilet and got on
my knees. I became hot throughout my body. I begin to
throw up. My body became weak. I was to sick to stand up.
I tried to crawl back into the room. I was very faint.
So, I laid on the bathroom floor trying to conjure up
some strength. I was able to pull my body up.

I got onto my hands and knees. I started to crawl out of
the bathroom into my bedroom. I crawled to the door. I
reached up and opened it. I continued to crawl into the
hallway. I passed Neferata's room. I slowly crawled to
Jake's door, and I was out of breath. I fell flat onto my
face. I rolled over onto my back. I kicked the Jakes door
with my foot. At that moment, everything went black.

I felt someone shaking me. I was able to open one eye. It
was Jake. He was standing over me. "Oh my God, Asasa,
what's wrong?" I heard Neferata door open. I heard her
voice. "Oh my, what happened to her, Jake?" Jake replied,
"I don't know, I heard a thump at my door. I opened it,
and she was lying here." Neferata looked down at me.
"Jake, bring her into my room, at once." Jake scooped me
up off the ground and took me into Neferata's room. I
heard the door close.

Jake laid me on Neferata's bed. Neferata ran some cold
water in a bowl. She dipped a towel into it. She placed
it on my forehead. I was starting to come around. I could
hear Jake calling my name. "Asasa, please wake up!" I

begin to flutter my eyes and came back to consciousness. The light-filled my eyes and blinded them for a bit. Neferata sat next to me on the bed. "Asasa, can you hear me?" I slowly flickered my eyes. Then I opened them completely. I tried to talk; my voice was crusty and low.

"Yes, Neferata, I can hear you." Neferata Looked concerned. "What happened to you Asasa?" I took a deep breath. "Well, I was brushing my hair in the mirror. All of sudden I got this urge to throw up." Neferata looked over at me, and her eyes seemed concerned. "Have you been drinking Asasa?" I took a deep breath, "No, not at all." Neferata turns and looks at Jake's face. "Jake, is there something you need to tell me? Before I read both your minds?" Jake takes a deep breath. "I don't know if this has anything to do with it.

But, we were in Tiranog!" Neferata eye's widened. "Tiranog! Jake, have you lost your damn mind?" Jake tried to explain. "Neferata, I go there all the time, alone. Just to think and take a load off. I only wanted to show Asasa how beautiful it was." Neferata touched my hand. "Asasa, please tell me, you and Jake…. didn't, do what I think you did? Not in Tiranog!" I looked over at Jake and then back at Neferata. Then back at Jake. I felt my face become flush. I sighed deeply. "It makes no sense to lie. You can read our minds if you want.

Neferata became silent. "Asasa, you are pregnant. I sat up from the bed in amazement. "That's Nonsense Neferata; vampires cannot get pregnant." Neferata smiled. "Oh, but Asasa, you weren't a vampire in Tiranog. It is the land of eternity. You gained a soul when you trespassed on their land. I'm sure you noticed." I went deep in thought for a minute. "Yes, Neferata, I did, but it's been so long since I've been a human. I forgot about those types of things." I looked over at Jake, and He looked stunned. "Neferata, are you sure Asasa is Pregnant?"

Neferata smiled. "You think you're the only vampire couple who has stumbled into Tiranog? Of course, I'm sure… you cannot stay here, Asasa. You have to go back to Tiranog, or the baby will die." Hearing the word "Die" was alarming. "So, I can't stay here?" Neferata touched my hand. "No, you'll only have to go back for a week. That's nine months in Tiranog. But, the baby will not survive here. When she is born, you may bring her back. Your home is here

Neferata paused for a moment. "I'll have to pull a few strings to get you and Jake to be able to stay in Tiranog safely. The fairies won't like this at all." Jake looks over at Neferata. "If she stays at kindred, she could lose the baby?" Neferata shakes her head. "Yes, Jake, she will go back into full vampire mode at any minute. You must go back! But before you do, let me talk to the fairies. Neferata left the room. A servant girl walked in with more cold rags. She walked over to my bedside. Replaced the old rags with fresh cold ones. She looked concerned. "You can't have the baby here at Kindred castle. The ghouls will eat your baby. My eyes widened as she placed a cold towel on my forehead. I grabbed her arm mid-way. "Ghouls? What do you mean by Ghouls?

The servant girl dropped the cold rag into the bowl. "Yes, madame, the hunters for the fledgling lab are ghouls. They live off the dead and flesh from the wastelands. But, they are known for eating fresh newborn babies." There was a knock at the door. Ada rushed in. "Oh my God, Asasa! What have you gotten yourself into?" I felt a strong urge to sit up. "What did the fairies say about Jake and I staying in Tiranog?" Ada sat on the bed. "Well, we spoke to Spirit; she is the only reasonable one. She will hide you from the other fairies for a week. Spirit will keep you safe. I must warn you; she is only doing it because of your baby. She is part fairy Asasa."

I paused for a moment. "What do you mean, part fairy?" Jake interrupts before she could answer. "Asasa… if a baby is consumed in Trianog, then the baby is automatically a fairy. Not fully, she will also be a vampire, and goddess, plus fairy. This is actually a great thing Asasa. Our child will be so powerful. In all of the land." Ada starting packing a few things quickly. "I came to help gather your things. You must go now! The baby will not survive in your vampire state.

You have to stay for a week. That's nine months in Tiranog. You will have the baby and come back to Kindred. You are apart of the pack, and you are family. You and your child may stay here for as long as you like." Ada kissed me on the cheek and hugged me. Ada and the servant girl scrambled to pack more clothes for me. Neferata enters the room with Spirit. "Spirit is here Asasa, she will protect you and keep you safe. She is not like the others." Spirit walks over to the bed. "Have they explained to you, Asasa. That the baby will be part fairy?" I nodded my head yes. "Yes, yes, they have". Spirit glared at me with a grin. "Good, that's the only reason I'm doing this for the child. She will be an Omega breed, which is rare in all the lands. Much, much more powerful than a vampire, God, or fairy put together.

She will be worshiped like a queen. Her beauty will be like nothing you've ever seen in any land. "Spirit, why do you keep referencing the child as a "She?" Spirits smiled was removed from her face. "I have seen her prophecy; she will be a girl. A very powerful woman. We must go now!" Jake helped me off the bed. We grabbed my things and followed Spirit off to Trianog. Spirit led us to a small cottage deep in Trianog. The cottage was pink and resembled a mushroom. Spirit typed a code into the door. The lock released as the three of us entered.

Spirit walked in first. "Come in; you will be safe here from the others. This is a secluded spot deep in Trianog. Most fairies don't come past the waterfall banks. Once they lure the humans in, that's when they attack." Jake walked in and dropped his bags. "Thank you, spirit." Spirit grins, "Don't thank me yet, not until this whole ordeal is over. I hope you know this goes against my land. I could have my wings chopped off."

I looked over at Spirit. "Oh, Spirit, I would never want that to happen. You're doing a good thing by saving my child's life." Spirit walks towards the door. She opens it and walks out. I sat down on the couch. It was hot pink. It felt like leather. I looked around the cottage. It was very colorful. Orange, green, pink, red and blue. Nothing really matched, but it was beautiful. I started to feel a bit homesick. I missed Beatrice, the smell of my grandmother's house. I even missed my brother. I was quite confused. I never thought that I'd be a mom. I looked over at Jake. Jake was smiling at me, he grabbed my hand. "Let's get married, Asasa, and you will be my queen."

I like the thought of being a queen. But it saddened me. I knew at any moment, this realm, my existence here, could be all over. Jake continued to speak. "Asasa, since the day I met you in the fledgling lab. I knew there was something special about you. As if we had already met in another world. Like our spirits were catching up on old times. I wouldn't be marrying you just because of the baby. I've wanted to marry you since the day we met." I smiled at Jake. I didn't know what to say. My life was so complicated.

Jake smiled, "We are going to have a huge wedding, when we get back to Kindred, I promise. A wedding made for royalty." I smiled on the outside. But the feelings of sadness deepened inside me.

The Return

Chapter

The days went by extremely fast. Jake and I spent our days. Swimming nude in the waterfalls. Taking journeys through the tall color changing grass, running through pleasure rains, relaxing in the caves, under the falls. I looked down at my belly, and it was huge. It had been a full seven days as we were out running in the grass. I felt my first contraction. Jake begins to panic. He rushed me back to the cottage.

"Lay here on the bed. The contractions will get worse. I need to run into the enchanting forest." He fled out the door in a hurry. I laid back on the bed. I was very uncomfortable. My contractions were getting worse. I took a few deep breaths. Jake was gone for a good five minutes. I was starting to worry. The pain wasn't helping. Jake rushed back through the door. He laid down a cloth on the bed. He opened the cloth up. There was a bunch of tiny golden mushrooms. "Asasa, eat these, they will stop the pain." With no hesitation, I grabbed a handful and began eating them.

The pain started to fade quickly. There was a knock at the door. Spirit walks in. "Sorry, I couldn't get here faster. I had to throw off the other fairies. I didn't want them to follow me here." Spirit looks over at my face. She touches my cheek. "I can see you have given her the golden mushrooms." My head started to fill hazy. The colors in the room started to glow. These mushrooms were magical. I glanced up at Spirit. "I feel fine" Spirit placed a towel on my forehead. I started to feel tingly all over. It started at my forehead first. Wait a minute. This wasn't the mushrooms. I knew this feeling. I knew it very well. I begin to panic. I reached out to Jake. "Jake, it's starting again!"

Jake felt the cool winds hit his face. He looked up and saw the whirlwinds forming. He immediately threw himself in front of me. Spirit stood to the side, in amazement. Jake threw both his hands into the air. He fired his bolts, one after another, after another. Until he was out of Breath. Spirit rushed over. She put her hand up to the whirlwind. Spirit shouted, "Kela Mit, Sheuleh e von dust!" A bolt like a silver lasso shot out of her hand. It wrapped its self around the whirlwinds. I felt the baby crowning and slipping out. I reached down and pulled her out as Spirit, and Jake fought the whirlwind. I lifted her up and laid her on my chest. I hugged her. I looked up, and the whirlwinds were stunned, frozen in place. Jake looked over and saw the baby on my chest. Jake stared at the tiny creature in full admiration.

The baby shakes as if she shaking the water off her body. Two little purple wings appear. Spirit walks over, and she doesn't take her eyes off the frozen whirlwind. She glanced down quickly to look at the baby. She smiled. Jake picked the baby up off my chest. He stood next to Spirit. They both smiled at her. She was beautiful. I closed my eyes for a moment. The tingles were beginning to start again. I panicked!! "Jake!" At that moment, I felt a zap. My body was sucked into the ceiling of the cottage. I glanced down. I saw Jake holding the baby and Spirit. At that very moment. I was gobbled up into the whirlwind and whisked away.

"Noooooooooooooooo!" I blacked out. I opened my eyes and found myself lying in bed. I was still at my grandmother's house. I sat up and looked around. I grabbed my forehead and began to cry. Beatrice was sleeping on the couch near the bed. My cries woke her up.

Beatrice saw I was awake. She jumped up and ran over to the bed. "Oh my God, you've been out for two days. Are you ok? What's wrong?" I pulled the blanket back. I swung my legs over the side of the bed. I caught my breath.

My hands were shaking, and I was hysterical. Beatrice just stared at me. "What's wrong ty, what happened to you? Was this trip bad? I've never seen you like this." I looked down at my stomach. "My baby... my baby, I had a baby… I had a baby girl!" Tears streamed from my eyes. I wiped my face. I saw a light flickering above me. I looked up at the bookcase. It was the soul of Amaya flickering in the jar. I became angry, and I jumped up from the bed. Beatrice glanced at what I was looking at. She caught me in mid-air. "TY! What are you doing? We just got her back in. Two days ago, when she brought the whirlwinds.

Beatrice held my arms tightly. "NO, Ty!" I broke free of her hold. "You don't understand, I have to go back! I have to go back now! Beatrice stared deep into my eyes. "What happened to you there? You never fight to go back! Hell, you never want to go back to those places." I calmed down a little bit. There was a knock at the door. Beatrice looked at the door. "Come in". The door slowly opened. It was my brother, and he was carrying a cup of tea. He smiled, "I figured you'd be up soon, and you'd want a cup of tea. I heard the screaming, are you ok?" He walked over and put the tea inside my hands.

I held it in my palms, it smelled of lavender. I immediately became a little calmer. I looked down into the cup. My brother smiled. "Its green tea with a little lavender and honey." I sat back down on the bed and sipped. I sipped some more and a little more. It made me feel better. I smiled and looked up at him. "What else did you put in this tea?

He smiled back, "Nothing, I promise… Are you ok? What was he yelling about?" I looked into my brother's eyes. I sipped some more of my tea. "I need to consult the ancestors. I need answers about what happened this time." I started to tear up again. Beatrice looked at us both. "I'll give you guys a little privacy." Beatrice walked out of the room. She closed the door behind her. My brother looked into my eyes. "I'll go with you if you'd like." I nodded, yes. He walked over to the bookcase and grabbed a few pieces of moldavite. I finished my tea. I placed the cup on the end table, next to the bed.

He handed me a piece, and I laid back on the bed. So, did he. We both placed the moldavite on our foreheads. I relaxed and pierced deep inside my mind. My racing thoughts begin to fade. My mind went solid black. The purple flame begins to dance in the darkness of my mind. I drifted quickly into the subconscious realms. I opened my eyes. I was sitting in my usual spot. I glanced over, and my brother was next to me. "We made it at the same time." He smiled, "Yes, I often come for clarity." As we sat in the darkness. The glowing white light shined down upon us. We were sucked into the mothership.

The doors open as we slide in. We walked through the doors. The ship looked empty. I walked towards the center. Elta was sitting at the motherboard. She looked up as we walked in. She smiled, "I was expecting you. Didn't think you would come so fast." I immediately pulled out a chair and sat down. My brother sat on the couch across from us. Elta looked over at him. "I see you brought your brother." Elta looked over at him. "It's Tyrone." He glanced at her. "Your name, your birth name, that your mother gave you."

He smiled, "How did you know? I was just wondering what my real name was. I often wonder from time to time. So, I'm a Tyrone? Interesting." I smiled, "Tituba and Tyrone make since. Now I can stop calling you, My brother. I didn't want to call you Bruce. It just didn't fit you." Tyrone looked down at his feet, then back up. "I like Tyrone, and I will honor it." Elta smiled, "Tyrone, make sure you visit your spirit guides as well. We are all in the same soul family. But, you are assigned to your special guides.

Elta turned and looked at me. "What do I owe the pleasure of seeing you here today, my child?" I swallowed deeply. "I got sucked into another realm. But, only this time, it was different." Elta touched her chest. "How so, child? I've been busy in the realms. Talk to me." I licked my lips. "I stayed a lot longer than usual. I met a man. I…. I got pregnant, and I gave birth to a baby girl." I started to tear up again. I couldn't hold back any longer. I felt the little wet drops bust from the sides of my eyes. Elta looked concerned. I looked deep into her eyes. "Elta, was it real?" Elta took a deep breath.

She walked over and sat next to me. She touched my hand. "Tituba, you know as well as I, that what happens on other realms, are real. If you had a baby girl, in that particular realm. Then, she is still there. We travel to different realms in our sleep. Whatever we experience in that realm is real. Just because it's not in the material world, you live in. It doesn't mean that it isn't real. If you would like to go back, talk to the Naga, what's her name? I wiped my eyes. "Amaya". She grabbed a tissue off the motherboard. I took it and wiped my eyes.

I looked at her. "So, what's my lesson in all this"? Elta looked at me. "Everything isn't a lesson Tituba. But, now you know, what happens in a realm, stays in a realm. You can travel back and forth if need be. It will take some practice. And, you will need to speak with Amaya. I nodded my head. "I didn't even get a chance to name her." Elta smiled. "When I was an earthling. I had several, what's called a vanishing pregnancy. I would get systems like I was pregnant. I'd take a home pregnancy test. It would read positive some weeks down the road. I'd go to Drs. They would give me their test. It would read negative.

This happened to me at least three times. Those babies never vanished, you know. I was impregnated in different realms. I didn't know it at the time. But, I would travel in my sleep as we all do. Go to different realms. Have sex with the men or aliens. I finally got to meet those three children. When I came here, they told me I would visit from time to time now that I'm here. I see them all the time. We are very close. You're not alone, Tituba. It happens to everyone. Most people are not connected to their subconscious side. You are, you remember most of your journeys. Most people cannot.

Or, they just brush everything off. You know, as just a dream. Dreams, they can't even remember upon waking. You have a gift, being connected with the subconscious realms. If you want to visit that baby. Right now, at this moment. You have to ask Amaya. If she doesn't permit it, you will visit from time to time on your own. But, you won't be able to control it until you learn how to get back to that particular realm. It can take some time.

I smiled, I stood up. "Thank you Elta, I figured the realm was real. I just needed confirmation." I leaned in and hugged Elta. I looked over at my brother. "Let's go…Tyrone." He smiled, Elta stood up. "Tyrone, don't forget to visit your ancestors. They will give you clarity. Tyrone nodded his head. "Of course, I will haven't been in a while. Tituba and I, share the same gift, amongst other gifts. And gifts we haven't even unwrapped yet. Tyrone hugged Elta, and we walked off the craft as the doors opened to let us out. The light beam rode us down to our spot.

We closed our eyes, and within seconds, we are back in grandmothers' room. We both woke up on the bed. I sat up and looked at my brother. "Well, at least I know". Tyrone got up. "How often do you go out like that? Beatrice and I were worried." I took a deep breath. "It's Amaya, and ever since we've had her, she keeps sending us into other realms. I saved you guys from being pulled in with me. I can handle it, or… at least I thought I could." There was a knock at the door.

Beatrice popped in. "Hey ty, I know you've been through a lot. But, are we still on schedule for my procedure?" I had been out of it for so long. I forgot, after Candy's follow up. Beatrice wanted to be next. I stood up from the bed. "Your right, that was this weekend. I mean, of course, if you're ready." Beatrice smiled, "Yes, after seeing candy's results. I am truly ready. I took off an extra day at work, just to get this done. You were out for two days, so I lost some time. I have to return to work on Tuesday. Today is Sunday; I wanted a few days to recuperate if needed."

I noticed I was feeling fine. I wasn't dizzy when I stood up, and I actually felt revived and full of energy Which Usually happens after mediation. "Sure, why not. I have a favor to ask of Amaya anyways." Beatrice stared at me. "Oh, really, like what?" I sighed, "I found out, the dimension I was in, was in fact, real. I had a baby girl in that realm. I just want to go back, from time to time to visit her. See how she's doing. Sadness started to rise inside me again.

I swallowed it back down. Beatrice noticed, "I'm sorry, Ty, I know how much you've been tortured in those realms. I'm sure she is beautiful. Did you name her?" A tear squeezed from the right side of my eye. I wiped my face. "No…I didn't get a chance." Beatrice had a look of concern in her eyes. "Are you sure you're ok to do this?" I shook my head. "Yes… of course, I'm fine. Let's go into the office." I walk towards the door. Tyrone and Beatrice followed. We walked down the hall and into the office.

Amaya was on the desk, inside her crate as usual. I glanced over at Beatrice. "Any issues out of her, since I've been gone?" Beatrice thought about it for a moment. "No, not at all. She went back to sleep. I woke up to eat for a while. Then back to sleep." Beatrice shrugged. I looked around the room. "Ok, cool, well, it's going to be Tyrone's first time witnessing what we do." Beatrice looked confused. "Wait, who's Tyrone?" Tyrone laughed. "Well, Bea, while I was in the realms with Ty. I found out my real name. It wasn't Bruce Diamond. It never was, my identity has been changed too many times to count. With my memory being wiped cleaned so many times. I never knew the biological name my parents gave me."

Beatrice's face saddened. "I sorry to hear that, Tyrone." I noticed Beatrice had a crush on Tyrone. I could smell the lust protruding from her pores when she looked at him. Lust wasn't a bad odor, just strange. But I could identify it very well. "Well, Beatrice, relax on the couch, I will prep Amaya with the spell." Tyrone looked alarmed. "Spell…you have grandmother's spellbook, don't you?" I was surprised that he even knew about the book. "Yes, how did you know?" Tyrone grabbed his forehead. "I…I don't know, when you said, "Spellbook" it trigged something in my mind."

"I guess I knew about it as a child." I fell into silence for a moment. "Interesting". I walked over to the bookshelf and pulled it out. The book started to glow green. Tyrone's eyes lit up. I looked over at Beatrice. "Once I do you, I want you to do me." Tyrone looked at Beatrice and then back at me. "What type of procedure is this? I know you said, you guys run a beauty spa." I walked around to the chair behind the desk and sat down.

"It's actually a youthful, rejuvenating, immortality spell. It will erase about twenty years off your appearance. Plus, tighten your body where things sag." Tyrone rubs his chin. "So, where does the rainbow serpent come in at?" I licked my dry lips. "Amaya, our rainbow serpent, lays eggs and when those eggs are swallowed. They make you youthful and immortal." Tyrone smiled, "What are the side effects?" Beatrice chimed in. "So far with our research, there aren't any. But, some minor precautions are given to the client during the procedure. As far as we are concerned, this is an all-natural alternative to dangerous plastic surgery."

Tyrone smiled again. "Minor precautions, like what?" I stepped in to save Beatrice. "Like, death!" Tyrone's eyes widened. "You're kidding me right." I smiled, "Look, you're a Dr. you know the risk of any medication or procedure." Tyrone laughed, "I told you, "I'm not a real Dr. I'm programmed. Just like software on the hard drive of a computer. Also, my specialty is infection control. Not plastic surgery or natural rejuvenation. So please enlighten me on how death can occur?" I sighed. "Well, once the snake is inserted into the client's mouth. They have to hold still for a full sixty seconds. They can't move, they can't bite down or gag. If any of these things happen during the procedure, death can occur."

Tyrone rubs his hands together. "And how many subjects have you guys ran trials on?" Beatrice and I looked at each other. I cleared my throat nervously. "Um, one". Tyrone's eyes bucked. "One, wow!" Beatrice was chiming in again. "We are so proud of this natural procedure. We are testing it on ourselves and using ourselves as Guinea pigs. We stand behind this procedure. We take before and after pictures. We use them in our portfolio.

You know, to show people results. People will do anything to look more youthful and feel younger. This procedure will be world-renowned. People all over the world. Will come to our youthful rejuvenation spa and hotel." Tyrone shrugged. "Well, you guys seem to have it all figured out. I guess eating snake eggs is considered all-natural." Beatrice smiled, "not eat, you swallow them whole, like oysters." I got up from my seat, and I found the page in my grandmother's spellbook. "If you guys don't mind. I would really like to speak to Amaya before the procedure." Beatrice got up from the couch. "Will leave you guys alone for five minutes. And then, we are coming back in.

So, wrap it up in that time frame." Beatrice and Tyrone stepped outside and closed the door. I raised my right hand and summoned Amaya with the spell. Amaya's crate started to glow. She started to increase in size slowly. The crate top begins to lift off. It fell onto the floor. The glowing light now filled the room. Amaya grew into full human size. Top half women, bottom half snake. Her long dark hair touched the floor. The sound of her rattling tail filled my ears.

The glow from her eyes faded as her deep dark brown eyes priced into my soul. Amaya's voice echoed as she spoke. "You summoned me? How can I help you?" I sat down on top of my desk. "Let's skip being cordial here. The realm you sent me to last. I need to go back. Maybe not today, but as soon as possible. Amaya smiled. "Yes, madame, but only under one condition." I crossed my arms. "And what's that?" Amaya smiled, "I will work for you for one year, your time. After that one year, you will return me to my environment. I will grant you one of my eggs to keep and to hatch. That baby rainbow serpent will continue your work here.

I need to return home. The longer I stay here. The longer I fade away from my true home. The new serpent will only know the life you give her here inside of a cage, like a pet. I was wild and free before they captured me. And handed me over to you. I must go back to my freedom." I sighed. "You know about Kindred, don't you?" Amaya's snake tail rattled, as her voice echoed. "Yes…how did it feel, to give birth to a child?" I licked my lips. "You did this to secure your proposition." Amaya smiled, "yes, I went deep into your soul. I tasted your most prized desires how you wanted to be loved by a soul mate and produce a child.

It wasn't happening here in the material. So, I produced it for you in the subconscious realms." I became angered but kept my cool. "So, you'll just give me one of your babies?" Amaya's tail rattled as she spoke. "I will give you an egg. That will turn into a baby snake, yes. You will be its mother, and you will take care of her and feed here. Nourish her as if she were your own. If you abuse her in any way, I will know. I have scanned your body of emotions. You're not a bad person. Although some of your business deals have not been smart."

I stared into her glowing eyes. "Listen, Amaya, when we originally read the spell. It said to get a rainbow serpent. We didn't know you were stolen from the wild. I thought you were cage grown. I bought you from a man we barely knew. I will make this right. I think your anger is coming from you, being uprooted from your home. I didn't know this. I also didn't know you could grow into human form and communicate. I apologize for any inconvenience that we have caused you. I will honor your deal. After a year, I will let you go. You will leave me a baby snake that will continue the work. Here at the youth spa."

I felt like an apology was needed. I never stopped to think that she was ripped from her home. I really thought she was a pet snake. I should have asked the guy about her background. I was just so happy to be able to find a rainbow serpent locally. This still didn't take away the hurt. And all the realms I was swept into. And the things I had to do, to get out of them. Amaya's eyes were still glowing, tail still rattling. Her tail finally calmed down. "So, is it ok to proceed with the procedure tonight?" Amaya bowed her head. "That will be fine, madame. I will stick to my part of the bargain."

I sighed in relief. "Very well, I will go get Beatrice and Tyrone. I'll be right back." I walked over to the door and opened it. Beatrice and Tyrone were leaned up against the hallway wall. Having, what looked like a deep conversation. They didn't even realize I was standing there. I cleared my throat. "Ahem!" The two looked startled; they both headed towards the door.

I gave Beatrice an unapproving glare. They both walked in. Tyrone's eye's widened as I closed the door behind them. Amaya's tail started to rattle as we entered the room. Tyrone looked over at me. "Where did you find her? What is she? "I've seen creatures like this when I was living in a cage myself." Amaya's tail rattled louder. Amaya's glowing eyes became fixated on my brother. "I am a Naga, and my name is Amaya. Why were you in a cage? You look fully human to me." Tyrone looked over at me for approval. I nodded my head.

"I was kidnapped as a child, and I have special abilities." Amaya's voice echoed. "Really…what kind?" Tyrone thought about it for a moment. "I can feel people's emotions. I can see in my side mind. Like, a movie, what happened to a person in the past. I can feel when danger is around. I can draw the future. Amaya smiled, "Those are natural innate abilities. Of course, most generations of humans have been put to sleep. Those abilities have not been awakened by most. You were born with all of your DNA activated. Not normal for this day and age. So, I will say that yes, those are special abilities.

So, why were you in a cage." Tyrone smiled, "The people who stole me from my parents. I wanted me to do bad things for them. I wouldn't do it, and they tortured me as a child. They locked me in a cage. They were also afraid of what I could do to them. If I got angry enough, I could start a fire with my mind. I was pyrokinesis as a child. They were afraid of me. Especially when they tried to make me use it, they wanted me to set poor animals on fire. I wouldn't do it. So, they shut down that part of my DNA. I haven't been able to use it since I was a kid.

Amaya's tail rattled. "I see you are a kind human. Thank you for sparing the animals." Tyrone nodded his head. "I've seen hybrid creatures like you while living in the lab. You're natural, as well. Not like those demonic human-made animals and humans. They made some in the lab. Tyrone went into deep thought. He walked over to a chair and sat down. I think the conversation was too much for him. I stepped in, and I glanced over at Beatrice. "Beatrice, are you ready for the procedure?" Beatrice nodded her head. "Yes, I'm ready."

Beatrice walked over to our reclining leather chair. She sat comfortably. I used the remote and brought the chair up higher. I looked into Beatrice's eyes. "Ok, you know the drill. No moving, no biting down or gaging…please."

Beatrice nodded, "Ok, yes, I know, I have sixty seconds while she's in my mouth, then swallow. I know the procedure." Beatrice breathed in deeply and exhaled slowly. It was apparent she was nervous. But was trying to play it off.

I glanced over at Amaya. She begins to shrink in size. Tyrone watched, he was amazed. I quickly grabbed my phone. I got a few before pictures of Beatrice. Amaya was now tiny. I walked over and placed Amaya inside my hands. I looked over at Beatrice. Her eyes locked with mine. "Now! OPEN YOUR MOUTH!" I raised Amaya to Beatrice's mouth. As she climbed in, I grabbed the stopwatch off my desk. Amaya swirled Inside Beatrice's mouth. She made herself comfortable. I started the stopwatch.

Beatrice's eyes became big. I got worried. I walked over and beamed calmness into her eyes through mine. She finally calmed down. The seconds were ticking away. One whole minute never felt so long. Beatrice closed her eyes and stayed still. She didn't gage or bite down. The time was approaching thirty seconds. Amaya's green glowing eyes went to red. The eggs dropped onto Beatrice's tongue. Beatrice's eyes lit up again. I whispered in her ear. "You are halfway done, when she slides out, just swallow." I watched the time clock. Amaya was starting to move again. She slithered from the back of Beatrice's throat towards the front of her opened mouth. Amaya's head peaked out of Beatrice's mouth. The stopwatches had ten seconds on it. Amaya continued to slither out. When Amaya was completely out. I gave Beatrice the look of approval to swallow.

Beatrice gulped them down. She made a strange face. A look of disgust. She opened her eyes and closed her mouth. I took Amaya and put her back inside the cage. Tyrone stood up from his seat and walked over. We both stared at Beatrice. The dark circles under her eyes disappeared. The long crease coming in on her forehead wiped cleaned. The slight sag in her breast perked up. The small pouch in her belly went flat. This was all happening right before our very own eyes.

Beatrice started to smile. She stood up from the leather recliner. "I have this crazy boost of energy. I don't feel tired at all." She walked over to the long gold antique mirror. She got really close as if she was going to kiss it. She stared with disbelief as she admired herself. She touched her face with both hands. "This is amazing, I mean… look at me, Ty." Beatrice spun around, and she was gorgeous before the procedure. Just looking a bit tired over the years. Plus after having Cameron, she never lost the small pouch in her belly. Now, she looked flawless, energized, her body was perfect. Her waist also shrunk, back to the size when we were teenage girls. Her skin looked airbrushed.

Tyrone chimed in. "I can't believe it. You guys are going to make a fortune. It seems all-natural. Just swallow some snake eggs." I smiled and then swallowed. "There are some risk you know?" Tyrone's smile went away. "What kind of risk?" I sighed. "If, during the procedure. Someone moves, gags, or bites down before the eggs are dropped. Death can occur." Tyrone's mouth dropped. "Wow, yeah, death is a hell of a side effect."

I laughed. "I mean, as you can see, if the person stays still, doesn't gag or bite down for 60 seconds. They are pretty much home free. With a whole new youthful look. And as the legends say, immortal." Bruce's eyes bugged. "Immortal?" I took a deep breath. "Well, as the legend has it. It goes along with looking youthful again. The soul also regains its youth and cannot die. Were not sure of that part yet. I mean, if a person is in a car accident or something. I'm sure death will occur. But, if they live a long healthy life with no accidents. The body will remain alive after the age of one hundred and beyond. That is what the book of Nigron says. Grandmother's spellbook."

Tyrone looked intrigued. "I've seen that book before when I was a child. It was grandmother's go-to for everything. Of course, she wouldn't let us children touch it. She always said, when you older." Beatrice was still admiring herself in the mirror. She finally turned around. "Well, Your next Ty! When's the big day? I laughed because I was nervous. I knew that was coming. "Yeah, well, let's do it next week after your follow up. I have to go back to work this week. You took days off. So I will take it next week, in case I need it. But, you look like you're doing fine." Beatrice excited. "Ok, get the after pictures Ty. Look, I'm ready to move forward. Let's give the youth spa, an official name. Create some social media sites. And start posting before and after pictures. Let's get this thing moving.

I paused for a moment. I was unsure about moving forward. I shrugged my shoulders. "I guess we can." Beatrice was looking smug. "What do you mean, you guess? Let's get this thing popping, so we can move forward. Get you out of the DNA lab. Get me out of the cosmetics lab. Look, you think everything on the market has been through clinical trials? Um no, most natural stuff hasn't. But, it can still be sold. All we have to do is mention in the ads. Not FDA approved. Come on, People go over to Mexico and get these cheap, dangerous procedures done.

A lot of them don't even make it off the table. We have a better, more effective, safer procedure here. So safe, we stand behind it. And both of us have done the procedure. We both will be the face of the company. I think we should charge 10,000 a pop. That will include a couple of days stay here at the day spa." Tyrone and I looked at each other. "She has a point, Ty. There are many dangerous procedures and products out there that are far worse. Well from what I've seen. You guys are using an ancient way of becoming youthful again."

I stared at them both. "Well, I guess we can put underneath our results, that the FDA has not approved this procedure. Along with other warnings. At that point, they can enter a contract at their own risk. Beatrice clapped her hands together. "Great, well, you got the before and after pictures for Candy and me. We need to start loading them up on social media immediately. Even making the photos into a video and narrate the results.

We have to make this happen, now, Ty!" Beatrice stopped for a moment and smiled deeply. "Not only that, you have to do the procedure." I smiled, "I'll do it next weekend Beatrice. It's been a long journey for me. I was out for days, and I need to recoup. I'll be ready next week, promise." Tyrone jumped in the conversation. "I'll do whatever I can to help out." Beatrice's eyes widened. "Well, this isn't just a woman thing, you know. You could be our male model! You can undergo the procedure as well!" Tyrone smile transitioned into a worry. "Actual, I can't be a male model. I can't be advertised in any way."

Beatrice was looking concerned. "Well, well why not?" I glanced at Tyrone, and I saw how uncomfortable he was. "He can't Beatrice will have to find someone else. His identity and whereabouts are undisclosed at this point." Beatrice looked disappointed. "Ok, well, I'll proceed with making the slide shows for advertisement. Get them posted to social media and Youtube. And get things moving in the right direction. I'm going to gather my things. I have to go home tonight. I know Keith and Cameron are waiting for me.

Plus, I'll have to come back next week. To do your procedure. I'll go pack up now." Beatrice leaves the room. Tyrone glared as she walked out. "You do know she's married, right?" Tyrone looked shocked. "No, she never mentioned a husband." I smiled, "sounds like Beatrice. Well, she is, but it's none of my business." I sighed, "Listen, I have to go back to work, so I'll be leaving out tonight myself. The kitchen is fully stocked with food and drinks. I know you will be ok here. I'm sure; it's not safe for you to go back to Atlanta." Tyrone shook his head in agreement. "Are you afraid to be here alone?"

"No, I feel safe and protected here. I'll be fine, don't worry about me. I got Amaya here if I need company." I quickly glanced over at him. "You be careful with Amaya, she can be vindictive and untrustworthy." Tyrone smiled, "Ok, I take your word on that one." I smiled at him. "But, since your going to be here. Do me a favor and feed her." I smiled even bigger. "Please, I usually hall her back home with me. It will be nice having someone here. Grandmothers around, always, she may come to visit you." Tyrone smiled, "I'd actually welcome that."

I gathered my things around the office. "Great, I'm going to go pack. I usually stay in my grandmother's old room while I'm here. I'll be back next week weekend. I will be calling to check on you daily. Do you plan on going out at all?" Tyrone scratched his head. "Maybe outside for some fresh air. I'm trying to lay low if there's enough food here — no need for me to go into town. I'm fine, don't worry. I've lived through many horrible times in my life. Thank you for giving me this opportunity to take a break." I walked over to my brother and gave him a big hug. I could see the pain in his eyes.

As I hugged my brother, the smell of cinnamon and sage filled my nostrils. At that moment, I knew grandmother was here. I broke free from the hug. "You're going to be fine, and I know you will. But, I'm still going to call every day to make sure you're ok." I walked over to the desk and grabbed my things. Tyrone and I walked down the hall together. He veered off towards his room. I went into grandmother's room and grabbed the rest of my things. I locked up the bed and breakfast. I got into my car and headed back to Atlanta.

New Beginnings

Chapter 16

As I laid in the warm water of my soothing bath. I stared up at the ceiling. I knew a change was coming. I could feel it. I almost lost my mind in that other world. New beginnings always begin after a breakdown. After you've lost your mind. I was feeling like the death card in a good hand of tarot. The renewal was upon me. Something refreshing was coming. I so well deserved it. I sat up in the tub and pulled my knees to my chest. I was taking a cleansing bath. I filed the tub with bay leaf. Basil, white sage, Epsom salt, lavender oil, dried rose petals eucalyptus oil, Obsidian, pink Himalayan salt, and rosemary. I visualized in my mind, all the black goo being pulled out of my body and mixing with the bathwater. All the stress, all the confusion. I expelled it from my body and into the cleansing bath.

I soaked my soul for about an hour. I finally pulled my tired body out of the water. I grabbed a towel and dried off. I had work in the morning. It seemed like forever since I'd been back to that lab. I crawled into my bed and fell asleep. I immediately awaken to my alarm clock. Was it time to get up already? The spiritual bath knocked me out cold. It was one of the best nights of rest, and I had in a long time. I didn't resist, I got up, dressed in my work attire. I fixed my hair and headed out the door.

I walked in to work and headed straight towards my desk. I bypassed the coffee station. Said hello quickly to everyone and sat down at my secluded desk over in the corner. The lab floor was typically empty this time of the morning. I sat down at my desk. I turned on my computer, checked my emails. I got a social media alert on my phone. I glanced at my cell phone and turned my ringer off. Another alert came through and another. My phone started vibrating over and over again. Finally, I decided to see what was going on. I unlocked my phone and went into my social media site.

I had over one hundred alerts, and my phone was still buzzing. I scratched my head and looked around. No one was watching. I tapped on my nonfiction button. I was tagged in one of Beatrice's post. It was a video she narrated. It was candy and Beatrice's before and after pictures. I stopped and checked the views on the video. There were over 1 million! My eyes bucked, and I saw that number. I went under the video into the comments section. People wanted to know what the procedure was. How much it cost. The comments went on and on. Some people even said the result had to be fake.

I was in complete amazement. My desk phone started to ring. I looked at the call back number. Of course, it was Beatrice. I looked around first and then picked up. I whispered, "Hello?" Beatrice is super excited. "Ty is that you!" I laughed, "Of course it's me; what's up?" I could hear Beatrice hyperventilating. "Ok, so I went home last night and made a new video. I posted it today on social media with lots of hashtags. I woke up this morning, and the video went viral! I'm sure you can see this, I tagged you! My phone is blowing up. People all over the world want consultations. Now!"

I was excited but nervous about starting this new life. Leaving the known for the unknown, but it had to happen. "Well, let's book ten consultations now. And if they go well. Will book them over the weekend for the actual procedure." Beatrice paused for a moment. "Let's do phone consultations. This way, we can weed out who's serious and who's not. If they want to book, then they will have to put down half the money. You opened that business bank account, correct?" I sighed, "Of course I did, weeks ago."

I heard Beatrice clap her hands. "Great, then we are all set. Let's do as many phone consultations as we can. And book the first ten people. We have ten rooms to fill in. If they stay longer than two days, that's an extra fee. While Tyrone is there, do you think he can help out a little?" I smiled, "I'm sure he would love to help out. He offered his help in advanced. Make no sense to hire someone. We both have to be back at our jobs on Monday. If a client stays longer, Tyrone will be there." Beatrice sighed. "Ok, great, look, I have to get back to work. My supervisor is calling me over the intercom again!! Call you back."

Beatrice hung up the phone. I hung up the phone, as well. And went back to checking my emails for work. Then, Kent walker strolled in. I had forgotten all about calling him over the weekend. I completely forgot, with all this chaos going on, plus falling in love with Jake. Oh, and having his baby. He smiled as he walked over to my desk. "Hey, I never got that phone call. How are you?" I smiled as I placed my phone on my desk. "I'm great; I just had a lot going on this weekend. I apologize, I really do."

Kent sat on my desk. "It's cool! I just figured you got what you wanted. And you decided never to call me again." I blushed, and then I realized he was talking about the files on Tyrone. I slapped my forehead. "I'm so sorry. Thank you, though. That information you gave me, Led me to a long lost relative. I appreciate everything you've done for me." He nodded his head. "Well, I'd like to take you out again. When you're ready." I smiled, "I think I might like that."

Kent smiled back. "Cool, I'll give you a call soon." He touched my hand as he said soon. He stared into my eyes. Deeply, his dark brown eyes were piercing. I liked Kent a lot. I just really needed that file. So, I could find my brother. I just didn't want to get to close to him. When most guys found out who the real Tituba Jones was. I always got a weird card. So, I kept my conversation to a minimum. I didn't get all deep and subconscious on him. Although I am sure, he is a freemason. After that place, he took me to on our date. I am for sure, he is a freemason. Not sure what sector. But he's definitely a freemason.

The day went by quickly — my usual lab routine. I sent a few check-up texts to Tyrone. He responded each time,

which alleviated my stress about leaving him alone.
Beatrice sent me ten people. I had to give them phone
consultations. Once I got home around six o'clock. I
walked in, played with Gretta and Giselle for a bit. Hit
the shower and started making phone calls. Finally, I
finished calls around 10 pm. Out of ten people, five of
mine were scheduled for this weekend coming up. Payments
had to be made the day before the procedure. Or the
appointment would be filled by another client —
Beatrice's rules of course.

I climbed inside my bed. I got under the covers and
became hypnotized by the ceiling fan. I drifted off and
fell asleep.

Chapter 17

In the Beginning, There Was Greed!

Continued

Beatrice and I dug and dug and dug. Until we couldn't dig
anymore. Beatrice looked up at me. "I think the hole is
deep enough. Let just throw her in it." I eyeballed the
hole. It was just barely big enough. Mrs. Williams was a
thick lady. I gazed at her lifeless body. Beatrice saw
the way I looked at her. "Look, Ty, its nothing we can do
about it. She's dead, and neither of us is going to jail.
She signed the papers; she knew the risk." Beatrice
grabbed her forehead. "Let's go get Tyrone. He can help
us lower her body in."

I shot Beatrice a dirty look. "Hell no, I am not getting
him involved in this shit! I don't even want him to
know." Beatrice had a look of despair on her face. She
scratched her head. "Look, grab her legs. Let's just get
this over with." I quickly grabbed Mrs. Williams's legs.
Beatrice grabbed her arms. On the count of three. We
lifted her up a bit. And dragged her closer to the hole.
Then we rolled her inside the ground. We took our shovels
and buried her quickly. We quickly grabbed our utensils.
We walked briskly through the forest and back to the
house.

Beatrice and I walked quietly through the back door. We
tiptoed softly down the hall. Beatrice went into her

room, and I went into mine. The next few weeks passed. We saw more clients, did even more procedures. We were raking in cash. We were booked every week. We both left our jobs. We continued the beauty spa full time. Beatrice and I never really spoke about that night again. Until a month down the line. There was a knock at the door. Beatrice and I were just finishing up a procedure as I walked towards the door. Tyrone beat me to it. He looked out the peephole. He jumped back quietly. He tips toe over towards me. He leaned over and whispered in my ear.

"It's the cops, they can't be here for me. They wouldn't be dressed in cops' clothes." I looked at Tyrone. I whispered, "don't worry, I'll get the door." I walked towards the door and looked out. I kept the door closed. "Can I help you?" The cop put his badge to the window. "Yes, we're here to check out a missing person's report — a Mrs. E. Williams."

Magic Mysteries Of Gullah Isalnd part 2 is well on its way. Thank you so much for reading my magical book.

If paperback readers will please go to amazon.com and leave an awesome review, I would greatly apprecitate it. If you are reading an ebook, please click the link below, it will take you to the reviews.

https://amzn.to/2JQQb5f

Please connect with me

Youtube- Manifesting Moon

Facebook January Moon

Instagram- January Moon lite

Twitter- Urbanhorrorhuni

For question Please send an email- Jaquarymoton@gmail.com

Or DM on social media.

Made in United States
North Haven, CT
28 December 2021

13819670R00124